CONSUMED

All illustrations by Christiano Neves
Design by Casa Hamid

PART ONE

The man lying awake in the dark hotel room was named Romain Thomas Mariani and he was the world's sixty-third-best road racing cyclist.

Later today he had to ride one hundred and ninety-six kilometres and beat Hans Banquo, Herr Wunderschön, Hansi the Conqueror, the cyclist ranked sixty-two places above him, by one minute and fifty-one seconds.

If he did that, two tall beautiful women in short dresses and high heels would kiss his gaunt cheeks and then help him into a silver jersey, a crowd would clap, and he would be the winner of the L'Essence du Tour, the last and hardest one-week stage race in the professional cycling calendar. He would be ranked the world's twelfth-best rider, and for the first time in a number of years, be truly happy.

Bright early-morning September light knifed through the thin gap between the orange curtains. There was a smell of feet and warming carpet.

In the room's other single bed, a big-jawed man slowly opened his mouth and groaned.

'Hey, Hitler Youth,' said Mariani, 'time to get up.' Half-English, he spoke the language fluently and with only a trace of the guttural accent of his Eastern European homeland.

The groaning man, Mariani's teammate Dieter Grasch, kept his eyes closed and rubbed his dry lips together. '*Ja, ja,* Commie bastard.'

Mariani swung his legs, tanned from the middle of his thighs to his ankles, out of the bed. When he stood he put his left foot down first, one of several superstitions he adhered to. He was naked. There were indelible records of impacts with kerbs and tarmac and crash barriers on both elbows, left wrist and right shoulder. His torso, untouched by the sun, was pale and skinny as a boy's. He walked into the bathroom, urinated a little less powerfully than he would have liked, and then, as he did twice every day, stepped on to his 'U-Analyser' personal electronic scales. Seventy-three point five seven. He'd lost fifty grams in the night. That pleased him. With his big toe, he pressed a switch on the scales and the readout changed to tell him his body fat content: five point five per cent. He poked an index finger into both buttocks and told himself that this was the solid, lard-free ass of a man who could win a major bike race.

Mariani showered quickly, shaved his face (left cheek first, another su-
perstition) and then scraped the plastic razor over the barely there stubble
on his legs. He smeared antiseptic cream over the saddle sore on his perineum. The ceiling light buzzed and flickered once. He wound a thin white
hotel towel around his waist, put the lid down on the toilet and then sat and
thought about what he had to do.

He was nearly twenty-seven and knew that for most of his six years as
a professional, he had under-performed. In his first season, he had come
ninth and seventh in two of the one-day classics, Milan–San Remo and
Flèche Wallonne. A year later, he had won a stage of Paris–Nice and finished fifth in the three-week-long Giro d'Italia. For a short while he'd been
talked of as the next Banquo, interviewed, photographed. A Belgian non-
alcoholic beer company had paid him twenty-five thousand euros to be
their spokesman. Women had knocked on his hotel room door, and on a
number of occasions he had let them in. But then, after breaking an ankle
dancing in a Triblisi nightclub, and starting a will-sapping relationship with
a forceful French P.R. manager, his career had drifted. Mediocrity beck-
oned. Nineteenth place in the Tour de France the year before last was the
only recent result he wanted to remember.

But life had changed in the last twelve months, and so had he. A new
team, Gazin-Ségur PMP, a new no-carbs-after-midday diet, a new pedalling
technique. New recovery methods including ice baths, compression socks
and sunflower oil massage cream. A new girlfriend, Keira Ladoga, a level-
headed Swiss figure skater. At the start of the Essence, after sleeping for a
week in a hypoxic tent, he had found himself in the best shape of his life.

One minute and fifty-one seconds would take him from second to first,
also-ran to winner. In his mind, Mariani began to search for inspiration.
He thought of sledgehammers smashing into the Berlin Wall, of Keira's
carved shoulders, of the way Kevin Pietersen could effortlessly switch-hit
a cricket ball into the crowd. (Mariani's mother Jane had taught him to love
the game.) He visualised Banquo receding in the distance, the Austrian's
tongue lolling between his famously white teeth, face dripping with the
sweat of impending defeat.

At that moment Mariani realised how much he wanted to win this race, how much he wanted to make something of his life and not end up like his father. After three drug suspensions, Tanel Mariani, a willing, moustached *domestique,* could no longer find a place on a team and had returned, aged thirty-one, full of anger, to a fearful wife, two cowering young sons and a two-hectare pig farm in the second-most-deprived area of the second-most-deprived country in Eastern Europe, where he had lived and worked and raged ever since.

Mariani's pulse jolted as he pictured his father's fury and clenched fists. He sat back to let it drop closer its resting rate of thirty-five beats a minute. His heart had a lot of work ahead.

From the bedroom he heard the creak of springs and then a hissing intake of breath.

'My fucking knee,' said Grasch. 'My fucking back. This fucking sport.'

'Best sport in the world,' replied Mariani. He believed it absolutely, though on certain days it had seemed like the worst. Yesterday it had been thirty-eight degrees at midday and the forecast for the day ahead was no cooler. He thought about the sun roasting his skin and cursed his inherited English pallor. The back of his neck had burnt where he'd forgotten to put on protection and he touched it now and worried about cancer.

Grasch opened the door. He was in his grey underwear and black-framed glasses. 'May I piss?'

Mariani stood.

'Watch Mitchell on the final climb,' said Grasch as Mariani left the bathroom.

Mariani shrugged. 'He's an Australian,' he said, over his shoulder. Mariani did not like Australians and had no respect for rat-faced Trent Mitchell even though he was ranked second in the world and this year had not only won on the flat cobbles of Paris–Roubaix but also two mountain stages in the Tour de France. Mariani's disdain was returned by Mitchell, and with interest.

Mariani dropped back on to his bed and stretched out his long thin legs.

'Think I can do it?' he said, in the direction of the bathroom.

The toilet flushed. 'You beat Hansi and I let you have free use of my colonic irrigation machine often as you like.'

'Answer the question.'

Grasch came back into the bedroom, adjusting his testicles with one hand and scratching at his jaw with the other. He had a thick white bandage and gauze netting over his left knee, the result of a thirty-man pile up at a roundabout on the first stage of the Essence.

'What's your father doing right now?' he asked.

'Wearing a stupid hat and wading through pig shit.'

'You want to wear a stupid hat and wade through pig shit?'

'*Nein, Commandant.*'

'Then you'd better kick my half-brother's perfect Austrian ass.'

*

At three thirty-four that afternoon, after more than five hours of riding and with six kilometres remaining of the stage, Mariani rode up to the back of the leading group.

His arms hurt. His back hurt more than his arms. His legs hurt more than his back.

A drop of sweat fell off the end of his nose and splashed on to his knee.

He looked ahead. There were three others in the group. Name them, he told himself. Think about them.

Banquo. Banquo's main slave Xterrax, leading his master up the climb. And at the front, pushing hard, some mountain goat from Crédit Haussman. Through the radio taped to Mariani's left ear, his *directeur sportif* had told him the Haussman rider was de Vilde, but he found that hard to believe. De Vilde was no goat – he could not climb – and did not win stages.

Mariani relaxed for a moment. He reached round to the back pocket of his jersey and felt inside. Three of the Jelly Babies he liked. He put them in his mouth, chewed slowly. Even my teeth are tired, he thought. As he swallowed, he tried to guess the weight of a Jelly Baby. How many fewer grams was he carrying now?

Fuck Jelly Babies – concentrate.

All right. The group. Mariani. Banquo. Xterrax. Unknown goat.

Now, the road. Six kilometres. Average gradient of eleven per cent. Between fifteen and sixteen minutes of cycling. Twelve hundred turns of the pedals.

The aim. Ride those six kilometres one minute fifty-one seconds faster than Banquo.

Mariani spat.

He glanced out across the ancient Pyrenean valley, trying to put his objective into a wider context.

The lake silver-blue in the distance. Steeples. Dots of vehicles. Heat shimmer across the whole picture.

He looked down. The small silver GPS-equipped computer on his handlebars told him he was nineteen hundred and seven metres above sea level and that the temperature was thirty-seven degrees. How was that helping? He felt a burst of wrath for inanimate objects and an urge to rip the computer from its fixings and hurl it at the sky.

Sweat ran into his right eye. He unzipped his jersey.

Suddenly, he wanted meat.

A steak. Or, Jesus, yes, a bowl of *guhtruzi*, the stew of wild ram they served in his village. He could smell it.

These were cravings he could not control. His team doctor called this haphazard need for fatty protein his 'metabolic inefficiency'. But Mariani knew it was more than that. He wanted it as a comfort when he'd failed and as a reward when he'd done well, and the fact that cyclists shouldn't really have it at all only increased its allure.

He tried to sluice the desire away with a squirt from his bidon. It splashed through his oesophagus and into his stomach. The water tasted of warm plastic, exactly like Bink, the powdered food he'd been given as a baby. He gagged and threw the bidon on to the roadside.

The Haussman rider looked back. It was de Vilde. Face trying not to show the fear, the hope, the pain. Dirt smears on his chin. Lips cracked. Nose burnt red.

The pace lifted. Twenty-two, twenty-three km/h. The afternoon sun made white glints on the riders' dark wet skin. Mariani lost a metre, then closed the gap.

Banquo turned his head and showed his teeth. Armstrong had 'the look'. Banquo simply smiled, white crescent in a tanned, untroubled face: Hi... happy to beat you. On Banquo's ass, the red logo of *Schmackhaft!*, an Austrian liverwurst.

Mariani looked down at the chain spinning in the middle of Banquo's glinting rear block. What was he in? The sixteen? On a one-in-ten incline?

The roadsides were thick with people. Smashing their palms together. Screaming. Making frenzied gestures.

A fat man in a pink cap, tiny Speedos and boots shaped like bananas ran with the group, gut jiggling. He waved his hand above his head like it was on fire.

'*Allez! Vitement!*' After ten metres, the fat man stopped. He coughed and spat.

Mariani saw a beautiful red-haired woman eating a burger and wanted to slap her face.

The rutted road reared up to fourteen per cent. They passed a waterfall. The tumbling water looked good and cold and for a moment Mariani saw himself standing under it, lathering his armpits and singing a song.

He looked down. On the dusty grey-white road surface, his shadow, a half-size flattened version of himself. He smelled dust and salt on damp skin.

'One minute and fifty-one seconds,' came the shout in his earpiece. 'No one remembers the runner-up. Got to go take Banquo soon, Romain.'

Mariani invoked an old curse his father always used: 'May the Devil suck out your blood and replace it with that of a chicken.' He wished further terrible things on Banquo, the kind of terrible things that every cyclist in the peloton regularly wished on every other cyclist in the peloton. Banquo started to whistle.

Mariani felt a malign presence behind him. He looked over his shoulder. A bike-length back, Mitchell, his small sharp features partly hidden by yellow personalised glasses. Very quietly, Mariani said, 'Fuck'.

At the front of the group, de Vilde lifted his malnourished behind off the saddle, pumped the pedals and gained two metres. He was eighty-first in the *classement général*, the GC, could not possibly win the tour, but obviously wanted this stage. Xterrax followed de Vilde, Banquo followed Xterrax. Mariani had to follow Banquo.

'Banquo's going,' shrieked Mariani's *directeur sportif.*

No shit.

L'Essence du Tour was a new north–south race comprising seven of the Tour de France's most iconic stages. So far this week, Mariani had spent thirty-one hours in the saddle and ridden over eleven hundred kilometres. He'd burnt twenty-six thousand calories. He was sure now, as the group passed the five-kilometre sign, that the race, the first he had any chance of winning, was lost. But you never know, he said to himself, as he got back on to Banquo's wheel. Not until the flags fly and the anthems start. And not even then. Heras in '05. Landis in '06. Contador in '10. All major tour winners until the lab got a look at their piss and blood. Mariani couldn't believe Banquo would dope, not Herr Wunderschön, but the sport kept telling him that everything he thought was wrong. Whenever cycling was pronounced clean someone made it dirty again. So he gripped the bars and told the pain it didn't exist and focused instead on Banquo's wheel, narrowing his gaze down to the twenty-two millimetres of cellar-aged, hand-stitched black rubber that encircled it.

His speed went up to twenty-four km/h. He'd never climbed this section so fast. His heart rate read one ninety-seven. Five off his maximum. The programmed numerals on his computer's screen flashed red: danger, keep this up and you'll blow. But he didn't look at them. The saddle chafed the sore on his perineum. He felt a spasm of cramp in his left hamstring. He was certain a carcinoma was forming on his neck. He was suffering and he was going to keep suffering. That, mostly, was what bike racing meant.

Mitchell rode level with him. 'Oink,' said Mitchell. 'Oink, oink.' Mariani ignored the Australian, but imagined a live wallaby roasting on a spit and then wondered what it would taste like. He had to make do with warm sweat laced with factor-50 sunscreen.

De Vilde began to pull away.

'What's de Cunt on?' muttered Mitchell. 'I want some.'

Mitchell began to suck air with a rasp like he was wearing an aqualung. Mariani savoured the sound. You bathed in the anguish of your fellow man. That was also what bike racing meant.

Xterrax kept the group with de Vilde as they went towards the summit finish. The Spaniard was a bona fide climber, *un vrai grimpeur*. 5' 3", fifty-eight kilos in his socks. Legs barely thicker than his seat stays.

The riders went over their own names, chalked on the road. *Mitchell heart ass. Banquo merde.* Sheep nibbled on hillocks, unimpressed with these thin men in orange, cherry blossom-pink and topaz giving all they had. A helicopter slashed at the air overhead. A cameraman, hanging off the back of a motorcycle, tried to go in tight for the agony shot. De Vilde flicked an obscene gesture at him then spat a phlegm nugget on the lens.

Four to go. Mariani watched Banquo's bronzed legs, elegantly tapered, their action smooth and powerful as an expensive gun. No tension in his shoulders. Mariani looked inside himself for something that would enable him to ride away from Banquo and saw emptiness.

A fan in a surgical mask and green scrubs ran with him, offering him a syringe filled with what Mariani hoped was not real blood. The fan mimed jabbing the needle into Mariani's arm and Mariani elbowed him hard in the side of the neck.

He passed a furious male face, painted in the national colours of the country they both came from. '*Hydracxeki*, Mariani!' A donkey. He was riding at twenty-four km/h up a nine per cent gradient and the fan thought he was a donkey.

He gulped air. The sun-softened tarmac was sticking to his tyres. He imagined rain.

Three to go.

One minute and fifty-one seconds.

Meat.

'Go now or don't bother,' said the voice in his ear.

He stood and stamped on the pedals like he wanted them dead. Rocking from side to side, he went past de Vilde. He had three metres. Five. Eight. Ten. Then something seemed to leave his body. He watched his dusty silver shoes as their movements slowed. His socks were filthy. He had to sit. He had to stop. He tasted bile, made sweet and thick by half-digested Jelly Babies.

The others came past, Banquo unsmiling. Mariani watched the tarmac between him and them lengthen. One last effort, three turns of the cranks, but his legs were those of some old and wasted man. He shook with exhaustion. He wasn't sure if he would ever make it to the top.

The four other riders rounded the bend and disappeared.

Mariani watched the highlights of the day's stage on television that night. As he saw his legs weaken, his head drop and his hopes of winning fade and die, he dragged his hand down his face. He took a deep breath in and then let it out slowly. On screen, De Vilde crossed the line, arms raised, both index fingers pointing to the skies. When the picture cut to the press conference, the red-nosed Belgian journeyman thanked God and said that life was great.

Mariani knew little about de Vilde, just that he was a *domestique ordinaire*, *un bon chien*, a rider who'd given everything and won nothing, worked for fifteen years shielding the glamour boys from the wind and fetching their drinks and titbits. He was famous for riding into dogs – he'd killed two. What he did not, could not, do was ride away from Hans Banquo.

*

When Mariani woke up next morning, sore and stiff and disappointed, de Vilde's name was all over the media for a different and even more surprising reason. He was dead.

An hour later, Mariani listened as Grasch, thumbing his iPhone, read out online tributes.

'He liked pancakes, Assos crotch cream and the music of Foreigner… He once went head-first through a café window during a city-centre *kermis*…'

'Anyone say how he died?'

Eyebrows slightly raised, Grasch looked at Mariani.

When cyclists died in their sleep – and, in the last twenty years, as many as thirty had – the cause was always the same. Blood, thickened and slowed by an artificial increase in oxygen-carrying red blood cells, not reaching the heart. The colourless liquid that caused this effect, erythropoietin, was injected into the arm from tiny phials, kept refrigerated like miniature milk bottles. An artificial hormone, it had been developed to treat kidney failure and anaemia in cancer patients. It was effective. Riders using it would – if they remembered to set alarms – get up in the night and start the sludge in their veins flowing by pedalling for an hour on a stationary trainer.

Grasch's phone bleeped with the arrival of a text. He read it.

'*Roommate Pfaff came in at one-thirty with podium girl, but kept lights off and her moans in pillow. Pfaff didn't know deVilde dead until tried to wake him for breakfast. Podium girl under sedation.*' Grasch looked away from the screen. 'I would be also, if I'd let Pfaff boof me.'

Mariani laughed through his nose. Then he looked away and his shoulders dropped. Best sport in the world.

*

At the start of the day's stage, black armbands, always carried by every team, were distributed. Banquo had decreed quiet and dignity. The peloton set off at a funereal pace on the final one hundred and ten kilometres of the professional season. The organisers, following the tradition of the Tour de France, had envisaged this last day as a celebratory epilogue, with champagne handed to the riders: there would be no racing for the overall lead, though the stage victory would be contested by the sprinters.

The champagne stayed on ice.

Mariani sat in the pack and listened to what he knew were shocked euphemisms.

'Brain haemorrhage.'

'Heat stroke.'

'Liver exploded.'

As the peloton rolled quietly through the countryside, Pfaff freewheeled next to Mariani, saying nothing, dark glasses covering his eyes, looking like a dejected insect.

Mariani rested his hand on Pfaff's upper arm for several moments.

The Lithuanian's stare was fixed on the road. His thin shoulders were slumped and his dark legs looked listless.

'Fuckin' Triesmaan,' he said.

'Triesmaan?'

Pfaff shook his head and said nothing more.

Triesmaan? Mariani hadn't heard of him for years. When he'd first turned pro, an eyebrowless man wearing a tweed jacket and a small fishing hat with a feather in it had come up to him in a café, introduced himself as Bennett and quietly offered the services of his employer, Dr Alann Triesmaan.

'What?' Mariani had said. 'He's a what?'

'A healer. Yes?'

'A masseur, you mean?'

'No. You're not quite getting this, are you, old cock? Goodbye.'

All Mariani had understood was that Dr Alann Triesmaan's services would cost a lot of money, more money than he could afford.

Later, he'd questioned his teammates. Most responded by making circles at the side of their heads with an index finger.

'*Loco*,' said Sanchez. 'No good. He has that *domestique* who calls you a penis all the time. *Old cock*.'

'He has the seriously weird stuff, boy,' said the greying veteran, Tishland Speyer. 'The freaky shit. Understand?' He mimed spiking a syringe into his arm, hung out his tongue and made his eyes rotate wildly.

The team medic, Henk Potts, simply said: 'Triesmaan? A vuckin vucker.'

'He's a proper doctor?' asked Mariani.

'Who knows what he is? Always used to wear a white suit, like John vuckin Travolta.'

Mariani had seen Bennett's pale smooth face under its strange hat many times since, but the man had not approached him again. What he had for sale, nobody knew. Or rather, nobody would say. Certain riders appeared to have an arrangement with him, but the *omerta* that shrouded bike racing meant that Triesmaan's methods were all innuendo. Mariani had forgotten about him.

*

The outside of the town hall was decorated with miniature flags of the twenty-seven nations represented by the riders in L'Essence du Tour. A podium had been positioned at the bottom of the building's main steps. At the top, a twelve-piece band played a version of 'Climb Every Mountain'. The musicians wore green uniforms and were conducted by a man with a black patch over his right eye.

Mariani waited at the left-hand side of the podium. The music stopped. The sun went behind a cloud and then a loud happy voice came over the Tannoy. He heard the word '*troisième*' and then his own name. The band began the marching-feet introduction to his national anthem, 'We Are Here', a piece of music never before heard at an international sporting event. He came forward and stood on the lowest part of the podium. He half raised one arm as the applause rippled round the square and then pulled his team cap a little further down his forehead. The tall, pretty women in the short dresses he had hoped would be zipping him into the winner's silver jersey instead gave him a small stuffed giraffe instead, which he held by its left front leg. This was his prize for coming third, along with a cheque for twenty thousand euros, which, tradition dictated, he would share equally amongst his team. He pulled the brim of his cap down further. He tried to smile and to remind himself that he had beaten everyone except the two best cyclists in the world.

The runner-up's name was announced and from the right-hand side of the podium Mitchell stepped forward. He had finished fifty-eight seconds ahead of Mariani on the mountain stage, three seconds more than he needed to go past him on the GC. Mitchell winked at Mariani, oinked at him and then stood on the podium. His giraffe was bigger, as was his smile. He pumped his small fist and then with an index finger, tapped his narrow chest. Mariani suspected Mitchell had padded out his shorts at the front. The band played 'Advance Australia Fair'. Mariani suddenly wished he were deaf.

Banquo's giraffe was the biggest. His smile, when he stepped on to the podium, was the biggest too, though because he was Hans Banquo and knew what was required of him, he curled down the ends of his mouth to add a fitting sense of melancholy. The band played 'Land of Mountains' and Banquo, head slightly bowed, sang along. He then unshowily raised both long arms, waved the giraffe in a slow, dignified way, turned to Mitchell, shook his hand, and then shook Mariani's with slightly more enthusiasm. His sideburns, Mariani saw, were exactly the same length as his ears. An official gave Banquo a microphone, and in good French, he made a speech. His words were bland and well-chosen and he got the minute's silence he asked for at the end of them.

During the quiet, Mariani looked at his feet and wondered what he would do when it was time to stop doing that. Third. He would go back to his home in the village of Çigi and drink a lot of shocking coffee at his friend Svarik's café and walk in the wet woods. He would arrange to see Keira and try not to see his father. Third. He would not take calls from his agent, Serge Hamptons. After several weeks, he would begin again. He would ride the quiet roads he knew like his own face and gradually allow his love for the wind, air and trees to replace the cramped, sour-sweet and confusing feelings he had now. He would forget about cyclists dying in hotel rooms. He would forget about Banquo, forget about Mitchell. He would try to forget about the moment on the mountain when he'd realised he had nothing inside. He would forget about third, except perhaps to work out how he could turn it into a different number. He had been close to victory and would very much like to get closer.

The silence ended. Applause followed. The sun came out. The cameras clicked for several minutes, and then the three riders were politely ushered off the podium by the blazer-clad race director.

Wearing a cerise velour Feraz-Hi:Gen Pro-Racing team tracksuit, Mitchell's mother, Nikki-Jo, hurried over to her son. She kissed him, half cheek and half mouth and turned to Mariani.

'What was it like down there? Shit view, hey?' Her voice like a crow talking.

'Australia were 76 for 8 last time I checked,' said Mariani, looking at her steadily. England was on the verge of an easy victory in the deciding one-day international.

Mitchell's mother narrowed her mouth, turned away and linked arms with her son. They walked off hip to hip. She was twice his width and several centimetres taller.

Mariani stood still, uncertain what he should do next.

Banquo glanced at him. 'See you in the spring.'

Perhaps this was his cue to leave the square, but if it was, he did not take it.

Instead, without quite knowing why, he took half a step closer to Banquo. When he had, he began to feel an odd heat that had nothing to do with the air temperature. It was energising and seemed to take all the aches away from his body. He realised it was the aura of fame, made up of money and power and thousands of electrical pulses, each one representing the appearance of Banquo in a fan's thought pattern.

To Banquo's right, his security guard, an ex-Sumo wrestler, big and fat in a white 'Hansi' brand tracksuit and mirrored sunglasses, turned his head questioningly in Mariani's direction, but the Austrian seemed not to notice Mariani, or not at least to be disturbed by his presence. It was as if Banquo was letting Mariani feel the glorious sunshine of adulation. Banquo looked regally at the mêlée of fans, journalists and photographers standing behind the crowd-control barriers and gently nodded his head.

From out of the VIP enclosure, with a small white-blonde child in each firm, tanned arm, Banquo's wife approached her husband. As she neared, Mariani, overcome perhaps by what was occurring, had the peculiar sensation that she was his wife, not Banquo's. He blinked hard. Then she was standing directly in front of him.

She handed one child to her husband, took off her sunglasses, and with the manicured nail of her left middle finger, pushed a stray lock of her short hair behind one ear. Mariani had only met her once before at an event she'd organised for *Kinder und Leben,* a kids' charity she was involved in. The entire peloton had been obliged to go. Her hair had been longer then. All he knew about her was that she was a photographer and that he liked the unripe raspberry colour of her lipstick.

'Romain,' she said. 'How are you?' Faint creases around the sides of her mouth and between her eyebrows. She sounded concerned.

'Hello. Fine, thank you.'

'You had a great tour. And a good season.' Her green eyes considered him. 'Have a long rest.'

He found he could not meet her gaze. He was not used to being looked at by the beautiful wives of world-famous multi-millionaires. But then his eyes moved to her face again. He began to feel he was being acted upon by a force beyond his will.

'Here.' Mariani handed his giraffe to the smaller of the Banquo children. Claudia smiled at him. Her lipstick really is a lovely colour, he thought.

Her husband turned to him. 'Would you care to go away now?' he asked, eyebrows raised.

Suddenly exhausted, and with emotions shifting in unfamiliar ways, Mariani finally left the square and went back to his hotel room.

*

He sat on the bed, his feet in travel slippers, eyes on the cheap print of a poppy field that hung on the wall. In one hand a stubby bottle of unopened beer from the mini-bar, and in the other his phone. He was waiting for Keira to answer. Mariani wondered where she was. Maybe at the physio's, getting rehab on the knee she'd damaged so badly four months previously, rupturing the cruciate ligaments. He remembered when he had first seen her on the ice. Wearing navy tights. Spinning on one leg, the other pointing to the skies, a one-eighty-degree split. No man could be immune to that.

Her breathless voice brought him back to the present. 'Hi. Sorry. Hi. I was in the bathroom.'

'That's OK.'

'Everything all right?'

'Yes. Fine. You didn't watch?' Mariani stared at the poppies on the wall, imagined their red heads shaking in the wind.

'What?'

'On TV? You didn't see me get my giraffe?'

'It's happened already?'

'Twenty minutes ago.' He tried to keep the hurt from his voice.

'Oh. What time is it there?'

'Just past four.'

'Oh God. Is it? I'm sorry. I got my zones mixed up. It'll be on again later, for sure. On a sports channel. I'll see it then. How was it?'

'My giraffe? Fine. Nice soft ears.' He laughed.

'You sound disappointed.'

'I'm not. I wanted to win. Thought I could. Dreamed I could. But third is...' He coughed. 'Third is pretty good.'

'It's great, Romain. I'm so proud of you...Romain, hang on, Dad's trying to get through...don't go anywhere, OK?'

The line went dead. Mariani kept his eyes on the poppies. He opened the beer and took a pull. Gastein, Keira's father, had an extraordinary knack of phoning at the wrong times. She always took his calls; seemed unable to tell her father that she'd phone him back. Mariani began to time the interruption by his usual method of tapping his right foot on the floor at an even thirty beats a minute. The record was eighty-seven foot taps. He took another pull on the beer and made a growling noise in the back of his throat. He had never met Keira's father, simply knew he was a big name in the telecoms industry, rich, two metres tall, an ex-Olympic swimmer and very possessive of his daughter. In fact, he realised now, as the count reached fifty, he didn't even know Keira that well. He'd spent less than two weeks in total with her in the year since they had first met. They were always either travelling, competing or training. Even when Keira was injured, she'd had to spend time in America for surgery and post-op and now needed physio almost every day. Mariani hadn't seen her for over six weeks. As his foot taps went into the nineties, he felt his irritation rise. He'd got to ninety-six when she came back on the line.

'Sorry, Romain. Once he starts...'

'So. How's the knee?'

'Sore. Bandaged. Useless.' She sighed. 'When are you going home?'

'Tomorrow.'

'You'll get a hero's welcome, for sure.'

'Yes.' Mariani put on a mock-triumphant voice. 'Congratulations, Second Loser!'

'Romain — come on.'

'Just joking.' His fingers tightened on the beer bottle.

'Call me when you get in. You'll be drunk tonight, I guess.'

'A rider died. De Vilde.'

'Oh, God. An accident?'

'No.'

'How then?'

'In his sleep. No one is sure.'

Keira said nothing for a moment. Then: 'I don't like your sport, Romain.'

'I'll call you tomorrow.'

'OK. And you were brilliant – all right?'

Brilliant. Mariani knew that over the coming weeks, journalists would attach similar adjectives to his name. Why then was he so restless, so uneasy? There was still this emptiness in his guts, a need. Not just for food. Something had not been satisfied, but what it was he did not know.

As he rang off, there was a double-knock on the door. A voice outside, loud and pleased.

'Romain! I've got people, Romain. Nice people. People who want to improve your life.'

He shuffled to the door and opened it just enough to see Serge Hamptons's bleached teeth grinning back at him.

'What you doing in here?' asked the agent, stepping from foot to foot. 'Can I come in?' His solid, smooth forehead shone. He stroked it, happy with the effect of recent Botox treatments.

'I was just– '

'This is no time to be all Eastern European,' said Hamptons. 'No dark nights of the soul, please. Not today. Come downstairs and smile at certain people. Do that for thirty minutes and your kids will forever grateful. C'mon.'

'Is this bullshit?'

'Bullshit? No. Bullshit is moping about in your slippers, breaking wind and watching TV.'

Mariani laughed. 'I'm not watching TV.'

'Within half an hour, you could be the ambassador for Holland's second most-popular-brand of energy drink.' Hamptons reached into the inside pocket of his white linen jacket. He brought out a gleaming black Mont Blanc pen. 'It's new. Let's go break it in. Write some zeroes.'

'Some? How many is some? Two?'

'Two is two better than none,' said Hamptons, and smiled. His teeth were very white. 'Be happy, Romain. It's important to be happy. It's even more important to be rich.'

'I am happy. And I wouldn't mind being rich. It's just...de Vilde, you know. Makes you think.'

'Sure. Sure. Yep. Well, can you be happy downstairs?'

'I guess. Five minutes, OK?'

Eleven minutes later, Mariani pressed the lift-call button with the knuckle of his index finger, a hygiene safeguard against virus transfer that he'd learnt as soon as he'd turned pro. The lift came and he got in. Frowning, he watched the floor indicator as it went from three to one, the reverse of his fortunes during the last week. The doors parted and he wandered into the private room of the hotel. He was wearing a Gazin-Ségur PMP T-shirt with the names of seven other European companies on it.

For just over half an hour he drank champagne and ate smoked salmon and quail's eggs, none of which he particularly liked. He shook hands with two florid-faced Dutch marketing men and told them he thought their energy drink was the best on the market.

'That's great,' said one of them.

'Lekker is a great product,' said the other.

'Yes,' said Mariani. 'It is.'

He had never drunk a sip of Lekker.

When Serge Hamptons took the men from Lekker to a Michelin two-star restaurant, Mariani went with the other members of his team, the *soigneurs* and the mechanics to the swimming pool at the back of the hotel, took off his clothes and jumped in. Thirteen men, naked, drunk and happy, in a pool the size of a garage. They sang The Doors' 'Riders on the Storm', at the end of which several of them, overcome by comradely spirit and a sense of themselves as battling, tragic heroes, were tearful. They drank tepid champagne from the bottle. They reminisced about the season. Mariani was told a number of times that he would soon be working for Hans Banquo and asked twice that if he managed to sleep with Claudia Banquo, would he please make sure he had some kind of camera in the room? Frank, the hairy mechanic, threw up in the water and then apologetically baled it all out. The air was warm.

Mariani and Grasch found some space and floated on their backs, staring at the clear night sky.

'Do you think de Vilde is up there now, listening to 'I Want to Know What Love Is'?' asked Grasch.

'Wherever he is, I hope the pancakes are free.'

Grasch spouted water upwards from his mouth. 'I met Triesmaan once. Three years ago.'

'Why?'

'I was in a bad place. No form. Shocking legs. Remember? *Lanterne Rouge* in the Tour that year. I wanted to see what he had to say.'

'And?'

'I realised I wasn't that desperate. Or that brave.'

'Good.'

'It's easy to do the wrong thing,' said Grasch.

'When you're in a bad place, yes.'

'When you're in a good place, too.'

'Yes, then too,' said Mariani and remembered the sensation of standing close to Banquo in the square, transfixed by the blast of power and money and fame.

'You'd never dope, right?' asked Grasch, idly kicking his feet.

'Never.' Mariani flicked dismissively at the water. 'Look what it's done to the sport. Look what it did to my father. Ruined his career. Ruined his marriage. Ruined him.' He sighed angrily. 'Stupid old fart.'

He half-closed his eyes and saw a yellow-green bolus flying towards him in slow motion, felt it slap, semi-solid and warm, against his left cheek. He pictured the black-haired knuckles jabbing into his kidneys, the punch in the side of his neck and the rubber inner tube whipcracked across the back of his legs. Under the water, he clenched his fists.

Grasch stood up and looked around. He grinned at the chlorine-scented bacchanal and then put his hands on the edge of the pool and levered himself out. Mariani stayed where he was, looking up at the stars and wondering how many of them were like de Vilde: dead.

A minute or two later, he got out and put on his tracksuit. When the team passed round the traditional end-of-season cigarette, he took a puff. He was sick in some bushes. Then he went to bed.

The plane, decaled in mud-brown and bruise-purple, the national colours of Mariani's homeland, came in low over the dark forests and slow grey river. Rain spotted the windows. Crosswinds made it lurch. Mariani had to hold down an acrid belch. The pilot landed onto the more decrepit of Airport Central's two runways, and the jolt caused a plastic panel in the plane's ceiling to fall into the aisle. As they taxied, the vibrations caused by the pitted tarmac forced open the doors of three overhead compartments. A child's doll tumbled from one of them and hit the floor with a soft thump.

'Goodbye, sir,' said the potato-shaped hostess to Mariani as he left the plane, 'and thank you for flying with us.' She smiled, revealing a front tooth dabbed with dark orange lipstick. It had taken a moment to understand her. For over three months, he had hardly spoken the language of his birthplace.

'Thank you,' said Mariani. He had a hangover and felt terrible.

As he came past the yawning customs officials and into Arrivals, he imagined that his father might be waiting for him. A knot of apprehension formed amid the queasiness in his stomach. Tanel would find something spiteful or demeaning to say and Mariani was not in the mood to hold back.

'Romain...' A male voice, but not his father's nicotine-soaked bark.

A white light exploded in his face. He winced.

'Romain...over here...'

More cameras.

There were journalists too.

Mariani stood for a minute in his beanie, zip-up jacket and jeans and squinted at the flashpops. He smiled shyly and blinked his tired eyes. The journalists asked him how he felt. No man from his country had ever asked him that before. For many centuries his nation had favoured rule by paranoid autocrats. The most recent, 'Papa Jhö', Norgejhö Lihgrinjhi, was the last of the old guard of Communist dictators and had clung to power – and in truth, been allowed to do so by his subjects – long after his fellow Eastern European tyrants had been deposed. His malign influence was still evident: he had been publicly executed over a decade ago, but still no one felt comfortable talking openly. Public statements about personal feelings were regarded with suspicion.

So Mariani did not answer the journalists' questions. He thanked them and moved away. He looked around. He had called Herzy to let him know the time of the flight, but there was no sign of his elder brother's fleshy, wind-battered features.

Mariani shouldered his bag and walked towards the exit. Two cops patrolling the airport shook his hand. They both had ancient Soviet pistols in their holsters. The shorter man was mildly hunchbacked.

As he passed the news stand, Mariani saw his own face looking back at him from the cover of *Cycliska* magazine. He decided against buying a copy, thinking it would be immodest, but then, as he went through the main doors, wished he had. His thoughts were moving backwards and forwards. He had a feeling that a transition was coming and welcomed it, but sensed it would need careful handling. Actions had consequences.

He walked towards the taxi rank, bypassing the group of middle-aged prostitutes who had worked the airport for as long as he could remember.

'Suck it for two hundred?' asked the one with the red leather mini-skirt and varicose veins.

'Pick n' mix,' said the short, fat one in the blonde wig and mismatched tracksuit. She opened her red mouth, yawned and then half-heartedly rotated her thickly made-up jaw, making the same action with her pelvis. 'One hole for three hundred, two for five, three for six-fifty.'

Yes, he was home.

He climbed into the first of two waiting taxis. The driver, paunchy, mid-thirties, balding, and with a lush moustache, was listening to folk music and eating a cheese and meat *broshkt*.

'Çigi, please,' said Mariani. He could smell animal fat and tobacco.

'Çigi?'

'Take Road C. You turn off just before Grihgji.'

A large black crucifix on a beaded string dangled from the rear-view mirror. A piebald yellow-clawed *gruhkyk's* foot was somehow attached to the dashboard. Mariani lowered the window. Although his hangover was making him sweat, he pulled the beanie down to his eyebrows and put his jacket collar up. He hoped the driver did not recognise him or want to talk.

'Welcome back,' said the driver. 'We thought you'd keep second at least. What the devil happened?'

Mariani shrugged. 'I didn't eat enough.'

'Ach!' The driver handed back a grease-spotted bag of *broshkts*. 'Well, eat now. My lovely wife makes them.'

Mariani's stomach turned over. 'I had lunch on the plane. Thank you anyway.'

The driver put the car into gear and accelerated hard.

'And to lose it to the Australian mother-lover... Must hurt like the Devil's piles?'

'Worse.'

'See, it was the time-trial that did for you. You went too hard. Left too much on the road. You were in the real big meat. Wounds of God! What was it, the fifty-four eleven?'

'Yes, but— '

'I'd have been on a fifty-three twelve. Nothing bigger. Even on that girl's chest of a course. Those fifty-fours, those dinner plates, they're for the freaks and the dopers. Grasch, thighs like his, he'll churn it 'til St Konstantin's Day. But not you. What d'you weigh, seventy-four?'

'Seventy three point six.'

'Body fat? Six per cent?'

'Five point five.'

'Added together, that's seventy-nine point one total. You're under eighty total, you never go bigger than a fifty-three twelve. That's my law. The law of Stepan. That's me, hey? Stepan.'

The driver pulled another *broshkt* from the bag and ate it thoughtfully.

Mariani knew how quickly the people of his country – himself included – could slide into obsession, particularly in the decade since the death of Papa Jhö. They needed something to believe in and weren't too fussy about what.

'Chimney?' Stepan was pointing a crumpled brown soft-pack of Kleptas at Mariani.

'No, thanks.'

'Good boy.' Stepan shook one from the packet and lit it. 'You could win a big one,' he said, through the smoke. 'You've got the equipment. Your father never had that.'

Mariani nodded, shrugged and opened the window further. In his head, he repeated Stepan's last comment. He could not suppress a smile.

'Read this?' asked the driver, holding up *Cycliska*.

'No.'

'Bit of a hatchet job, questions your consistency, but not bad. Here, on me.'

He threw the magazine onto the back seat. 'Bad news about the Belgian, too. Hooched up, was he?'

'No idea, sorry.' Mariani did have an idea, but it was not something to be discussed in public with strangers. Anyone outside the sport found it difficult to understand the tradition within it – mostly drugs-spawned – of denial, intrigue and paranoia.

'Dah,' said Stepan dismissively. 'Can't ride fair, you shouldn't ride at all.'

Mariani was happy to agree with that statement and did so.

The taxi sped along Road C for another ten minutes, swinging between the two lanes without indicating, beeping non-stop at the vans and lorries. They passed two accidents: the car involved in one of them looked to Mariani as if it had been flayed and its innards strewn across the carriageway. Neither incident was attended by the police. Stepan hummed along to the folk music on the radio and smoked. He belched now and then. Grey-black mountains appeared ahead, snow splattered on the top of several. The rain thickened.

'Nice day,' said Stepan.

'Beautiful,' said Mariani. The pale grey sky was easy on his eyes after days of being blasted by sunshine. His gaze drifted down to the gaunt ruins of the collective farm, abandoned for nearly ten years. 'You want the next right.'

They turned off the highway and on to the long, twisting road that led up to the village. The woods became denser. The occasional retort of a rifle echoed. Ramshackle, lurching houses became visible between twisted mediaeval oaks. Forest people standing outside them, the Giûrgïu.

Mariani had often passed them while walking in the woods. Their primitive brown faces were lined as bark, and their clouded eyes barely moved. They seemed fashioned from the earth. Mumbling cadaverous hags. Male bruisers with black, toothless mouths. From a distance, he'd once seen a small crouching boy pull the pelt off a hare in ten seconds. On another occasion, he'd been surprised by the sight of a pair of girl twins, beautiful in ways forgotten now, sitting on a branch ten metres above the ground. They all wore shapeless clothes in shades of soil and silt.

Stepan slowed to look across. '*Jeszu*, this country's gone downhill. Worse than Albanians, that lot. Real scum. Everywhere, too. No better than their dogs.'

These were *dorneis,* bad-tempered, big-shouldered mongrels, rumoured to mate with wolves and bred to bite. Lumbering and sniffing and slavering, their dull eyes flickering nervously towards their owners. One of them howled at the car.

'You'll be in the pot tonight,' yelled Stepan. He put his hand out of the window and made the three-fingered gesture of ridicule. 'They eat those mangy curs,' he shouted back to Mariani.

From behind a tree stepped a blockheaded dwarfboy. He stared at Mariani who raised his hand in greeting. The boy smiled hugely and then waved, moving his arm metronomically from the elbow as if polishing a window.

'You know that *spacker*?' asked Stepan.

'Hangs around the local café.'

'Hope he doesn't do the cooking.'

Stepan accelerated and the wheels slipped on the old and crumbling tarmac surface. There were no warning signs on the sharp bends. From time to time, the side of the road just dropped away.

'You train on this?' asked Stepan.

'Sure.'

A sudden left-hand bend had him braking hard. Mariani was jerked forward into the back of the passenger seat.

'Shit of the devil!' said Stepan. 'Apologies.'

'Curse Corner,' said Mariani. 'Everyone swears here. You need to know this road.'

'P'haps you could use some of the loot from your new contract to have it resurfaced?'

'Yes. Though I want to pay off the national debt and install a hydro-electric dam in the valley first. Oh, and build a new hospital,' Mariani deadpanned.

Stepan nodded and then shook his head: the *lijzki* was the national gesture that communicated appreciation of humour.

He drove on, just avoiding a filthy green transit that came hurtling towards them on the wrong side of the road, the spare wheel wobbling on its left-rear axle.

It was gone six-thirty by the time they arrived at Çigi. The clouds had faded and a slanting light threw gentle late-September sun on to gardens and plots. Shadows stretched.

'So, what are your plans for next season?'

'Do better. Eat more. Next left, please.'

Mariani's house was at the top of the village. Built from dark local stone, its roof was two shades darker, almost black. The front door was painted white. He was happy to see the place. He wanted to sleep in his own bed and watch his own TV and wear his old slippers. He would lie in the hammock and listen to the wind and for a few weeks at least forget the whole crazy circus.

'The luck of St Konstantin to you,' said Stepan. 'A big one next year, remember.'

'Thanks for the magazine.'

Mariani paid and tipped Stepan thirty *chõp*, a quarter of the fare. He walked up the path and unlocked the front door. The house was chilly inside and he stood for a moment, feeling the cold air drift around his face. He put his bag down in the hall and then wandered from room to room: he'd been away for nearly three months. Spiderleavings clung to his face.

No one would have known a professional athlete lived here. Mariani kept the trophies he'd won as an amateur in a cupboard in his training room. There were no photographs on the wall. It was not time to look back yet. That was for later, perhaps, when he was retired. One hundred kilos and twenty-five per cent body fat. Face the colour of his cock end. A pullover, elastic-waisted slacks and a little dog called Eddy.

Svarik, the owner of the village café, had left him a tin of coffee and a litre of milk in the fridge. A note with them: 'Free beer for a ~~month week~~ month.' Svarik's wife Varta looked after the house while Mariani was away. She had filled a bowl with fruit and put lilacs in a vase, polished what little furniture he had and placed his battered leather slippers, the colour of ox-blood, at the bottom of his bed. His mail was arranged neatly on the kitchen table, utilities bills opened and unfolded, the 'pay by' dates ringed red. Mariani liked living alone, but was not good at it. There was often no food in the fridge. 'Your head only works when there's a helmet on top of it,' Varta would say. As always, she'd left him the last fortnight's issues of *Fair and True* and Mariani looked quickly through the headlines, all of which belied the newspaper's name. The paper, with little else to write about, fanatically sustained the country's rural and urban myths and regularly featured stories of malicious adolescent snoop The Listening Girl, Nanniçkh the Mad Monk, and the legendary Golgotha, the omnivorous feral hog with human eyes. Nanniçkh was now stalking the cities allegedly: outside Dringl's nightclub he'd supposedly carried out a frenzied sexual assault on a middle-aged woman while simultaneously begging her to forgive him. Reports of Golgotha had been fewer in recent years but, Mariani noted as he flicked through the pages, the beast seemed suddenly to have become more active, and only last Tuesday, claimed the paper, had killed and eaten a bull. Mariani felt an odd, almost electric, sensation trail down his spine.

Once, when they were boys, Herzy claimed to have seen Golgotha feeding on a freshly slaughtered dog's warm and steaming entrails. The thing was a brute, he'd said, like the Devil's pet, and as it lapped and chomped it had grunted happily, its tail twitching and its blue eyes wide with pleasure. Whether his brother was lying or not, Golgotha had always seemed to Mariani to have more substance than these other chimeras. He had sometimes visualised the beast while riding in breakaways or time-trials, and tried to siphon some of its nightmarish power into his own body. He carefully read all the latest details of its savagery and appetites: the tone of the pieces appeared almost awe-struck. It seemed to him that the animal was being turned into something of a celebrity. For a moment, Mariani imagined himself and Golgotha together as some kind of national double act. He smiled and shook his head at the craziness of the thought.

He picked up his bag, went into the bedroom and sat on the dark grey eiderdown that covered the bed. He knew it was sentimental to keep the house, but he would never sell. He'd bought it when he'd turned pro. Price six hundred and fifty-five thousand *chōp*, fifty-five thousand euros. Well over his annual salary at the time. How often was he here…fifty nights a year? Next season he would have to buy somewhere in Spain or France and stop renting apartments with Grasch. This house had four flights of stairs, unthinkable for a cyclist: stairs were evil, unnecessary effort and notoriously bad for your knees. The treads here creaked loudly, as if warning what they might do to his patellae. Although Mariani had moved his bedroom to the ground floor, his bathroom was still on the first. 'How do you manage?' Grasch had asked in all seriousness. 'Wash in the kitchen sink and dump in a bucket?'

It was very quiet in the house. His headache was fading and his stomach had settled. He unzipped his holdall and emptied the contents onto the floorboards, which were stained the colour of strong coffee.

Yawning, he got up. He kicked his washing into a corner and left the bedroom. He unlocked the back door, the key sticking in the corroded mechanism. The wood was warped and he had to shoulder it open. Outside, Varta had cut the grass and strung up the hammock between the two cherry trees. If it wasn't raining this would be where he would spend tomorrow. The early-evening light was beginning to fade. The sun seemed far away and he liked that. A purple lid of cloud hung in the east and let through just a few soft rays. The breeze stroked his cheeks and brought with it the smells of cooking. He was suddenly hungry.

*

Mariani ate dinner at a chipped, unsteady wooden table in Svarik's café:

hogget – year-old lamb – medium-rare with *matjkes,* chestnut and garlic dumplings. He drank half-litres of strong black Vighü beer, brewed by the bearded silent monks of the local monastery.

After two months of rice, chicken, pasta, egg, pureed fruit, this rich, dense food felt sinful. He had missed red meat with an ache. It was, he reflected, like a drug to him. Varta watched as he wiped the crimson-brown poolings of blood and fat off his plate with a slice of heavy black-brown seeded bread. The air was fugged with tobacco smoke and carbonised animal protein.

Mariani sat back with the happy sensation that he was home. He had inherited more English genes than his dark-skinned, cricket-hating brother Herzy, but had always seen England as a very foreign country and knew he would never cut himself off from the land where he had been raised. Not that this tiny, toe-shaped nation of just over one million people had much to boast about. Grasch called it a pisspot, and in many ways it was worse than that. The unemployment rate was thirty per cent. There was rain on two hundred and fifty days of the year. Last summer, they'd even had a small earthquake. But, Mariani thought, as he licked grease off his lips, the hogget was the best in the world.

Nothing had changed in the café. There were always *matjkes* to eat and Vighü to drink. There were always three other men sitting at a table quaffing clear *sotinko* liquor, calmly and solidly, all at the same workmanlike rate. They always wore undershirts and slippers without socks, as if they were sitting in their own front room. There was always a woman in a patched housecoat trying to talk to one of them, and she was always ignored. Svarik always had an unlit cigarette slanting from his mouth.

'We had a Giûrgïi in this afternoon,' said Varta. 'Wanted to sell us a stereo. Bang & Olufsen, he kept telling us. Five hundred *chõp.*'

Mariani laughed. 'Probably made it themselves.'

'It was purple and orange.' Varta shook her head. 'The stuff they've got. "We Giûrgïi. You want anyffin, we get it,"' said Varta, impersonating the harsh-edged, choppy accent of the forest people.

'Yeah. I read in *Fair and True* they'll sell you a baby for a thousand – not bad,' said Mariani. He was already quite drunk.

'Hey. I'm running for Area Sub-governor,' said Varta, as she took his plate.

'But you're not sixty-five, obese and a crook.'

'All we do is complain. Thought I'd try and do something instead.'

'Careful. That's an unpatriotic statement.'

'You sound like Svarik. Sometimes I think he wishes Papa Jhö were still alive.'

'Who says he isn't? I saw in the paper he was spotted yesterday at a cattle show. Still wearing that cardigan, too.'

'Ach. Will we ever be rid of him? He's a wound that never heals. Why can't we move on? We're all just floating in this limbo. No direction. No wonder we lap up all this nonsense. I heard some idiot has even set up a website for that pig thing…for sightings and God knows what.'

Mariani looked up. 'For Golgotha?'

'All this rubbish from the past…' Varta sighed.

Mariani forked the last of the hogget into his mouth. He thought he might Google that website when he got home. On the internet he had found many 'Golgotha' postings, almost all of which were, disappointingly, teenage boys' blurry homemade videos of their dogs running around in distant fields, set to thrash-metal soundtracks.

'Seen your father?' asked Varta.

'Who?'

She clicked her tongue. 'And Herzy?'

'He called earlier. He meant to come tonight but there's a problem with a pregnant gilt.'

Varta took his plate and brought back a bowl of *franzyxk*, cream pudding with chestnut custard.

'I'll burst,' said Mariani.

'All right.' Varta lifted the bowl off the table.

'*Jeszu*, put that back!'

'One more beer?'

'Since Svarik's paying.'

'Then coffee?'

'If I must.'

The previous Christmas, Mariani had brought Svarik a Brasilia Opus Sublima coffee machine.

'The only one in the country,' he had said as Svarik hesitantly untied the red bow. 'Makes the world's finest espressos.'

Svarik had yet to master it. The coffee still had the consistency and colour of creosote and for some reason, the endocrinal tang of Varta's speciality, *gruhkyk* pâté.

After three cups, Mariani walked the long way home, through the silent dark village. His stomach felt swollen and his mouth was claggy with yeasts, sugars and fats. For a moment, he was a pig farmer on his way back from a night with his pig-farming friends: he should stagger home now and slap his wife before passing out in front of the fire, loyal bloodhound at his feet. In fact, he reflected, he would quite like a dog, but it would be impossible.

Thoughts swept through his mind on a wave of strong beer.

Hans Banquo had a dog. And a wife. He wondered if that marvellous couple were kicking back with a plate of wurst and a stein or two. No. Probably eating macrobiotic tofu on a sun-kissed island with Chris Martin and Gwyneth Paltrow. He wondered if he should get some tofu. He'd have to order it over the internet. He remembered how Banquo's wife had looked at him. She was one of those icy beauties, a bit scary, arms like wire, made her husband look fat. Wasn't she heiress to some Swiss fortune or another? Chocolate, was it? Banking? He couldn't remember. 'Maybe chocolate money?' he murmured with a smirk. He wondered what her photographs would be like. Landscapes? Self-portraits? Nudes? Self-portrait nudes in landscapes?

A clear space opened up in his blurry head. Why, when she crossed the square, had he felt that she was his wife? Strangely, he didn't find her very attractive. It was rather that for a moment, he had imagined that it was he, Romain Mariani, who was the world's best cyclist, not Hans Banquo. That nipping, nagging sensation returned, just behind his navel. Hoping to quieten it, he rubbed his hand across his stomach. He remembered the conversation in the swimming pool with Grasch. *It's easy to do the wrong thing...*

He blinked and, with an effort, shifted his thoughts. He pictured Keira.

Lovely Keira. The softness of her skin just below her ears. The way her calf fitted so perfectly into his hand. The hardness of her vertebrae against his tongue.

He hadn't called her, though. He took her for granted. That was bad. He hadn't done a lot of other things, either. Last month, he'd forgotten Herzy's birthday. He hadn't been to his mother's grave for three years. Or patched things up with his father. He hadn't even paid his slate at the café: he must owe thousands now. He should try harder to think of other people, not just himself and cycling. Cycling, cycling, cycling. He made a 'Pffft' sound and sighed: now he was maudlin. A bike jockey. Was that all he was? A damn bike jockey, a set of gears for a brain? Per-haps – because now he couldn't help but remember the other thing he hadn't done: gone up a mountain faster than that *trejanzk* Mitchell. The thought stuck. Now he wasn't maudlin. He was angry.

'Loser!' he said to himself, suddenly and helplessly furious. 'Wel-come home, Second Loser!' He shouted the words into the big, empty night.

The sound faded. The village was silent. Mariani began to wonder if there was something wrong with him; probably too much Vighü on top of too much sun.

The church bell rang weakly. He stopped to look at the frescoes on the turret, of peaceful saints and cavorting animals. They were bleached and pitted. The graves needed tending, lichens grew on the stones. His mother was lying in one of them. He slowed, thought about going in but did not. Under his heart, he felt a stab of sorrow. He could still smell the fresh, damp soil and the flowers and his father's cigarette smoke, the sour tang of drink on the priest's breath. He could still picture her lifeless and strangely relaxed face. He growled and shook his head, trying to clear it. The growl seemed to mutate into the angry snort of an irritated boar and he wondered if that was the sound Gol-gotha made.

He walked up to the path to the house. The window in the front room glowed pale yellow.

Mariani frowned. He hated leaving lights on. He went to open the door, but it swung back before he could put the key in the lock.

'Hey…wha– '

'Late. Drunk. Reeking of garlic. Once a pig farmer…'

He grinned and followed Keira inside. Now he was neither maudlin nor angry.

He did not fall asleep in front of the fire.

'You were moaning in the night.' Keira sipped the coffee Mariani had just made.

'Bad dream.' He kicked off his slippers and got back into bed. 'Shouldn't eat *matjkes.*'

'So weird,' she said, staring at his white torso and burnished arms, the hewn face and neck. She drew back the covers, looked at all of him. Knee to hip just slabs of protein.

'Will you put on much weight now? You're like an anorexic chicken.' She ran a finger up the ridges of his ribs as if playing an instrument. 'Is that your liver I can see?'

He covered himself with the sheets, momentarily ashamed.

'You're hardly any better.' He put his thumb and finger around her wrist. It felt as fragile as a child's. Yet he'd seen her strength: she could do vertical push-ups, her body as straight and rigid as a bike's top tube.

'What were you dreaming about?'

'Anorexic chickens.' In fact, he'd dreamt of pigs, screaming for their food. Their mouthfroth, the crazed greed in their tiny glittering eyes. The sense they gave that they would eat anything at all, nuclear waste, anything, just didn't care, as long as their guts were filled and they could live another minute longer. And somewhere in the background of all these visions was a huge black shadow, silhouetted tusks curling from its mouth, never truly showing itself until a final sudden split-second close-up in which its slavering chops and curved yellowing teeth were plunging into a ghastly mass of meat and blood, the nature of which was somehow obscene. The animal's big round blue eyes stared laconically, and its gnashings and slurpings were so real to Mariani that he'd woken with a lurching heart, gagging, and frantically wiped his tongue and the inside of his mouth on the pillowcase.

He resolved to stop reading stupid stories in the paper: that damn hog was giving him nightmares.

Keira looked pensive as she sipped her coffee.

'Romain, what happened to the rider who died?'

Mariani's face tightened. 'He stopped breathing.'

'You know what I mean. Drugs?'

He shrugged.

Keira nudged him with her elbow. 'You must have an opinion?'

'I don't know the facts.'

'I'm not a journalist, Romain. I don't have a tape recorder under the pillow. If you tell me you won't be… what do you call it?'

'Spitting in the soup.'

'Exactly. Well?'

'What would you like for breakfast?' Knowing he had nothing.

She frowned at him. 'Romain – you don't take anything, do you? Romain?'

'What would you like for breakfast?'

'Romain!'

He looked into her eyes. The fleck of black in the green iris of the left one. 'I have never doped. I will never dope. Doping makes monsters. It takes over your soul. Now – breakfast,' he said, and licked her breasts.

He hoped Svarik's was open. It was. Keira only wanted a plain roll. As he walked back, thoughts about her replaced his bad dreams. He worried she didn't eat enough: she'd also spent a long time locked silently in the bathroom before they got into bed. He thought of the vein in her bicep. It was hard and evident, a blue cord. Her breasts felt smaller. Her ass was disappearing. She continually mentioned food but hardly seemed to eat. Mariani frowned: did she have 'issues'? Grasch had told him that German female cyclists seemed to believe that throwing up was now an essential part of training: if you missed a 'session' in the bathroom you were seen as unprofessional. But Keira had always seemed so calm, so content, rare in an athlete. Did she secretly feel the need to punish herself in that way? He wondered if the injury might be getting to her. He resolved at least to make her have butter on her roll – and then remembered he didn't have any.

*

Keira had to leave in the afternoon. She had an appointment with her surgeon in New York on the next day and had to catch a flight to London that night to make the connection.

Mariani called her a taxi. As they waited, still in bed, leaving it until the very last moment to get dressed, they talked about their fathers. Mariani detailed Tanel's violence, his hate-streaked ambition for his son and his twisted attitude to the sport and drug use in it. When Keira described her own father's smothering love, how much he needed to see her and talk to her, Mariani realised that the relationship was in many ways a benign reflection of the toxic one he had with Tanel. She kept pictures of Gastein on the gold phone his company produced, while Mariani had to turn to Google for images of Tanel. ('You look quite like him,' she'd said, to his disappointment.) For her last birthday, her twenty-fifth, she had received a five-carat diamond and a Warhol illustration of a pair of court shoes from her father, while for the previous seven years, Tanel had not even sent his son so much as a text. But when she confessed that she thought her father was moulding her into some ideal he carried in his head, the perfect embodiment of the rich man's daughter, Mariani knew that Gastein and Tanel, one wealthy and tall, the other poor and short, were more alike than they were different. He and Keira were both tied to ogre-like men.

*

A dusty blue Gourovsko estate with a bald tyre and a one-eyed dog in the back took her away to the airport. They hadn't said anything about seeing each other again; there seemed to be a mutual trust, deepened by their conversation about their fathers.

Mariani watched the taxi disappear. Sadness bloomed inside him. He wanted to see more of her, but knew that he did not need the distractions and difficulties of a full-time, long-distance relationship. It would be unfair on Keira to pretend he did. He felt he was on the verge of some kind of transition in his sport and he had to keep that foremost in his mind. All the truly successful athletes he knew or had read about were the same. He closed his eyes for a moment and brought his fingers to the lids. His eyeballs seemed to be vibrating. It felt as if new connections were being made inside him.

There was a deep grumble of thunder. Rain, fine but heavy, began to wet his face. He had planned to spend an hour cloud-watching in his hammock, but instead he went inside.

He lay on the couch, closed his eyes and listened to the rain. His legs were tired, his mind more tired still. Forty-five-thousand-kilometres-in-a-year tired.

Once, his body had been a mystery to him. Now he understood most of the signs and could decode the signals. It was still a war, at times, between what he wanted his body to do and what it would agree to. In last week's time-trial, he'd felt unstoppable, his legs like a turbine powering him to a surprising victory. When, as stage winner, he went to give his sample, he'd seen knowing headshakes – 'like father, like son'. But then, on the mountain, five days later, the spirit had skulked away and he was left on the road like carrion. His body could still confuse him. Lie to him even. He didn't know what to make of that 'inefficiency', his craving for protein. It irked him that he couldn't master it.

Outside, the light began to lose its soft bullion lustre and slowly he followed the world into darkness.

He woke six hours later. The phone was ringing.

He reached over and picked up.

'You wasn't going to call me?'

Mariani's fingers tensed on the handset. 'Tonight.'

'Is tonight.'

'Later.'

'Liar.'

'As you like.'

He heard his father mouth-breathing. Then the crackle of burning tobacco as Tanel took a hard suck on a cigarette. Was he still smoking Nistanjhi? The cigarettes so addictive they'd been classified as a Class-C drug and were available only on the black market.

'Anyway,' said Tanel, and coughed, 'you fucked up gigantic. Wounds of God! What happened on the climb, eh?'

'Search me.' Mariani tried to make his tone indifferent.

'You let yourself down. This ain't criticism. It's the truth.'

'Maybe.'

'You need to hear it. The old team managers would shred you alive for cracking like that. Nowadays, you all think you're celebrities, hey? Untouchables. All out for yourselves. Think you shit gold turds. Look at that kraut ponce…'

'Banquo's all right. And he's *Austrian*.'

'Austrian ponce. Helicopters. Those bloody adverts. Ach! For the love of St Konstantin.'

Mariani's composure began to break. 'Your ass is on your head. How much have you had?'

'Don't be like that. Hey?' whined Tanel. 'How about you buy the old man dinner?' He coughed thinly. He sounded consumptive.

'Think you can bear to be seen with me?'

'I'm proud of you. I want you to be a champion. Ach! To see my son in a yellow jersey, I could die happy.'

'Yellow jersey? Oh, that's so easy.'

'Make it quick, eh? I ain't got long.'

'Don't talk that way.'

'Fifty-three. Then I'm God's. Or more likely the Devil's. Two years.'

'I'll order the stone now, then.'

'Don't bother. Save your loot. Ach. Just feed me to the pigs.'

It was the old conversation, the old wounds. Round and round they went, like bitter opponents in some old-style criterium race, no time limit, last man still on his bike wins. Why couldn't he simply forget Tanel? After all the years of his father's self-pity and self-delusion, his cajoling and humiliations, his fierce defence of his drug use – 'That was what we did. It was part of being a rider, part of the tradition. Clean riders are traitors!' – and his arguments for his son to do the same: 'You can do it if you dope. Why be less of a rider than you could be, hey? Anyway, they're all still on it – you'll kill yourself trying to keep up!' Mariani still could not shut out Tanel's hoarse, grating whisper. As he listened, the familiar cold hand reached out from the past to grip his heart.

'Buy me a nice dinner.' The tobacco-crackle again. 'Take me to Hoxtia. We'll share that leg of roast kid they do – with that sweetbread sauce. We'll work out a plan for next season. Eh? Together. Like we used to. Hey?'

Mariani shut his eyes. He was on the mountain again, every cell exhausted.

'All right. No shouting this time.'

'I shouted because you wasn't listening…'

'I wasn't listening because you were talking donkey shit…'

Later, Mariani lay in bed. A cool silent breeze that had carried the scent of pines south across the Russian steppe and then over the cold high mountains came in at the window. Despite it, he was hot and lay awake.

FiVE

Mariani had been fourteen the first time his father had talked about drugs. Many banned riders, even in retirement, protested their innocence. Tanel did not. In a way, Mariani gave him credit for that.

'To win, you got to charge. To even compete – you got to charge. We all charged. Nice guys, arseholes, kids, veterans. All lit up, full headlights. When I first started nobody made a fuss. It weren't illegal. There was no controls. You took it the same way you'd wipe your ass with bog roll. How the hell else was we supposed to ride those tours and classics, hey? At those speeds, hey? You ride pro, you need drugs like you need a fucking bike.'

Mariani had looked at his father as he talked. Tanel's eyes were moist with pasty rheum. Though he now had a half-football paunch, he appeared fragile and his arms were thin-skinned and spidery.

'With your talent, you'll get noticed. You'll get a contract, place in a team. You'll want to perform, belong, be accepted, earn your money. Hey? But you'll keep coming in last. Why? Shit of the Devil! You can't understand it. You know you've got the strength. But suddenly you're no good. Those kids you're tearing the balls off now – they're tearing *your* balls off. Ach! You'll get looks. You'll hear whispers – another cream cake rookie. If you're lucky someone might help. A *soigneur* might take pity on you. "Here," he'll say, "here's the difference between a nice career in the best sport in the world and running a pig farm. Choose, rookie. Good money, banging your choice of podium girls, respect from the hardest men on the planet? Or a life spent knee-deep in stinking shit?" And in his hand will be a little white pill. It won't kill you. It won't harm you in any way. It'll only do you good.'

They were in the car, the clattery old bile-green Gourovsko four-door, coming back from a junior race. Mariani had crashed out in the final sprint. There was still grit in the gleaming wound on his elbow. Road rash on his lower left leg. His head hurt. Thin thighs, pale and cold, stuck out of ripped, soaked shorts. Both bike wheels were in his lap. The kinked frame was on the back seat. He was starving.

'You could be great. Trust me, hey? I rode with LeMond. Fignon. I know what the best look like and you look like that. You could be up there. Champs-Élysées, say, ten years from now. On top of that podium, raising your arms, the national anthem playing, dah-dah dah-dah-dah, the winner of the biggest, toughest sporting event in the fucking world! My son! Imagine, eh? Ha ha!'

Tanel steered the car with his knees, lit a Nistanjhi full-strength filterless, and with his other hand pensively scratched his crotch.

'It's tricky now, though. When I started it were Tonton and Tintin, nice little blasters…in the ass, boom! Make you chatter like a woman, go like a wild boar with its balls on fire. Beautiful. If we wanted something special, we'd club together and get Mr Sixty to break into a hospital and filch us a few treats. Hah! Mr Sixty — that were his haematocrit level, highest ever recorded! Genius burglar, too. These days, it's like chemical warfare. Human Growth Hormone today, the Devil knows what tomorrow. Still, that's progress, eh?'

Tanel cackled as he put his hands back on the wheel and turned the rattling Gourovsko down the rutted path to the farm.

*

Mariani sat at Hoxtia's best table. He picked a second bread roll to pieces and continued looking at the stuffed animals displayed at various points on the floor and walls. The *gruhkyk,* a large and vicious stoat, stared back at him with empty eyes.

He checked his watch. Ten minutes later, he pushed back his chair and stood, angry only with himself for turning up.

He retrieved his jacket from the cloakroom. As he went out through the restaurant's door, Tanel was outside coming towards it. He had a cigarette in his mouth. He didn't see his son. Mariani banged into him, hard.

'Clumsy fuck,' said Tanel.

'You're late. And drunk.'

His father swayed in the dim streetlight. The industrial grey smoke of a Nistanjhi drifted from his mouth. His face seemed more wrecked than ever, falling in on itself. He looked like a drunken bat. 'I'm here now. Lemme finish my chimney and we'll go in. Let's get at that kid. Hey?'

'I'm not eating with you.'

'No? Brought dessert, too. See?'

From his pocket Tanel produced an ampoule of clear liquid. He held it up to the light. The glass sparkled.

'Hey?' whispered Tanel. 'Special delivery from Mr Sixty. Only the best for my boy.'

Mariani turned, walked away. Tanel stumbled after him.

'Wassa problem? Only a *pot belge*...little heroin, little cocaine, coupla other goodies...it'll take that frown off your face. C'mon, let's break your cherry, eh? I'll light you up. Issa present for being a hero.'

Mariani kept going. Then he felt a bang against his ear as if a door had been slammed on it. His vision blurred. His knees softened. His neck muscles seemed to have disappeared.

'Don't walk away from me, boy. Ever.'

Tanel stood, flexing the fingers of his right hand, his lips twisted, Nistanjhi still in his mouth.

Though only semi-conscious, Mariani still heard the faint plea in the serrated voice. Tanel stepped towards him and put a hand on his shoulder.

'Hey, son... Romi. Hey. Is me, your old dad, eh? No need for us to fight. Eh?'

Fireflies in team colours were still dancing in front of Mariani's eyes. His father was patting his shoulder, rubbing the skin through the shirt. Mariani saw Tanel transfer a small syringe, its plunger pulled back, from his left hand to his right. His brain had a moment's clarity: it found the truth of what was about to happen difficult to accept, but told him to act.

He brought his left forearm up hard, straight into the underside of his father's nose. Tanel dropped the syringe on the dark slick cobbles and put both hands to his face. He moaned and bent over. The nub of his cigarette dropped out of his mouth and then he vomited weakly. He spat bubbled strings.

Mariani stepped on the ampoule, heard it crunch and walked away.

He went home, undressed and had a long hard piss, imagining his father's face just under the surface of the water in the toilet bowl. When he'd finished, he shook, and then spat into the bowl. He slammed the lid. He couldn't imagine speaking to Tanel again, though this was probably the tenth time he'd had that thought.

He sat on the edge of the bath until his head had cooled. Then he stood on the U-Analyser. After two weeks of *matjkes* and indolence, he was up to eighty point three kilos and just under nine per cent body fat. He looked at himself in the mirror. His legs weren't just sinew and bone veneered with skin, they had a depth of flesh. Already he was beginning to feel the urge to spin pedals round the cranks and speed blood round his veins. Feel the thud of his heart against his ribs and see the numbers climb on the power meter. One more week and he'd open up the training room. Thoughts of a new season and potential success cleared Tanel completely from his mind.

He went downstairs into the front room and flicked through the day's edition of *Fair and True*. The wife of Jinchi Nil, the country's most famous footballer, was filing for divorce after receiving evidence from The Listening Girl of her husband's obsessive love for a rent boy. Nanniçkh had followed a Macedonian woman into her hotel room and forced her to apply red lipstick to her nipples as he read aloud from the *Book of Revelations*. And there had been another Golgotha sighting, this time no more than forty kilometres from the house.

This screwed-up country, thought Mariani, and then imagined coming face to face with the animal: he pictured it snorting, with scraps of gore on its chops and nothing at all in its big front-facing blue eyes. The thought excited him and a hot thrill wired through his stomach and then shot into his throat. It was as if the thing was starting to haunt him. Thank Christ he'd never found that website.

He got into bed and, after jerking awake several times, fell asleep to night sounds. Feral cats fighting. A black owl making its soft, fluting call. A sudden squall of rain splattering against the windows. Creaks of the hammock's fastenings in the pulsing wind.

He awoke to a loud mechanical clattering. It came from the skies and sounded like an invasion had started. He frowned and looked out of the window. The din passed away into the distance, then stopped. He got up slowly. In the kitchen, he started to make coffee. As the kettle was boiling, there were three polite but solid taps on the front door. Mariani mumbled curses, tightened the cord on his dressing gown, went to the door and opened it.

'*Guten Morgen.*'

A man dressed in a yellow tracksuit and tangerine trainers. Buzz-cut, dark coppery hair. Around his shoulders a belted green collarless jacket. Mirrored, white-framed sunglasses. A soft black leather holdall in his hand.

'I was passing.'

'Yes?' asked Mariani. He stood in the doorway for a moment, his own thickly-stubbled face and unruly early-morning hair reflected in the mirror lenses. Then the man smiled with no humour. Mariani's mouth went dry. Why, he thought, was Hans Banquo knocking on his door at nine o'clock on a Tuesday morning?

'I parked in a field at the bottom of the village.'

'Parked?'

'I won't get a ticket?'

Mariani opened the door wider and then led Banquo into the kitchen. He wished he were not wearing his dressing gown and slippers. He ran his hand across his head, patting at the springy tufts on his crown.

'Coffee?'

'For sure.' Banquo looked around. 'Nice place. Quiet.'

'Thank you.'

'You live alone?'

'Yes.'

'I'm never alone. I have forgotten what it's like.'

Mariani gave his least chipped and biggest mug to Banquo and poured coffee into it. 'Breakfast?'

'I don't have much time.' Banquo went to drink from the mug, but something, the aroma perhaps, put him off. 'We'll have this and go, yes?'

'Yes, all right.'

Mariani waited to be told his destination. There was a short silence.

'Have you been on the bike?' asked Banquo.

'No.'

'Nor me. I have been doing some water-skiing. And swimming. I swim round the island.'

'The island?'

'The island I have.'

Mariani nodded. 'Is it nice?'

'I like it. It's where I breed my mini-horses.'

Mariani nodded more slowly. 'Is it a big island?'

'It suits my needs.'

'Do you eat tofu there?'

'What?'

'Oh, nothing.' Mariani shook his head. He didn't always think straight in the mornings. Should he be making jokes at the expense of his sport's most powerful figure? Probably not.

Banquo put the coffee down untouched and looked quickly at his big steel watch.

'Shall we?' He began unzipping his holdall.

'Of course,' said Mariani. He waited to see what Banquo would take out of his bag.

'I need to be out of here by one. So…three and a half hours.'

'That's fine.'

'Going in your dressing gown?'

'Oh. No, I was…'

Banquo brought out a pair of his 'Hansi' brand bike shoes, in white. At least Mariani now understood what he was supposed to be doing. Why was a different question.

'Let's say one hundred and twenty kilometres. No more than five hundred metres of climbing.'

'Fine. Er, you have a bike?'

'In a minute.' Banquo took an iPhone from his jacket pocket.

Mariani went out of the kitchen and into the hall. His mind began to work.

He picked up a key from the small table by the front door and then un-locked the stripped wooden door at the back of the hall. He pushed it open. Inside was a bare room. French doors that once opened onto the garden, but whose lock was now solid with corrosion. In the centre of the room stood a bike attached to a stationary trainer, a blue sweat mat under it. The trainer was linked to a computer. Three more bikes hung on the walls. On a bench, six pairs of cycling shoes. On a shelf, ten different saddles. A metre-high pile of tyres on the concrete floor.

Mariani hadn't been in here for nearly four months.

He took a jersey and bib tights from the drawer and changed as quickly as he could, took a bike from the wall, rapidly pumped both tyres and wheeled it back into the hall. Banquo was waiting by the open front door. Apart from his shoes his kit was dark grey, anonymous. Outside stood a bike in the same colour; the fifty millimetre-deep rims on the wheels also matched. Mariani decided not to ask where the bike had come from.

He had not even brushed his teeth. Or eaten. Was there time? Banquo was already free-wheeling down the path.

Mariani filled bidons with water and put an apple, the only portable food in the house apart from a grey furred lemon and five potatoes, in the back pocket of his jersey. He grabbed his keys, pushed his bike out of the front door and jumped onto the saddle. The extra kilos he was carrying did not make for an easy landing. There was little wind and in the far distance he saw dark clouds dense with rain.

six

Spinning an easy gear, he led Banquo through the village. Svarik, in paint-splattered football shorts and an oversinglet, was opening the café. He was staring at the 'Vote Varta' posters his wife had placed in the window and frowning as if he did not understand their two-word message.

'Hey,' said Mariani as they passed. Svarik raised one hand hesitantly in return and looked quizzically at Banquo.

Mariani glanced over his shoulder. The Austrian had his hands off the bars and was thumbing his iPhone. Who was he talking to? Who else was he bending to his will? What could his life possibly be like? Did he have holes in his socks, pick his nose, have sex? Very briefly, Mariani saw Claudia on all fours, her husband behind her metronomically thrusting while he checked a digital device for messages. Claudia noted the time on her Rolex and then began to pant over-dramatically. Her lipstick was perfect.

They left the village going east. Mariani had in mind his figure-of-eight route which at the halfway point would lead them back to the village. Then he could get something from Svarik. A cheese roll, maybe. From there, the descent down to the highway, followed by a final long, easy climb home. One hundred and twenty-one kilometres. Only the descent could be de-scribed as challenging.

The first loop was through undulating countryside on dark ribbons of roads. Vineyards, empty now of the *tgreszv* grapes that made the local black-red wine. And at the furthest point the still, deep waters of Lake Rig, from where Herzy had once pulled a sixty-pound carp that had the jaws of a pike. Two children had gone through the ice there the winter before last. On a steep slope to their left was a trudging horse harnessed to a plough held by a boy with a rifle slung over his shoulder. Horse, plough, boy seemed one.

Mariani tried not to think about why Banquo was here. The Austrian did nothing without a reason. Not a second of his life was wasted. Mariani hardly knew him. How old was he…thirty-four? Seven Grand Tour titles: three of those celebrated on the Champs-Élysées with the *maillot jaune* on his back. He'd also won one-day classics, including Paris–Roubaix, riding away from everyone across the cobbles, finishing before the next rider had even entered the Velodrome. Mariani had watched the DVD of the race.

Banquo had had time to slow down, receive his newborn child from his wife in the crowd and then ride across the line with the cooing infant nestling in one arm. His V02 max was rumoured to be in the low-nineties, his body shifting oxygen to his muscles at a rate only LeMond or a cross-country skier could have equalled. He spoke four languages. Mariani could not recall him ever getting a puncture. He seemed to be a different category of person: you had to be to wear that tracksuit, thought Mariani.

A single dark bird, high in the sky, followed the two riders. For thirty minutes Mariani kept the pace just below mid-tempo, thirty-five km/h. After more than two weeks of rest, and still not fully recovered, he was uncomfortable. His hamstrings were tight and he had begun to sweat. Banquo sat on his rear wheel, invisible. Mariani felt somehow that he was being examined.

They came round a corner and a line of black-faced sheep was moving out of one field, across the road and into the field opposite. The two riders braked hard and stopped. The shepherd stood in the road and looked at Mariani without blinking. He was dark and massive, with matted hair and beard. In one corner of his thin slash of a mouth glowed the nub of a cigarette. A sheep, bloodied and broken, was slung across his shoulders.

'Two concerns,' said Banquo while they waited.

'Yes?'

'One. Performance-enhancing products. With your father's history and that time-trial performance, suspicions become aroused.'

'It's not an issue for me. I don't dope and never have. Can I ask why you're asking?'

Banquo ignored the question. 'Two. Your metabolic irregularity.'

Shit of the Devil, was there anything Banquo didn't know?

'I'm working on it. It can be answered.' A twinge in his heart at the half-lie. But he felt it was vital not to show any weakness around Banquo.

'Explain it to me.'

'It's... It's like my need for protein is over-developed. Particularly at exhaustion levels.'

'Why?'

'I don't know.' He adjusted his sunglasses. 'It's not serious.' As he said them, Mariani hoped his words were true.

The last woolly backside disappeared through the gate. The shepherd spat a brown wad and followed the animals into the field.

Mariani pushed the crank down and set off. What game was Banquo playing? These personal questions were making him uncomfortable. What would he ask next? Mariani's sperm count?

Banquo rode up alongside, only several centimetres between the bikes. Mariani noticed once more their similarity in size.

'Every year I go to my borders and advance into unknown territory,' said Banquo. 'I've been happy to do it. But next season will be my last. My wife told me that although you and I are not alike, she sees something of me in you. I am not sure what. Perhaps it is not definable. Or laudable.'

Even though they were riding along a flat road, Mariani felt his heart begin to thud.

'So,' said Banquo, 'I am retiring.'

Mariani nodded and tried to control his breathing.

Ahead were the dark silver waters of Lake Rig. A breeze rippled the grass on the banks. He turned to start an anti-clockwise lap. It seemed that an opportunity for the future was about to open up, but strangely he was thinking of his past. As a boy, he'd ridden ten circuits of this lake twice a week, Tuesdays and Thursdays, as a time-trial. The same thing over and over. At first on a three-speed heap of shit he found tyreless in the forest. Then on one of Tanel's cast-offs. Doing something he'd found he was good at. Better than good. Going under thirty. Then twenty-nine. Twenty-six eighteen point three three was his record. He'd done that on his seventeenth birthday. Beaten his father's record by twelve seconds.

'Your agent has been contacted,' said Banquo as they went past a hunched, hooded figure sitting on a lump of wood and gutting a large bream. 'An odd man. But he felt negotiations could be progressed.'

'I see. Yes.' Mariani tried to keep his mind perfectly clear.

'He was told not to approach you. I like to do these things personally. While riding if possible. It seems appropriate. This is a striking lake. Unrefined.'

They'd almost finished the lap before Banquo spoke again.

'I will miss it – these contests of strength and will. The freedom of the mountains and the valleys. It is the most noble, the most life-affirming of all sports. Yes?'

'Yes.'

'I mean, imagine being a golfer.' Banquo shook his head. 'You will be lab tested – you must hit certain levels, physically and psychologically. But I am told you have a haematocrit of forty-seven and watts-per-kilo at threshold of six point one. These are promising numbers. Let us push a little harder for one more circuit.'

Already Mariani was feeling the ache of hunger. He wondered if Banquo had anything with him, even an energy gel. But if the Austrian was about to offer him a contract now was not the time to show he was anything but perfectly prepared and completely professional.

He let Banquo lead as they started the second lap. He wondered how to play this. His powermeter showed three-eighty watts. Already they were doing forty-two km/h. Mariani felt a twist of cramp in his hamstring. He shifted into the thirteen and braced himself for what was now inevitable: two minutes of terrible suffering. Banquo went down onto the drops and increased his cadence. His ass tightened.

On his powermeter, Mariani saw four-fifty. Then five hundred. The air began to roar in his ears.

When he was seventeen and circling the lake, he had tried to become one with the natural world around him. The deep cold water. The flitting fish. The shifting grass. The enveloping air. He would try to get to a place where the agony in his legs and the booming of his heart and the rasping in his lungs were just aspects of the environment, the same as a plover flapping its wings or cirrus drifting.

He tried it again now as he saw Banquo's chain jump into the smallest cog and heard its alloy steel begin to whine. Fifty km/h. Fifty-two. Fifty-five. Mariani went past the rock that he'd placed ten years ago to mark the halfway point. Banquo flicked his elbow for Mariani to come through. He watched a thousand appear on his powermeter, fifty-seven on the speedo. He could hold this for maybe another forty seconds. He tucked in his arms and dropped his head as far as he could, reducing drag. He ground his teeth as he went past Banquo. You are just molecules, he thought. Just water and air, mud and stone. The pain is a bee's buzz, a leaf falling, a wriggle of a worm.

Six hundred left. Tactics were pointless now. Numbers irrelevant. Movement was all there was. Knees. Calves. Feet. Flashes of the world in his peripheral vision; grey, green, silver. Feeling the power transfer. Trying to make the chain scream. A dark red bubbling behind his eyes. Wanting to see Banquo crying, helpless: *Have my millions, my contracts, take my little children, sell them to a Serbian sex beast, just please Romain...Mr. Mariani...sir, stop the torture!*

Two hundred to go. Fourteen seconds. Both gasped like dying men. They didn't look at each other.

They were together. Their cadences were the same. Their positions on the bike. The rhythm of their bobbing heads.

Banquo edged half a tyre's width ahead with fifty left and Mariani knew that he'd proved whatever he'd had to. He fought down the thing inside him that wanted Banquo to be just a smear on the tarmac. He clicked back into himself. He was a slightly overweight starving hungry twenty-six- year-old pro cyclist who hadn't brushed his teeth and everything was hurting, but it didn't matter because he'd shown Hans Banquo exactly what could be expected of him. He eased back two per cent and Banquo took it by half a bike length.

Once he'd got some breath, Mariani ate his apple. Flesh, stalk and pips. It would have to do until they got back to Svarik's. They took the right turn back towards the village.

Banquo looked at his watch. 'Let's talk further.'

Above them, the black bird hovered as if unsure where to go. Eventually, it wheeled and followed.

SEVEN

Banquo wanted Mariani to join him at Team Cavasoglu Super-Pro. If Mariani's first season was good enough, and he showed the correct character, he would then take over as leader after Banquo's retirement. He mentioned money: initially, it would be twice the eighty-five thousand euros Mariani was currently getting. If he became leader, that would treble.

Then Banquo went on to what he called 'stipulations'.

He wanted Mariani to marry Keira because married riders were less distracted: he had a number of charts that proved this. But they were not to have children for another four years. Riders under thirty with children were more distracted: again, he had charts that proved this. Divorce would be granted only in the most extreme situations and not before six months of marriage counselling. He wanted Mariani to get a podium position in a Grand Tour during the next season. He would need to drop three kilos and submit to a non-negotiable training regime. A team would be constructed around him as capable and strong as any that had shepherded Armstrong to seven yellow jerseys. Certain beverages and foodstuffs would be prohibited, dependent on dietary analysis, but he would not be drinking fizzy water or eating tomatoes again. He would also need a decent haircut.

'What is decent?' asked Mariani.

'Don't interrupt me,' said Banquo.

Mariani would be fired without recompense if there were any evidence of him using illegal performance-enhancing products. Recreational drugs, including legal highs, would incur the same punishment. Certain doctors were blacklisted: consulting them meant instant dismissal. They included the Englishman, Alann Triesmaan, who, Banquo said, should be on a blacklist all of his own.

'Was he involved with de Vilde?' asked Mariani.

'He supplied de Vilde with certain products, but nothing was found in the autopsy.'

'Meaning?'

'Meaning nothing. He is a blight on the world and I will talk of him no further.'

Banquo returned to his stipulations. Mariani would have to move to one of three approved French villages. He was not to ski, run or dance. Or scuba dive. Grasch was a bad influence with his espresso-drinking competitions and his homemade colonic irrigation machine and should not be seen socially. Banquo never saw him, he told Mariani, even though he and Grasch shared a father, if not a nationality. Mariani would receive a full contract within a week. It should be returned, signed, within forty-eight hours.

They were quiet for a kilometre. Mariani knew that riding at his level was as much about planning and professionalism as the simple desire to ride and win. But the higher you rose, the more you resembled a politician running for election. He had not fully realised the person he might have to become. Banquo's diktats revolved in his head.

Svarik's café appeared in the distance. Mariani felt cold drops on his face. The rain had not stayed away. He looked up at the sky. His mind seemed to slow. He thought of what might be waiting for him. 'Well,' he whispered to himself, 'well, well.' It was what his mother would say whenever she was happily surprised.

'I must get something to eat,' he said. 'You?'

Banquo shook his head.

They stopped. Mariani dismounted. Banquo stayed on his bike and pulled out his iPhone. Mariani went inside the café. Svarik was smoking while slicing bread. He quickly stubbed out his cigarette.

'What's to eat?' asked Mariani.

'Not much. Rolls. Blood sausage. Bit of liver soup.'

Mariani glanced outside. Banquo was checking his watch. The rain was getting heavier. On the forested mountains lay a heavy grey-green mist, as if the trees were puffing on Nistanjhi.

He was going to sign. Of course he was. He wanted to lead Team Cavasoglu Super-Pro and earn half a million euros a year. Of course he did. Who would not? He remembered the giddy waft of power and fame that he'd felt standing next to Banquo in the town square after the Essence. Great shifts were about to take place in his life. His chest seemed to expand of its own accord. He thought, strangely, of Golgotha, rampaging across the land, blue eyes cold, its heart pumping rivers of hot blood to its tireless muscles.

Mariani chose the blood sausage and a dark brown roll. He cut two chunks off the sausage, chewed them and swallowed. He tore the roll in half, put one half in his back pocket and the other in his mouth.

He nodded at Svarik, then turned and walked out. He got back on his bike. Through the window, the dwarfboy waved goodbye.

*

If Hans Banquo had a weak point, it was descending. Mariani saw it now as they dropped down towards the highway.

The Austrian locked his back wheel going through a left-hander. Mariani watched as the bike seemed to twist and flex. Banquo pulled it round, put his foot down on the tarmac and slowed. Mariani accelerated and rode beside him.

'Want to follow me?' He wanted to add 'Or go back?' but thought that might sound insulting.

Banquo nodded him ahead, tight-lipped.

Just keep it steady, thought Mariani. Don't show off. Don't get Banquo killed. He glanced over his shoulder. The Austrian was already three bike-lengths behind, but waved him on.

Don't think about what he's been saying. Don't think about the contract. Don't think about getting an accountant's haircut. Don't think about the salary. Or marrying Keira. Or having Hans Banquo as a boss. Just ride.

A tight right bend. Road surface in tatters. He looked over his shoulder again. Where was Banquo? Had he stopped? Punctured? *Jeszu,* he hadn't crashed, had he? And what was that in the distance, crashing through the forest? A *dornei…*? No, too broad and squat. By forcing each eye to the furthest corner of its socket Mariani tried to look to the front and to the back at the same time. He squeezed the brakes. Whatever was running in the forest slowed too. He turned his head and shoulders, trying to see back around the corner. His mind told him that he needed to brake and to keep his eyes on the road in front. The instruction became more urgent with every passing metre.

Banquo appeared. Relieved, Mariani turned and increased his speed. It was a bad decision. With a jolt, he realised he was at Curse Corner and then, in the next instant, understood that he was not going to make it. He felt suddenly very cold and filled with a dreadful sense of failure. From somewhere quite close, he heard his father's harsh voice telling him how badly he had fucked up. He grabbed at the brakes. He whispered the word 'shit'. He saw a flash of the dwarfboy waving. Then the bike was on the ground and so was he and together they were heading for the edge, and then he and his bike and his life were falling.

Voices. Murmurs about his skull. Lights. Numbers pulsing on displays. Hands touching him. Attaching and probing.

Wrong sensations. Nerves subdued by chemicals. All feeling removed. No suffering.

A smashed thing, still and bedbound. Horizontal for days. Confusion flaring. Sudden shouts thrown from his mouth.

This place of hope and dread.

The repeated whish-zip of curtains. From behind them apologetic murmurs and then the defeated silence of stunned men.

The long blue-black nights.

All these illnesses. Greenish faces and yellow arms. Things furred and blocked and kinked. Scraped breathing. New categories of anguish. Whimpers he didn't recognise. Agonies of the soul provoking movements like some bizarre dance.

His capacities dwindling. Muscles wasting. Lungs shrinking. Heart atrophying. Blood thinning.

Not himself any more just scabs and sutures. Veins needle-pricked. Flashbacks of a thick hard hurt in his head. Jumbled footage as he slept of whatever had been running in the forest, chasing and waiting, waiting and chasing, assuming a half-familiar shape, then disappearing: there, not there.

Familiar faces. His father, silent. Herzy's squinting eyes. Grasch fooling around, but face heavy with worry. Svarik with a tin of coffee. Varta with a book. Keira: her warm soft hand on his.

How was he? How was he? How was he?

He was OK. Getting there. All right.

The unspoken except.

*

The spokes of the wheels glinted in the strong morning light. Mariani paused and blinked. He was out of breath and sweating. The early-winter air was thin and sharp. The sun was warm on his face as he looked down into the valley.

Keira waited behind him, watching and smiling.

'Ready?' she asked, after a minute.

He nodded.

Keira put her hands on the chair's grips and pushed him the rest of the way to the hired MPV. He'd managed nearly a hundred metres on his own. The hospital porter, a cycling fan, followed close behind.

The two of them lifted Mariani into a passenger seat and the porter folded the chair and put it in the back.

'Thank you,' said Keira.

'Good luck.' The porter gave Mariani a raised-fist 'power' salute. He returned it feebly: he still could not properly lift his arm or close his fingers.

Keira put his seat belt on and then started the car. 'Let's go home.'

The sixty-metre fall down the side of the ravine had left him with three doubly fractured ribs, a fracture of the left femur, an open fracture of the right tibia, fractures to the right ulna and radius, a punctured lung and lacerations to his back, neck and face. He'd undergone three operations lasting a total of seventeen hours. His femur was held together with a titanium rod and eight screws. You're lucky to be alive, the doctors had told him. On certain days, when the pain relief wasn't doing its job, he'd wondered if that was true. There was a deep ache building now and he knew he'd soon need the liquid morphine that Keira was carrying in her handbag.

He had other problems too. He'd suffered a contrecoup injury, his head shunted from the rear and the brain smacking into the front of his skull. There was uncertainty about the white dots and blots on his frontal lobe. There had been no bleeding and his motor functions were fine. But Mariani knew. Something was missing.

He sat in the seat and looked into the big blue sky as if the answer might be there.

'It's like that feeling when you know something needs to be done but you don't know what,' he'd explained to Keira. Then the absence overwhelmed him and he'd begun to cry.

The six weeks of specially constructed computer games and brain exercises at the hospital here on the eastern edge of the Austrian Alps had changed nothing. Every morning he awoke with hope, to be disappointed seconds later. Then the panic would start and he would have to talk himself down, remind himself what he'd been told, that the brain worked to a system no one truly understood. Nothing was definite, but he could expect his perceptions to narrow and his moods to swing in an instant. He might have trouble concentrating and remembering. He might believe things that weren't true. His worst traits might be exacerbated, his preoccupations intensify.

Mariani was silent as Keira drove down the mountain road, through the village and towards the autobahn that led east and south. They had talked a lot in the past few weeks, though not about the accident. He had told her many times that cyclists did not discuss their crashes and that they were always dismissed with silly euphemisms. But Keira and he had become intimate in a way neither had foreseen. She had told him she loved him and he'd echoed her words. During the long quiet hours in the hospital, they began to understand more of why they were drawn to each other.

One rainy afternoon she became distracted, said, 'Can I tell you something?' and then quietly talked for nearly twenty minutes about her obsessive-compulsive attitude to food and her bouts of bulimia.

'I don't know why, but I thought you'd understand,' she said. 'Dad doesn't know. Or anyone else.'

Mariani took her hand and applied gentle pressure. He felt like a selfish fool. 'I wondered if you had a problem. I'm sorry, I should have asked you.'

'It got worse after my injury. All that stuff about getting back control. Plus, when you can't train, you worry about the weight...'

'I know,' said Mariani, who on the scales that morning had been shocked to see he was now nearly eighty-two kilos. 'I often think I'm on the verge of something myself. The amount of hogget I can eat...' He shook his head and moved closer to Keira. 'How do you cure it? Is it serious?'

'Well, it's not cancer. But I'd like it to stop. Who *wants* to be colour coding the contents of their fridge? Sometimes it seems the only time I'm not thinking about food is when I'm eating it. It's like being held prisoner.'

'Are there specialists?'

'Oh, there are lots of people to see.' She put her free hand on top of his and gripped it very tightly. 'But I wanted to tell you first. Is that all right?'

Mariani knew he was not the most warm-hearted of men. But when Keira turned to him with an expression that held its small hopeful smile of enquiry for a moment before slowly starting to fade, he put his arms around her and told her that whatever she did was all right by him. Then he talked about his own strange and erratic need for red meat, and about his electronic, computer-friendly, multi-function U-Analyser; on his laptop, he showed her the charts he had constructed from its downloaded data: she was fascinated.

Keira had more to tell him. On the day before he left the hospital, she tearfully confided that her athletic career was all but over. The graft from her patella to form the new cruciate ligaments had left her with chronic tendinitis that the physio was not reducing. She faced at least another year of rehabilitation and possible further surgery. She didn't know if she wanted to put herself through it. As Mariani listened, it seemed to him that despite the tears, she was relieved. She had doubts about the true level of her ability – before the injury, she had been struggling to make the national team – and about her dedication. She looked at him, she said, and knew she was not driven by the same forces. There were other things she could do; she had already talked to a cable TV channel about presenting sports programmes. She might even open a restaurant: together, they wrote potential, though very different, menus.

They talked then about Mariani's future and he, roused by Keira's belief in him, began an impassioned monologue about the kind of rider he would be when he returned. His words quickly became loud and malevolent and Keira had to tell him, laughingly, to keep his voice down and mind his language.

He did not tell her he had exaggerated that malevolence because he was worried it was not there at all.

*

Fibroblasts gathered at injury sites. New bone cartilage bridged fissures.

Three months later, Mariani opened the door to the training room for the first time since the accident. It was a day he had both longed for and dreaded. He felt bulky and misshapen in his kit, inflated: he was nearer ninety kilos than eighty and his stomach swelled the front of the jersey. He was unshaven. He had the beginnings of a double chin. When he poked his backside, it wobbled. His eyes were caved and red-rimmed.

He had crashed many times before, sometimes badly. Every pro had a collection of X-rays and scars. The clangs and crunches, rips and tears, the pistol shots of exploding tyres and the soft wet squelches of flesh hitting tarmac, the cursing groans, were sounds as familiar as the whir of wheels. At least five times a season you were going to come off and it was going to hurt. A one-in-four chance it would be a *chute grave,* serious enough to put you in hospital. If you couldn't make that part of your life then you could kiss a career in cycling goodbye, no matter how many watts you could churn out. You fell off, you were put back together and you got back on.

He studied the machine on its stationary trainer for some minutes. Bike, his mind told him. You sit on it and you pedal. That's your job. He nodded.

His eyes scanned the room. He remembered the hours spent in here, replayed the sessions, imagined the power outputs. He slipped his feet into his shoes and tightened the straps. Steadying himself with the crutch, he put one leg over the top tube. He put the hand of his strong arm on the bars and pushed up and back, at the same time levering himself upwards with the crutch. He did not use enough strength and the tip of the saddle jabbed into his buttocks. He fell forward, testicles slamming into the top tube.

'Shitting cunt *matjkes!*' he shouted, his damaged brain scrambling words and concepts and languages. The pain made him close his eyes tight and grab himself by the scruff of his neck. His therapist had suggested a gym bike be set up in the training room, but Mariani had refused. At this moment, he wished he hadn't.

When his breathing had slowed and he felt less like throwing up, he tried again. He managed to land on the saddle, but as he did, the bike wobbled and, for an instant, Mariani thought the bike and the trainer and he were going to topple over. He jammed the crutch against the floor and the set-up steadied.

He clicked his shoes into the pedals and put the crutch within reach on the bench beside him.

He swallowed. His head felt flabby and numb.

Words came back to him: damage difficult to ascertain…behavioural changes…recovery time uncertain.

He felt nothing.

He took a breath and began slowly to turn the cranks. The garden outside was snow-covered, a featureless white rectangle. He stared at it as he did the twenty minutes his therapist, with instructions to 'just give the blood a nudge', had allowed him. Then he did ten more.

When he stopped, he looked at the read-out on the powermeter. He'd averaged eighty-seven watts, the statistics of a six year old. He climbed off unsteadily, put his crutches under his arm and levered himself back to his bedroom. He lay down, placed his hands on his paunch and closed his eyes, breathing deeply, trying to quieten the voices that told him he was finished.

He was about to get up to wash when the phone rang.

'Commie,' said Grasch.

'Hitler Youth.'

'Guess how many espressos I drank yesterday?'

'Espressos?' Mariani blinked. He could not put a meaning to the word.

'Espressos. You know. Coffee? Small? Black?'

He knew coffee. He understood small. Black, yes, he could see that. But espresso was what? A train, perhaps? 'No. Sorry.'

'Never mind. So. Still in pain, cupcake?'

'Pain?'

'You remember. Your *toothache*.'

'I'm OK.'

'Shall we ever see your ugly face in the peloton again?'

'Six months.'

'Six?'

Mariani gripped the phone more tightly. 'Five and a half.'

'Right. Rumours are my half-brother's announcing his retirement next week. He been in touch?'

'I have a Get Well Soon card. His wife signed it too.'

'The Frau Supertits. Pfaff says when she fucks in his dreams, she holds a syringe to his throat. Nothing in that card about joining Hansi's team?'

'No.'

'Maybe he'll wait for you.'

'I don't think so.'

'You think he'll take... *Mitchell* ...instead?'

As the Australian's name entered Mariani's consciousness, the lesions on his frontal lobe provoked the emotional maelstrom that Grasch had listened to many times since the accident. 'That fucking spunk-headed bastard cunt son of a cock-loving whore?'

Grasch laughed with delight. ' *Ja*, that's him. The guy sleeps with his *mutti* but he's good. Though not Hansi's style. He'd have to clean up his sick and illegal lovelife. Lose the mullet. And those tattoos. Me, I'd wait for you.'

'You're too kind.'

'It's good sense. What's another year to Hansi? Another yellow jersey, another ten million euros, another private island? I might say a word. Put him straight. Or maybe to the Frau. She likes you.'

'Tell her I have to wipe my ass left-handed. That impresses women.'

'Maybe in your country. Your power company still got donkeys hitched up to water wheels?'

'Power? We don't have power here.'

Grasch hesitated. 'Is that a joke?'

'Yes.'

'You know your country has power?'

'Yes. Of course.'

'Of course. Yes. You tried to ride yet?'

'Just today. Indoors.'

'And?'

'It was OK.'

'Good to be in the saddle?'

'It was OK.'

'Well, I can see you're all overcome with emotion. When I have nothing else to do, I'll call again.'

'Thanks.'

'Oh, I meant to tell you. I'm boofing Keira. She wears her ice skates.'

'Yeah?'

Mariani's mind had tired and he couldn't think of anything to say, so he cut the line and got up. He needed to urinate and did so in one of the two chamber pots he kept under the bed. His therapist had suggested a commode, but the thought of the thing with its spidery legs looking at him when he woke up every morning, reminding him of his weakness, was too much. He carried the pot to the kitchen, thought about emptying it down the sink, but then opened the back door, and in a weak arc, threw the hot piss onto the snow, where it joined several other yellow splashes and some curled turds. It hadn't snowed for a few days. He thought he should probably try and find the bathroom again soon.

He took off his kit, filled the sink with water, and from a bottle standing on the drainer, squeezed in shower gel. He put a towel on the floor and stepped on to it, but then quickly became interested in his pallid jiggling flesh and the worm trails of the scarring. After examining himself for several minutes, he came to the belief that his shower was over. He reached for another towel and wrapped it around his waist. A rope of fat lay proud above the towel's edge. He forgot to empty the sink.

It was just before ten o'clock. Keira was flying over tonight for a few days. He had been bad-tempered with her recently as he nervously edged towards testing himself on the bike. She'd had two presenting auditions at SwissSport TV and already terms were being discussed. She was moving on. By comparison, Mariani felt he was drifting, buoyed by little more than hope, and a furious if unfocused memory of what, for a few short months, he'd believed he could be.

He sipped his coffee. Now he had eight hours to fill before Keira arrived. He wondered why he still smelled sweaty. He picked up the paper and for the fourth time that day, though he thought it the first, looked for stories of Golgotha. There were none.

Two weeks later, Mariani sat at his usual table at the café watching his agent Serge Hamptons poke with a fork at the mound of steaming dark grey *guhtruzi* in front of him. Svarik was offering a special on this stew of local wild ram in sour cream and bogberries: six servings for the price of five. Presented indifferently on a chipped blue plate with slices of the ram's testicles, deep-fried. No decorative sprigs of parsley.

'So it tastes just like a bacon/beef type thing?' Hamptons gingerly dipped bread in the *guhtruzi's* sauce. 'It's very…meaty.' He brought the bread towards his mouth. The agent's plump forehead, pumped with muscle-paralysing toxin, gave nothing away. But his lips did not open. The bread stayed three inches from his mouth. Mariani noticed his agent had grown a postage stamp of beard on his chin.

'I'd love to, but…' Hamptons said finally. He put the bread back on the plate. His forehead shone. He patted it. 'Can't get my cholesterol below nine. My doctor says less meat, less dairy, more salad. Oats, lots of oats. Got me on these statins. Lipitor. The highest dose. Got to take 'em every day. Stop the liver producing all that bad shit that gunks up your arteries. Drugs. What would we do without 'em?'

'Die?' suggested Mariani.

'Yep. Drugs save lives. Just say yes! Here's to 'em.' Hamptons raised his glass of *tgreszv*. He sipped it and put it down quickly. 'So…how you feeling?'

Mariani straightened his shoulders. 'Fine. Excellent.'

'We hear good things from your therapist. You might be ready able to join the training camp in April?'

'Yes. Definitely.'

'Let them know you're still here. Be a presence.'

'I'm still here.'

Hamptons gave his forehead two quick strokes.

'You've been doing some easy sessions?'

'Yes. Perfect. No problems.'

'Good. Good. And what…maybe you'll get on the road in a few weeks? Couple of weeks?'

'Next week. For sure.'

Mariani knew Hamptons was here only to check on his condition and report back to whichever sponsors were still showing interest. He didn't care. He wanted Hamptons – and anyone else who would listen – to know that there was no doubt about him resuming his career.

'I'll be on the start line of the Vuelta.'

'That's…?'

'August. Third week. Spain.'

Hamptons nodded. 'OK. Well, that's a good thing to aim for.' He checked his shiny Breitling watch. 'I have a taxi ordered for eight-thirty.'

'Svarik has a room upstairs…'

'No, it's all good.' Hamptons glanced nervously to the corner where the Giûrgïu dwarfboy was sitting at a table and filling in a puzzle on the back of the day's edition of *Fair and True*. 'First flight back in the morning. I'm staying by the airport.'

'Airport Central?'

'Uh-huh. Is that the best name you guys could come up with?'

'Yes. It's an aiport and it's located centrally. It's that kind of imagination that's got this country to where it is today.'

'Coming through, the customs guy says to me: "Any weapons, pornography or Semtex?" And I say "Yep, all three," and he says, "Excellent. Welcome."'

Mariani laughed through his nose. 'At least they were awake. Did you hear from Banquo?'

'No. Means nothing. You know Banquo. Cards tight to his butt. They'll want to see you back on the road again, full medical report, before talking. Listen…I'm supposed to take some pictures, just so…just to show what shape you're in.'

Mariani leant back in his chair. 'What kind of pictures?'

'You know…pictures that show what shape you're in.'

'You want to photograph my ass?' Without knowing he'd done it, Mariani crossed his legs.

'I'm under some pressure here, Romain…'

Mariani turned to Svarik, who was watching a nature programme on the TV. A cow was giving birth and as the stunned calf exited the vagina, a man in a hat walked into frame, grinned and raised his thumb. His teeth were gnarled and yellowed.

'Svarik, how is the light in the toilet?'

'It works.'

'Is it soft and enhancing?'

Svarik *lijzk*-ied and went back to watching the cow lick birthing fluids off its baby.

Hamptons followed Mariani into the bathroom. The naked bulb shone hard and white.

'How do you want me?' he asked, nervously striking a model-ish pose and running a hand through his hair.

'Topless.'

'What?'

'Come on, Romain. You can't be Miss Shyboots here.'

'The weight – it'll disappear,' said Mariani, as he slowly took off his shirt and then the T-shirt under it.

He couldn't help but fold his arms across his chest.

Hamptons tapped his foot.

Mariani scratched at the side of his neck and looked down at the old and faded grey lino on the floor. He dropped his right arm to his side. He moved his left hand across his breastbone; the fat and tissue moved under his fingers, making him think of soft cheese.

'Romain…'

Mariani took his hand away. 'Fuck, Serge.' His face began to burn.

Hamptons aimed his camera. 'Nice tits. Don't worry. Kid at the office is a Photoshop genius.'

By March, the snow had melted though the skies were grey and cheerless. The wind moaned when it blew as if it too had caught the savage influenza that was tearing through the country.

On a day when the temperature just nudged six degrees, and the wigged, coughing TV weather forecaster told him there was no chance of rain, Mariani wheeled his bike out of the front door and along the path. He checked his phone, making sure the battery was fully charged. He looked at the *Good luck & FFS be careful* text he'd received from Keira that morning.

He took in lungfuls of cold air; passed a hand across his forehead, trying to rub away what felt like a dark stolid coating across his brain.

He had been posting decent numbers in the training room. His weight was down to seventy-eight. His cognition was better: he'd stopped having imaginary showers and shouting filth every time he saw or heard the words 'Trent Mitchell'.

A breeze gusted, stinging his fresh-shaven cheeks, and clouds scuttled through the skies. He thought back to that moment when he was winched up towards the helicopter, strapped to a stretcher, the china-white bone poking through the black material of his cycling longs. The memories were sharp. He winced. The screws in his femur seemed to tighten.

He shivered and zipped up his jacket. He checked his brakes for the third time. He had a final look at the power level in his phone.

The road out to Lake Rig had suffered in the heavy winter and Mariani felt every crack and bump. It seemed further than it used to. He kept checking the trip distance reading on his computer. There was no other traffic on the road. He kept his speed below twenty-eight km/h, putting no stress on his legs or heart. He tried to soak up the scenery he knew so well, the farm buildings and the tumbledown shepherds' huts, giant old trees in small copses, tried to use it to create sensations from the past. The air was still and quiet.

He felt his legs spin and the roadbuzz through the bars and the clean cold air in his mouth and nose. Everything was how it was, except for the edgeless, muffled response he had to it all. He rode on, waiting for it to disappear.

*

In four weeks, he rode to Lake Rig and back thirty-nine times, a total of two thousand three hundred and eighty-seven kilometres. He didn't consider any other routes. On rides nine and sixteen, Herzy accompanied him on a racer that had been lying in a farm outhouse for ten years. It had gear shifters on its down tube and an orange-brown rusted chain. The corroded cranks shrieked at every turn of the pedals. Herzy cycled in jeans and unlaced boots and brought a bottle of home-brewed beer for refreshment. He slung a rifle over his shoulder and fired at rabbits or hares as he loafed along. Mariani wondered if a passer-by would ever think they were brothers. But Herzy was good company and, Mariani realised, a hell of a shot. He finished each ride with three furry corpses inside his jacket, dried blood on his hands and bar tape. He chortled often and declared that cycling was fun, one of the reasons why it could never be classed as a proper job. Work, he claimed, was hard – that's why it was called work. Sport was not work. Sport was – well, sport. Mariani laughed and wished he and his brother were closer. At certain moments they had been, but they carried with them many unspoken grudges from the past. Mariani felt his bigger, stronger brother should have stood up for him against their father, and suspected that Herzy was somehow jealous of the attention that Tanel had given his cycling prodigy son. Like most brothers, their conversations consisted mostly of insults that occasionally referenced long-held resentments, but more frequently hinted at a mutual fondness and respect.

Mariani logged his numbers for each ride in his page-to-a-day diary. By the last, he had increased his average speed to thirty-six point two km/h at an average heart rate of one hundred and twenty-four. In the evenings, he would stare at the figures, seeing in their facts the athlete he had been slowly reappearing, like a figure out of a lump of clay.

The top of every page was also marked with a red G. Though he knew his obsession was entirely illogical, he'd become desperate to see the beast. He was disappointed not to have done so.

In April, he flew to Tenerife for the training camp. This was a week's preparation before the early-season Tour of Romandy. He went on long, easy rides with the team, and on the hard days obeyed his therapist and sat in the mild sunshine or rode a stationary bike in the air-conditioned gym. No one talked about the accident and no one talked about him going to Banquo's team. They were riding well and eating together, no splits in the camp, even the Dutch and the Germans were passing each other the salt. Vicek, 'The Vulture', smiled all day. He showed everyone pictures of his ugly new baby and demonstrated the improvements he'd made in his table manners. But the atmosphere of well being began to make Mariani feel tense and frustrated. He knew he was lacking something the others were not. He found himself wanting to pour paint stripper over the team bikes, and late one night, his urge to set fire to the team coach was only thwarted by his inability to unscrew the fuel cap.

He often caught Grasch glancing at him with with concern, but to talk about problems seemed to be tempting fate. On the last day, they climbed the Teide volcano together, ascending through the lava fields in the soft late afternoon. Mariani tried to lose himself in the churn of the pedals and the sight of smooth black tarmac cutting through misshapen grey landscape. He wanted to keep moving towards a des-tination. He felt that if he stopped to think about his life it would quickly unravel.

'Know when this thing last blew?' asked Grasch as they eased their way past a pair of puffing retirees on mountain bikes.

Mariani shrugged.

'1909.'

Mariani nodded.

'I read up on it. It's not active now. But it's unstable. It's got a fault.'

'Looks OK.'

'It looks OK, *ja*. But there is something not quite right inside it.' Grasch left the words in the air. Mariani adjusted his sunglasses.

'I am speaking metaphorically,' said Grasch.

'What?'

'I am talking about the volcano, but really I am talking about something else.'

'Hey?'

'About *someone* else.'

'Do me a favour, Grasch. Fucking shut up.' Mariani looked straight ahead.

Grasch let out a long sigh. 'So you think you'll be ready for the Vuelta?'

'Perhaps. I'll do a couple of local races next month. Just to see if there's form.'

'Local races?'

'There's one called the Hell of Hgruh. It can be challenging.'

'The Hell of Hgruh? *Hgruh?* My God, won't it be full of crazy donkey-fucking cross-eyed sons of bitches all desperate to take your head? You sure?'

Mariani looked up to the summit of the volcano. He swallowed and finally turned to Grasch. 'No. I'm not sure at all.'

He had won the Hell of Hgruh when he was twenty. It was the last time the race doubled as the national championship. The course encouraged what the national selectors called 'unfortunate' tactics. Combine that with its importance and the race could and did quickly become a free-for-all, a riot on two wheels: five riders were hospitalised that year, one with an amputated leg. But it was still an event in which every rider with pretensions – and a lust for danger – wanted to compete. Seeing a chance to cash in on its reputation, the organisers had opened it out to the public. The race had become the country's premier communal athletic event. Over seven thousand names were on the start list.

Mariani called the organisers and asked that his entry receive no exposure. Once on the start line, he knew the talking would begin, the mobile phones come out for pictures and the better riders would begin to plot and scheme.

Immediately he'd rung off, he thought: There's no need to do this. Grasch was right. There would be many angry farm boys and bitter factory workers, the could-have-beens, the if-onlys, who would look at Mariani on his ten-thousand-euro hand-built bike and just think: Jumped-up jerk. They would forget their sympathy for his accident, their admiration for him as a rider and their approval of his quiet, simple life. Instead, they would think about his sexy little foreign girlfriend. They'd convince themselves he was one of the Banquo set – he was riding with the Austrian *finkghz* when he had the accident, remember? They'd discuss the rumours he was moving to a five million *chōp* pad in Spain. He was a big shot who needed taking down a peg or two, if not three. They may not be able to ride faster than him, but they could certainly put gravel in his ass.

The day of the race was sunless, skies thick and grey as *cudhi* porridge. Riders gathered in the car park at the national football stadium. It was seven a.m. In front of the headless statue of Lihgrinjhi, decapitated at the exact moment of the dictator's death ten years ago, but for reasons no one understood kept in place and regularly cleaned, a band in denim and fringed leather played Euro-metal. The singer yelled motivational lyrics about hot blood, kicking down doors and triumph. Prizes, he wailed, were there to be taken, and by any means necessary.

Suffer, yes, we've suffered since we were in the womb

Came out screaming and with good reason

It doesn't matter how bad the bread

Don't let anyone take it from you

Even if you have to take their head

At the end of the last line, the band all pointed theatrically to the statue. No one clapped.

A thin wind picked up. Cans and wrappers and plastic bags danced and ran. The seven thousand riders waited nervously, slurping, chewing, making final calls to friends and loved ones, fiddling with gears, prodding tyres. The doors of portable toilets opened and banged shut.

Elites were not granted an early start. Riders went off in numerical order. With three minutes to go, Mariani, unshaven, in discreet kit and darkest glasses, wheeled into a starting pen alongside a dreadlocked nineteen year old wearing a horned army helmet and sitting astride a lime green white-wheeled courier bike, and a middle-aged man on a flat bar hybrid. The man looked pale and sick. 'Christ,' he said, and pulled down the front of his shorts and forlornly watched pale piss dribble from his shrivelled penis.

A sports channel had decided to provide television coverage. A two-man camera crew was moving among the competitors recording sound-bites. On the PA a presenter gave a cursory rundown of the rules. He then introduced a number of semi-pros and well-known local riders, after which he asked the crowd to please give it up for pro tour rider, national hero, the country's answer to Hans Banquo: Romain Mariani.

Heads turned. Necks craned. Mariani kept his eyes down and busied himself with the Ziplocs on the timing transponder attached to his handle-bars. The camera was suddenly in his face and he half-lifted a hand in acknowledgement. A surge of sour, vengeful testosterone seemed to rise in the air. Mobiles were produced, pictures taken. In the next starting pen, three of the semi-pros, lean men in Crédit Haussman kit, stared at him. He realised, with a tongue-click of disappointment, that he'd forgotten his Jelly Babies.

'Any chance of a draft?' asked the man on the hybrid.

The boy on the courier bike flicked a purple pill into his mouth.

The announcer counted down from ten, an air raid siren sounded, and the noise of thousands of cleats clicking into pedals rose above the shrieking guitar solo coming from the stage.

Mariani was in the second pen and within a minute was accelerating gently away from the car park and over the timing mat. He weaved his way through the field, unsure what he expected to prove. He decided to find a likely group to ride with, sit in and see. As he eased past a quartet of women on rickety mountain bikes and a pair of aged bearded twins on a tandem, he glanced behind and was unsurprised to see five riders already locked on to his wheel. The Crédit Haussmans were just ahead in a group of seven. Mariani pushed a little harder and within thirty seconds had joined them. He was now in a group of thirteen serious-looking riders moving at warm-up pace along Road G through the featureless outskirts of the city. His legs felt fine. He was breathing easily. This wasn't what he had come for, but it would do for now. He sat in the back five, rolled his shoulders and got comfortable. It was wonderful to be riding again.

'You're Romain Mariani?' asked the big red-faced man next to him.

He nodded and half-smiled.

'Then get to the front and do some fucking work. Hey?' The three others snickered and *lijzk*-ied.

Though he didn't hear it, Mariani knew that his name was already being passed through the rest of the group. He saw the front two look round and almost immediately increase their cadence. The pace picked up to forty km/h. From behind his dark lenses, Mariani examined the riders around him. All looked lean and fit, though none had the pipe-cleaner limbs and fat-free faces that distinguished the pro. Ages difficult to tell. These were probably the stars of the local clubs, disappointed men who just didn't have that extra two or three per cent necessary to move to the next level. Maybe they'd got distracted or crashed badly or found they couldn't tolerate the training or the pain or liked eating and drinking and being on top of women too much. One or two were probably overfond of Friday night fighting, releasing their cyclists' urge to smash other men by doing so with fists not wheels. Maybe they knew that genetics had slightly short-changed them and cursed their parents for passing on a mundane inheritance. But on the right day they would all be able to ride hard and fast for four hours. Mariani sensed they were thinking about how to beat him and already imagining the bragging rights.

'We used to race together as kids,' said a soft voice to his left. Mariani glanced round and looked into features that were chipped and scarred. 'Remember me? Slirick Fingh? I kicked your ass on the Junior Nationals when we were both fifteen. I bluffed you I was dying, let you do all the work.'

'How could I forget?' said Mariani. That defeat nor what happened afterwards: the car door slamming and then Tanel's phlegm exploding into his face.

'My best day ever on a bike,' said Fingh.

'What happened? I never saw your name again,' said Mariani.

'Got involved in the family business.'

'Yes?'

'Uh. Only been out of clink eighteen months.'

'Right.'

'Watch Rihli…the bearded bastard on the front. Won this last year. Thinks he owns the race. Ex- mountain biker. Mad as a *gruhkyk* on heat.'

Mariani could just make out the rider Fingh had identified. Silver hoops in his ears, all black kit.

'What you doing here anyway?' asked Fingh.

'Nothing on TV.'

Fingh *lijzk*-ied and then snorted snot onto the road. He took a drink from his bidon. He lifted his buttocks off the saddle and broke wind violently.

'Wish I could ride as hard as I can fart,' he said sadly.

'Horse,' shouted someone at the front and the group slowed to pass a wretched-looking greyish animal that was moving lamely, head down, towards them.

Mariani's group quickly overtook the rest of the riders who'd started ahead of them. The camera bike, a Honda 500 twin with rattling tappets and a number plate tied on with twine, had been moving back and forth, but now stayed with them.

'You're the leading group,' shouted the cameraman. 'Race faces, boys. Let's see some pain.'

Several riders tightened their mouths, flattened their backs and crouched lower over their handlebars. But after no more than thirty seconds, the camera bike's engine began to cough. From the exhaust came a dense bluish cloud. Within a hundred metres the bike had jerked to a stop.

Now they realised they were at the head of the race, and no longer going to be appearing at three a.m. on a free-to-view sports channel, the pace eased. Mariani looked at all the riders' numbers and placed himself third. Most had started with Rihli. If any of those wanted to win, they would have to attack. That was what Mariani wanted. They rode three more kilometres on good paved road before swinging left towards the dark shark's teeth of the Hgruh Mountains: incest capital of Eastern Europe. A marshal with an eye patch and smoking a white clay pipe clapped them through.

The road became a thin lane, a ditch, slush-filled, to either side. A fine brown dust of mud and dried animal excreta was thrown up by fifteen sets of tyres, coating nasal linings, palates, tongues and uvulas. Six kilometres of this. The group could not ride more than two abreast. Mariani sat with Fingh, who was concentrating on the wheel ahead of him, riding as close as he dared, getting maximum tow. The gradient gradually increased.

A roaring sound made Mariani look round. A kid, twelve, maybe thirteen, on a quad bike was following just behind, laughing, waving and flashing his headlight. Something hit Mariani on the shoulder. It was both soft and hard and also wet. He looked round again. Out of a bucket he gripped between his knees, the kid was picking yellow-reddish things and then throwing them. As another one flew past him, Mariani saw they were dead chicks.

The kid turned through a gate and into a field, where he drove round and round in circles.

They reached a hairpin and the road went through thick heavy trees. The light darkened. The gradient reared. The two at the front stood high out of their saddles but the gradient spiked up again to twenty per cent.

Their pace slowed to an old man's walk. The two behind were better climbers and their forward momentum forced them to brake. The ripple effect went back through the group and in seconds bikes were sprawling and men clutching and sliding and swearing. Sounds of thighs smacking down on tarmac. Grunts as air was forced through impacted chest cavities.

Fingh ran into Rihli's rear wheel. Both fell. Mariani, who'd seen this happen a hundred times, used his better bike-handling skills to stop dead. Six others had hit the deck. Red Face was in the ditch.

'You dopey prickend!' said Rihli and kicked out at Fingh's head. Rihli's cleats caught him in the ear. Fingh grimaced and then jabbed an elbow into Rihli's thigh.

The four at the front had crested the incline and were moving away.

'I'll smash you a new asshole later,' said Rihli.

'Your mother blows the Devil,' said Fingh. He got up off the tarmac and remounted. His shorts were torn and blood was leaking from a ragged hole in his knee.

'Fuck you looking at?' said Rihli to Mariani. Rihli's nostrils had widened and his bearded chin was thrust out as if daring Mariani to throw a punch.

Mariani shrugged. He dropped his eyes to the ground. No adrenalin rush, no whoosh of anxiety or fear. Instead he became aware of a hollow unease starting to leak into the back of his skull.

'Ride with fucking prison cum-swallowers and ball-tonguing tour slaves, this is what you get,' said Rihli. He swung a heavily muscled thigh over his top tube and pushed off, weaving through the three men still dazed and down.

Mariani and Fingh followed him.

'Pulled a flick knife year before last,' said Fingh. 'Said he'd stick anyone who didn't take their turn. Banquo ever do that?'

Rihli was pushing hard to catch the front four and Mariani could see he had the effortless power and smooth machine-churn pedalling style of a good pro. Class and strength. Shame he was a borderline psychopath.

ELEVEN

The course followed an old cobbled track across farmland for three kilometres and by the end of it there were seven left in the group. All three Crédit Haussmans, Rihli, Fingh, Red Face and Mariani.

No one had attacked. Mariani was still comfortable, taking short turns on the front.

A two-kilometre descent was next, on a hardened mud track that twisted around like intestines. Riders grabbed brakes. Back wheels twitched and jerked. Smells of hot rubber brake blocks on metal wheel rims. Cries of 'whoah' and 'urgh' and '*Jeszu*'.

They passed a farm two-thirds of the way down. Brown and black dogs, made frenzied by the sudden arrival of arms and thighs and asses, hurled themselves at fencing and howled for meat.

At the bottom, a five-metre-wide ford crossed a slow-moving river. The choice was to ride through the water or dismount and push the bike over a small wooden bridge.

A game of bluff began. Who would do what? It was difficult to tell the river's depth and the pebbled bottom was notoriously slippery. Mariani prepared to dismount and watched from the back as the others unclipped. The bridge was narrow but Mariani knew there would be no 'please, after you'. He hung back. The Crédit Haussmans and Fingh slowed.

Twenty metres before the bridge, Rihli clipped back in and accelerated. Red Face did the same. Both headed for the river. At the last moment, Rihli braked hard and, using a mountain biker's foot-down slide, changed direction towards the bridge. His momentum took him onto its wooden slats where he clipped back in. With three hard pedal strokes, he was across and away. He did not look back. Mariani had never seen a manoeuvre like it.

Red Face had charged into the river and was out of the saddle, trying to get maximum force through the pedals. But he'd misjudged the water's depth. His wheels were two-thirds submerged and he was struggling. Then it was as if someone had whipped the bike away from under him. He went down with a heavy splash.

Mariani, at the back of the riders walking across the bridge, glanced at Red Face who was sitting in the brown water, holding his elbow, head bowed, eyes closed, face white. His sunglasses were floating away from him.

The Crédit Haussmans led the short ascent away from the river.

They saw a chance. 'C'mon, boys.' 'Eat the pain.' 'Burn it!'

Out of the saddle, their three asses moved to the same tempo. Mariani watched them gain two metres, three, four, five. But it was as if they were just abstract concepts. He could not translate the gap into a need for positive action. He squeezed his eyes shut for a moment, urging processes to take place, connections to be made. Nothing. A dead zone. A challenge had been put down and it was as if they had asked him for the time.

At the top was a feed station. Marshals held drinks, energy bars and bananas. Mariani grabbed a bottle and shouted, 'Man down in the water.'

'Don't worry about him,' said Fingh. 'He deserves it. Bastard beats his dog.'

Mariani could see that Fingh was beginning to suffer. The Crédit Haussmans put their heads down. Their gap was now ten metres. The group sped through a village of no more than five houses. Outside the smallest, a string-haired woman in a wheelchair held up a purple-faced hydrocephalic baby and waggled it. The baby screamed. Encouragement or hate? Probably not even the child knew which. It just needed to scream.

Fingh shifted down a gear, gripped the bars and put in ten fierce turns of the pedals. Then he began to freewheel.

'I'm gonna puke.'

'Have some water,' said Mariani.

Fingh coughed. His bike wobbled. He turned his head to the hedge. A jet of vomit exploded from his mouth. He coughed again. Dry heaved. Shook his head. Slowed to a stop.

The Crédit Haussman at the rear looked back at Mariani. Two hundred metres later, he looked round again. Mariani could hear their voices. He knew they'd be confused about his tactics. Was he simply being snotty and refusing to ride with them? Was he messing with their heads? Did he have a mechanical? They'd know their level was some way below his. If he rode with them and took his turn at the front their average speed would increase and they might catch Rihli.

All three began to soft-pedal and within seconds Mariani was with them.

'Enjoying it?' asked Crédit Haussman One.

'Sure,' said Mariani.

'Want one?' asked Two, offering him an energy bar.

'I'm fine, thanks.'

'You all healed up now?' asked Three.

'Mostly.'

'You look really good,' said One.

'Thanks.'

'Want to work with us?' asked Two.

'Sure.'

'Take every eighth turn, if you like.'

'It's OK. I'll do my share.'

'Great. If you're sure? Sorry about our kit.'

'That's OK.'

'Gazin-Ségur PMP's our second-favourite team.'

'Don't worry about it.'

'Rihli can't be far ahead,' said Two.

'He's strong,' said Mariani.

'He needs to lose,' said Two. 'He butt-dipped my sister.'

'Right,' said Mariani.

*

The road to the Hgruh Mountains was long and straight. They saw Rihli's hard black shape in the distance. By the bottom of the climb, they'd caught him. He didn't acknowledge them, just kept working over a big gear.

The ascent was five kilometres into gathering mist. A hundred-metre stretch that required a horse's lungs to ride up. Almost immediately, Mariani could see that the Crédit Haussmans were going to struggle. He went to the front, Rihli in his wheel and the other three following on. He tried to keep the pace easy. The mist thickened. Rihli came up beside him.

'We drop these clowns and it's just you and me, uh?'

Mariani shrugged.

'C'mon,' said Rihli. 'You're not here to ride along picking your nose.'

He pushed ahead. 'C'mon, Wonder Boy. This is nothing for you. Kick my ass. C'mon.'

Mariani looked behind. The Haussmans had dropped back five metres.

'Wassa matter?' said Rihli, looking at Mariani as if he were a dried turd. 'Trying to bluff me, you sly wet cunt? Fuck you. I've heard your little girly gets double-holed by her daddy and her dog...'

On Mariani's second Grand Tour, his first Giro D'Italia, he had heard similar things. Ascending Mount Etna, he and a rider called Pronk had managed to get away from the peloton. Neither was a danger in the GC. The *maglia rosa* was already decided. Pronk, a party-loving Dutch prodigy who had been world champion at twenty, but spent most of the next four years trying to catch syphilis, was under heavy pressure from his team boss to claim a stage. He'd taunted Mariani all the way up, trying any kind of abuse to demoralise him.

Looking at Rihli's black-bearded face now, Mariani tried to recall how he had soaked up all Pronk's whispered filth and turned it into a fuel that became increasingly higher octane. He heard the accusations about bedroom activities with farm animals, his acorn-sized dick, how much his slutty English mother loved a gang rape, and with four kilometres to go, rocketed past Pronk. Which was what Pronk wanted. The Dutchman had sat behind Mariani, let that fuel blaze away, and then with five hundred metres remaining, eased past him, said 'Thanks, shithead', and claimed the win.

'Don't worry about it,' his team manger had said to a morose Mariani that night. 'You showed me what I wanted to see. I know that for a few minutes on that mountain, you wanted Pronk dead. You wanted to see his bleeding corpse left on the roadside for the crows. That doesn't make you a bad person. It makes you a good bike rider.'

The road up the Hgruh was old, grey concrete and looked as it had been imported from a war zone. Rihli weaved through the potholes, looking over his shoulder, muttering, taunting, waiting for Mariani's attack. Just the two of them ascending in the thick wet mist. Mariani kept his eyes on the shattered road. In his mind, vile curses and horror scenarios. Words.

Dead.
Kill.
Beat.
Destroy.
Smash.
Break.
Crush.
He repeated them. He sniffed. Rain began, cold hard pellets.

Before the Doberman had finished its work at the Malamute's throat, Mariani turned away and stared down at his shoes. They were dotted with flecks of sawdust and the toecaps were smeared with a dark matt slush. The basement he was in smelled of blood and body odour and cheap, harsh alcohol, and he felt if he took another breath of it, he would be sick. The crowd, fifty strong, roared the Doberman on.

Mariani's head wobbled. Neck muscles were always the first to go when you'd been drinking *sotinko*. From there the effects spread downwards to your feet, then somehow jumped back up to your brain.

'That dog's a world beater,' shouted Slirik Fingh into Mariani's ear. 'He'd do Golgotha. What do you think, Romain?'

Golgotha? It took Mariani a few moments to understand what Fingh was referring to. When he did he realised he hadn't thought of the hog for many days.

'Wanna stay for the terriers?' asked Fingh.

Mariani jerked a thumb over his shoulder. 'Get some air.'

'Sure.'

Fingh shook a lot of hands and then he and Mariani climbed up the concrete stairs and back on to the city's main street shopping street. It was dark and silent. The dogfights were taking place under a lady's outfitters.

'You all right?' asked Fingh. 'Having a good time?' He took a litre of *sotinko* from the pocket of his peach-coloured leather jacket and passed it over.

Mariani put the bottle of colourless, faintly oily liquid to his mouth, closed his eyes, and as the drink slid down his throat, thick and flavour-free, he remembered too clearly Rihli riding away up the Hgruh four days ago and his own blank response. The apathy. Not that he couldn't have stayed with Rihli, just that there was no desire to. No urge to fight, see Rihli in tatters, revel in his pain. He'd had to get off his bike then, as he felt his entire future fold in on itself. You're fucked, thought Mariani now, so you might as well get more fucked. He took three more gulps from the bottle.

'Good work,' said Fingh. 'Now – Dringl's.' He took the *sotinko* back from Mariani, returned it to his pocket and then reached inside his jacket and took out a pair of wraparound sunglasses. He put them on, began beatboxing the opening to 'Billie Jean' and slowly started to rotate his pelvis.

*

Strobing pinks and greens played over Mariani's face. The *sotinko* had reached his head now and it felt as if he had a cannonball on his shoulders. He sat slumped at the bar, his chin pressed to his chest. A metre in front of him, Fingh, his shirt silver and skin-tight, sunglasses still clutching his face, danced to Spandau Ballet with a frenzied bleached blonde. She had her bare arms around his neck. Her wattles of loose, fatty skin slopped over his shoulders, and she kept licking his ear. Through the fug of sixty-five-per-cent-proof alcohol, Mariani was beginning to wish that when Fingh had called him and asked him if he felt like an evening of fun in the capital, he had said no.

Wednesday was Cougar Night at Dringl's. The music was late-eighties English and American pop-rock with a slow ballad from local groups such as Cuhgji and Bved Liodri played every half-hour. Drinks were half-price for men under thirty, free for men under twenty-five.

Mariani felt an enormous lethargy come over him. His vision, which had drifted down to his half-unzipped fly, began to defocus. Just when he thought he was going to fall asleep, he felt a hand shake his shoulder.

'Hey,' said a female voice from what seemed to him to be the other side of the club.

He couldn't manage to raise his head at all.

'Hey, you're Romain Mariani,' said the voice. 'I used to teach you maths at school.'

A hand cupped his chin and lifted it.

Three women, all with the same greying hair, purplish eye shadow and prominent overbite appeared in front of him. Slowly, they merged into one single, jump-suited figure.

'Mrs Yeghklihi,' she said.

Dimly Mariani remembered her, in a floor-length grey skirt, chalking numbers on a blackboard.

'You're famous now,' she said, nodding.

'I'm fucked,' he said.

'Oh. Well, never mind.'

Mariani felt her hand begin to travel over the side of his face. Her fingers massaged his ear.

'You always were a nice-looking boy,' she said. 'You can take me home, if you like. I'll pay for a taxi. I've got a Jacuzzi bath.'

He felt sweat run down the middle of his chest. There was a smell of wet towels coming from Mrs Yeghklihi.

'You hit me on the head with a ruler once,' he said.

'Did I? Sorry.' She smiled and Mariani saw her big teeth and felt sad to his core.

And then, because it was the last thing he wanted to do, he put his hands on Mrs Yeghklihi's shoulders, pulled her to him and kissed her. His teeth crashed against hers. Her tongue wriggled and jumped around in his mouth, reminding him of a landed trout.

When he pulled away, Mrs Yeghklihi looked sad. 'You're a terrible kisser for a famous person.'

I'm fucked,' repeated Mariani, and as if to prove his point fell off his stool onto the floor.

*

It was past one a.m when the two men left Dringl's. Mariani, who had spent the previous hour in the reeking toilets, dry-heaving, pressing wet hand towels to his forehead and drinking stale-tasting water from the tap, was beginning to sober up. He took in big lungfuls of night air and thought about the logistics of getting home. But it occurred to him that the little house and the quaint village were like something from a children's story and irrelevant to the way he lived now. He felt he could easily wander the city streets for the rest of his life, growing a matted beard and living hand to mouth, his only friend a flea-infested mongrel on a string. That seemed a fitting response to a world that could so quickly and irretrievably shatter into fragments.

Fingh, who had not stopped drinking (he had moved on to *fkilm*, an acorn-derived liqueur), was on the phone. ''Course you wanna to meet him, honey…ah, come on, we'll be there in ten minutes.'

He took Mariani by the arm. 'Wanna check out the sweetest girl in Gkivk? In her nightie?'

He put an arm round Mariani's unresisting shoulders and piloted him into the night.

*

The flat was small and humid and smelled musky. The sweetest girl in Gkivk was a moody, willowy, full-breasted Bulgarian called Natalia.

She wore pink pyjamas and a matching silk headscarf. Her toenails were painted gold. On top of the television that dominated the living room, a small russet-coloured animal that Mariani thought might be some kind of monkey sat with its head jerking and tinkling noises coming from the silver bell attached to its collar.

Fingh introduced Mariani as 'athlete, friend to many celebrities and a symbol of all that's great about this country'.

Natalia, who didn't seem to speak much of the language, nodded and said, 'Ah.'

Mariani went to the toilet. The bathroom carpet was green and furry. The flush didn't work. He lay down for no reason, and unzipped his trousers and, to his surprise, took out his penis. He thought of Natalia's breasts straining at the cotton of her pyjama top. To his even greater surprise, his penis thickened. It seemed perfectly sensible then to masturbate. In less than a minute he was wiping his right hand on the carpet. He watched his quickly drying jism clump the man-made tufts.

When he went back there were lines of cocaine on the table. Natalia was looking at them in the way a cat looks at a sparrow.

Fingh was in the process of removing his trousers. His high-cut briefs were grey with an orange waistband.

After that, events took an increasingly confusing course. Later, Mariani seemed to recall that, in return for the cocaine, Fingh wanted Natalia to suck Mariani's cock, an event he, Fingh, would film on his mobile. He also wanted to sing a song during the cock-sucking, thus providing a live soundtrack for the resulting video which he would upload to the cycling section of the Eurosport website. Natalia had refused, Fingh had offered her handfuls of *chŏp*, but she had slapped him hard across the mouth, cursed Mariani and locked herself in the bedroom. Somehow Fingh persuaded Mariani to spend the night with him on the sofa. Fingh's wind was inhuman.

At six-thirty the next morning, Mariani levered himself off the sofa, thinking it could only be seconds before his head exploded. His bones felt soft and toxic. Fingh's bottle of acorn liqueur was on the floor, empty and capless. Lying next to it, stiff, with its tongue exposed, quite obviously dead, was the russet-coloured creature. Mariani stood still for a long moment and wondered what Hans Banquo was doing at this precise moment. He let himself out of the dishevelled and malodorous flat.

The Gkivk streets were grey and dusty. He wandered directionless, mouth and nose assailed by diesel fumes, cheap man-made fibres, dog and rat piss, uncollected rubbish, last night's meats, cement that was too dry and too old. He stood on a viaduct and looked down on to Vhiiojhi, the main north-south road, watching the Gourovskos and Yinczüs and the Dret scooters. An old woman in a red tracksuit and plastic sandals asked him for the time and then for a cigarette and then money. He gave her what he could. A big black bird landed on the stanchion of the viaduct's suicide netting and defecated.

Mariani wiped his palm across his mouth and walked off to find a taxi rank.

*

He woke at three a.m. the next morning determined to take matters into his own hands.

He went into the kitchen and then splashed water on his face. He opened a drawer and looked at all the knives, forks and spoons, glittering in the hard, overhead light. He picked up a corkscrew, put that down and then selected a sharpening steel. He'd never used it. Perhaps it would come in useful now. He put the tip to his ear and pushed gently, but it would not go in far. Perhaps it just needed more force. He touched his forehead, trying to imagine the site of the damage inside. He adjusted the angle of the steel upward and pushed harder. It really did not want to go in. He took it out again and explored the ear's canal with his finger. Not much room in there. He put his finger inside his nose instead. That was more promising. He brought the steel to his left nostril and began gently to prod around, searching for a way through. Just give the brain a poke, wake it up. Yes. But the nerves were too sensitive. Almost instantly, he had tears in his eyes and had to remove the steel. He dropped it in the sink; rubbed the side of his nose.

He felt his face to see if there were any openings he'd forgotten. There weren't. He had another idea. He lined up a suitable piece of kitchen wall and began to knock his head against it, softly to start with, just to assess the resulting pain. After three or four hits, the equivalent of light slaps, he tensed his neck muscles and gave the wall a reasonably firm butt. That hurt. He grunted. His head swam, his ears rang and his eyes unfocused. He retched. When the pain had subsided, he stood for a second, visualising his brain, checking his responses. He felt a slight buzz that hadn't been there before. Was this something? He felt compelled to find out.

He placed both hands against the wall and steadied himself. Slowly he drew back his head. He swallowed, then slammed his forehead into the plastered brick surface. As he staggered back, it was the noise that was most painful, as if he'd put his ear to a cannon as it fired. He fell to the floor clutching his head, feeling his skull might shatter if he let go. He began to hyperventilate. The pain was brutal and seemed to have depth and breadth and width. It felt evil and malicious. He'd experienced nothing like it, not even in the accident. He lay on the cold tiles for twenty minutes, foetal, drooling.

When he was able to get up, he went over to the sink and ran the tap until it was as cold as it could be and then put his head under it. He kept it there until the ringing, resembling an amplified, slowed-down car alarm, had begun to subside. Dripping water on the floor tiles, he stood, spluttering. He touched his forehead. There was a hard, tender swelling the size of half a small orange.

Go to bed, he thought. Just go to bed. And tomorrow make sure there are no power tools in the house.

*

Two days later, he was still in bed. In his socks and underwear. He couldn't think of a single reason to get up. The phone had rung many times – Keira, Grasch, Gazin-Ségur PMP's *directeur sportif*, several journalists – but he hadn't answered it and he hadn't checked his mobile. His head still had a thick, distant ache. He'd taken twenty-seven Paracetamol in forty-eight hours.

Finally, just as a grey light was beginning to creep into the room, he shifted himself out from between the warm and greasy sheets. He hadn't showered or shaved for nearly four days. He smelled of farmyards and hot salt, as if he'd just finished a hard tour stage.

Outside it was raining as it had been for nearly a day straight. Heavy and pitiless. The land slowly drowning.

In his flaccid dressing gown he slouched into the front room and turned on the television. He muted the sound and watched hours of cartoons, their acidic colours and incessant action in contrast to his inertia and the dank gloom of the house. He liked these misshapen mute creatures and their joyful never-ending carnage: they seemed realistic to him. He fell asleep on the sofa, remote control in his hand, the garish light from the screen playing across his pallid face.

At five-thirty he awoke. His tongue felt like it was about to crumble. He got up and went to the kitchen. He drank from the tap and then pissed directly in the sink. He looked out of the kitchen window and across the garden towards the grey mountains. Perhaps he should just get away for a few days. Cycling had been his way to escape this place, this life of silence, stillness and white cloud. But he was no longer a rider. He was a twenty-six-year-old brain-damaged uneducated joint heir to a run-down two-hectare pig farm. Perhaps he should sell the house, move to another country. And do what? What did washed-up cyclists always do? Open a bike shop? Run a café? Get fat, smoke cigarettes and when the days became too long and the memories too bitter, jam a gun to his head?

He put his index and middle fingers together and put his thumb up at ninety degrees. 'Handgun,' he said and snickered humourlessly. He put the fingers to the side of his head, then changed his mind and put them in his mouth.

'Boom.' He imagined his head snapping back and all his memories, hopes, dreams, desires, exploding out of the back of his skull. Then the darkness. He closed his eyes. *Ex-pro cyclist found dead aged thirty-nine. Did OK for a while.*

A tragic story. A dull story. Not his story.

He went to the phone and dialled. His lips were sticky and his palate felt like bark.

'Where've you been?' said Keira when she answered, her voice hard and hurt.

'Been? Nowhere. Here.'

'Are you sick?'

'I'm fine.'

'I thought you were going to call me after that race.'

'Yes.'

'What happened?'

'Nothing happened.' He looked at the floor and began scratching the side of his head with his untrimmed nails.

'Nothing?' She didn't say anything for a few seconds. Then, softer, realising: 'What do you want to do?'

'I don't know.' This was a lie. He wanted to do a lot of things. To touch her. To stop his life running away from him. To get a brain transplant.

'You could get a second opinion?' Her tone softer still. 'Maybe go to...I don't know, America or London.'

'I don't want to hear what they have to say,' said Mariani, though he knew he needed help and that this was why he was phoning Keira.

'I've done some research. New things are happening. New drugs for all kinds of problems, Parkinson's, Alzheimer's...they're making really good progress.'

'Those are diseases. This is injury.'

'Will you talk to my father? He has some contacts. He keeps asking me when he's going to meet you.'

'Should I talk to him about a new phone?' The words left a sour residue in his mouth.

'Stop it, Romain.'

'Sorry. I apologise.'

'All right. Listen, these chief executives, they're all in the Chief Executive club. He's bound to know someone in a drug company. There are so many round here: Cavasoglu, Sedaris, Hikke. Maybe find out what's in the...what do they call it?... the pipeline.'

'I don't know.' He shut his eyes. He felt uneasy even discussing the subject of drugs. But he had to do something.

'I just think you should know all the options. Let me speak to him. Look, why don't you come over for the weekend? I haven't seen you for nearly two months.'

'I know. It's just…'

'What?'

He sighed. 'I think my team contract is going to be cancelled. And not many companies are going to want their products advertised by a jobless man with half his mind missing.'

'If it's money you're worried about, I'll pay your airfare. It won't cost you anything while you're here.'

'I can't let you do that.' Accept it, he told himself. Let yourself be helped.

'Yes, you can.'

He sighed. 'I will pay you back.' What in, he thought then, piglets?

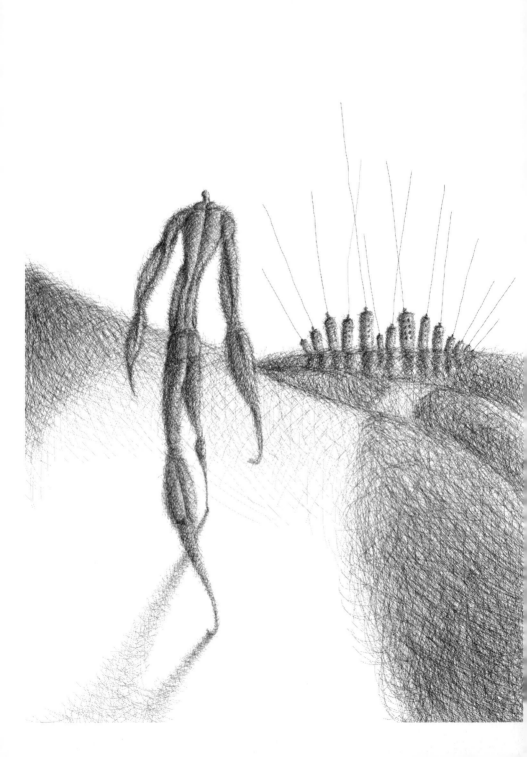

PART TWO

THIRTEEN

The clinks and chinks of cutlery and plates and glasses were the loudest noises in the dimly lit room. Mariani had never seen a man as perfectly shaved as the sommelier who was waiting, entirely motionless, hands clasped before him, for Gastein Ladoga's choice from the wine list.

'The Leroy,' said Ladoga. 'Ninety-six.' He handed back the red leather-bound volume.

The sommelier looked very happy and inclined his head. He went away.

'What do you think of the place, Romain?' asked Ladoga.

'It is...excellent,' he said. 'Very...excellent.'

'The chef is sometimes over-adventurous with his seasonings, but I still think it is the city's best.'

Gastein Ladoga made Mariani want to hide under the table. An ex-free-styler, Ladoga was nearly two metres tall. His shark-grey hair, two shades lighter than his suit, was brushed back from his face in a thick, gleaming wave. His skin was caramel-coloured and looked deep and soft. His elegant hands were huge, the fingers thin, long and hard, like the tines of a rake. Mariani thought of Tanel's etched, pouchy face and sunken eyes, the nicotine burnishes on his stubby fingers. Keira had told Mariani not to be fooled by her father's looks or by the facetious way he talked. In the last few years, she said, he had become so driven and hard-working that she feared for his health and could not understand why he wasn't a babbling wreck.

'I suppose, like Keira, you are vigilant about your diet,' said Ladoga. 'When I was competing, we ate what we liked. Things have moved on – though when I read about Michael Phelps's daily feasts, I must say it brought back happy memories. Ten pancakes for breakfast! Pizzas mid-morning! Now *that's* a diet. I mostly eat grilled fish now. Sad. Though if you ever get the chance, do try barracuda.'

A waiter offered Mariani a basket in which eight different breads were arranged. His fingers hovered over the choices, moving backwards and forwards until eventually he picked the darkest one. He sipped his water. As soon as he put the cut-glass tumbler down, another waiter softly topped it up to the prescribed level and thanked Mariani for allowing him to do so. He noticed the man's eyes flicker across Keira's arms and shoulders, exposed by her dress. Ladoga noticed it too and stared hard at the waiter's retreating back.

'You fly a lot for your work?' asked Mariani.

'Someone flies *him*,' said Keira. 'He has his own jet. A *black* one.' She looked at her father with loving mockery.

Ladoga smiled, showing wide, long teeth. 'An indulgence. A toy, really. A Gulfstream G550. But it reduces stress very effectively. My blood pressure has dropped considerably since I bought it. Without that jet, all my meetings would be in the great boardroom in the sky.'

He turned to focus on Mariani. 'Don't take this the wrong way, Romain, but *you* appear healthier than I expected. Apart from that nasty mark on your head. Cyclists usually look to me as if they'd snap in two with a puff of wind.'

'Well, I haven't been able to train too much. I've put on a few pounds.'

'To me they look as if they're undergoing torture,' said Keira. 'But they will never say what they know, never confess. Cyclists would make good spies. All that lying in the races too...ooh, ooh, I can't go on...oh, look, I've recovered and now I've won! Worse than footballers.'

'I think it's all that going uphill,' said Ladoga. 'Swimming's a nice, flat sport. You might reek of chlorine, and have to enjoy the taste of babies' urine...'

' Dad!'

' ...but at least you never have to go uphill. Anyway, Romain doesn't look dishonest to me.' Ladoga appraised Mariani with unreadable eyes.

Three more waiters silently appeared, each carrying a pristine white plate on which was arranged artistically sauced aquatic protein in a variety of shapes.

Mariani's waiter reverently lowered his offering on to the place setting and reminded him of what he'd ordered. He nodded, which he hoped was what he was meant to do.

Pale-gold wine was poured. He smelled rich, oily butter and just-ripe apricots.

'Well, nice to meet you at last, Romain.' Ladoga smiled. 'Why she's had to hide you away so furtively, I don't know.' The raised wineglass looked as small as an egg cup in his hand. 'Your very good health,' he said, and put the glass down again, untouched. 'Speaking of which, I made several calls this morning. I hope they may be of some benefit.'

Mariani tasted the food. He'd no more than rolled it across his tongue before it seemed to disappear. It was like a conjuring trick. That was typical of fish, dead or alive. The way they flitted around, there one second, gone the next. Herzy claimed that eating fish made you shifty and unreliable: he caught them, but put them straight back. He dismissed sushi as the food of the Devil.

'I know little about the pharmaceutical industry,' continued Ladoga, 'so I couldn't comment on their work. But these men – and one woman – have very good reputations. These aren't Frankensteins making potions in laboratories strewn with human organs.'

'We *are* eating,' said Keira, though Mariani saw that she'd hardly touched her food, simply moved it around the plate.

'Sorry, darling.' With one long finger, he stroked the back of her hand. 'And if they are, they're doing a good job of hiding it. Though as their vision statements endlessly proclaim, they are in business to push what is known, what can be achieved: rather like athletes, I suppose. As I am sure they would admit – though not on the record – sometimes their products don't work at all, sometimes they work too well, and sometimes they work in a way they weren't supposed to. Anyway…Very sketchily, mentioning no names, I went through the problem as Keira explained it to me. They were interested.'

'You should speak to them,' said Keira to Mariani, nodding.

'Thank you for making those calls,' he said and sat up straighter in his chair. 'It was very kind.'

'Obviously we all know how sensitive and, to use a business term, challenging this subject is for athletes. I still remember the East German swimmers with their hairy backs and absence of breasts. I stared too long at this enormous bear-like thing once, and she and two of her teammates threatened, as they put it, to beat nine shades of *scheisse* out of me. They seemed nothing more than genetic experiments. I believe the bearess finally went over to the other side. Had some items glued on. Petra became Peter. Works in construction now, I think.'

Mariani laughed. Ladoga was certainly not the pompous businessman he'd been expecting to meet.

'Some items glued on?' Keira gave Mariani an apologetic look. 'You wouldn't think he was a chief executive with an office the size of this restaurant and three personal assistants, would you? Is that how you talk to your shareholders?'

Ladoga winked at Mariani, and he had to stop himself from winking back.

They ate in comfortable silence for a short while, Keira exchanging secretive smiles with her father. Mariani finished his second glass of wine. It was heady and powerful and he wanted another.

'We were thinking of sponsoring a cycling team once,' said Ladoga. 'About three years ago. But it was too risky. For our reputation, you know. Tell me, are the drugs as rife now as they were then?' Ladoga looked at Mariani steadily, one grey eyebrow slightly raised.

Caught unawares, he cleared his throat and shifted in his seat. 'It's…It's very difficult to say. I don't think so…but there are people in all jobs who want to cheat, I guess. There's pressure everywhere to do better. Often results are all that matter.'

'True. Certainly, there are many people in the world of business who are enhancing their performance illegally. Some use computers, some plain old-fashioned bullshit. And on a more individual level, plenty I'm sure are doing so via narcotics.' Ladoga ran a long finger thoughtfully along the smooth line of his jaw. 'People often have to work all night and be alert the next day. One can only drink so much coffee. Stress levels have never been higher. Our HR department gets through more boxes of tissues than your average pharmacy. But the world expects more and more and we cannot disappoint: stock markets are unforgiving at the best of times, and I'm afraid we just have to knuckle down and somehow keep performing. Money – it's both a lover and a tyrant. I don't condone drug taking but I do understand it. It's a very complex issue. The laws here are the strictest in Europe, but patently don't work. We have a drug-related death a day in this city. Your father had a problem, no?'

Mariani blinked and then took a sip of water. Ladoga's words had unsettled him, but only for a moment. The man was very smart and obviously loved his daughter. He would have done his research on any male she brought along for dinner, especially one she had asked him to become personally involved with.

'Yes,' said Mariani. 'But we share a last name, that's all.' He thought that was a good and, in the way he'd meant it, truthful answer. He smiled with what he hoped was conviction.

The waiters began smoothly to clear away their plates. Ladoga was silent until they had done so.

'I would like to help you,' he continued. 'I like you already. Keira tells me she loves you.'

'And I love her,' said Mariani.

'I'm glad to hear it – and to see your English roots don't prevent you from saying what you feel. You'll have to explain cricket to me, by the way. And the House of Lords.' He looked at Keira. 'I don't want to embarrass her, but my daughter is the most important thing in the world to me.'

'Dad – you're so...soppy,' she said.

For a moment, Mariani thought Ladoga was about to cry and he thought again of Tanel, and the way that, when his father shouted, spittle would cling to the bottom of his moustache.

'Now,' said Ladoga, picking up his fork, 'public displays of affection over. Let's enjoy the rest of our dinner, shall we?'

FOURTEEN

Ladoga had to attend a meeting at ten-thirty, so at just after ten, Mariani, with four glasses of Corton-Charlemagne inside him, was walking unsteadily through the exit. Keira and her father had been stopped at the door by the maître d' for a last waft of charm. As Mariani stepped into the street, he saw two bored-looking photographers waiting in the shadows. They ignored him but, as soon as Ladoga and Keira appeared, raised their cameras and moved forward. Keira reached for Mariani's hand.

Flashes popped. Ladoga smiled and said good evening. One of the photographers, a pudgy-faced man, got too close to Keira and Ladoga froze. Something changed in his smile. His stillness seemed to warn of an imminent act of violence: on the end of the thick cables of his arms, just his fingers' last two joints were moving. Ladoga did not look at the offending lensman, or talk to him, but the man's face wobbled with concern and he moved back, lowering his camera apologetically. Keira glanced away, as if to avoid this sudden display of her father's darker nature, and held Mariani's hand more tightly. Both photographers faded into the night. By the kerb, Ladoga's custom-built black stretch Mercedes waited, its gull wing rising.

Once inside the car, Ladoga took his PDA from an inside jacket pocket and began to work the silver-and-gold device quickly and expertly. He faced forward, spread out across the dark leather seating. Mariani and Keira sat opposite. The chauffeur, his hairless neck white and thick, piloted the car into the evening traffic. Mariani's head felt tight and hot and he began to wish he hadn't drunk a third glass of wine, let alone a fourth.

'Work, work, work. Work and life have become almost the same things now,' Ladoga said as his thumb skittered across the keys. 'I haven't swum for three years. Perhaps we need a new word to describe what we do with ourselves all day. If I didn't work...well, it would be like losing a vital organ. Though I might not be twice divorced.'

Ten mostly silent minutes later, the Mercedes glided to a stop outside Keira's apartment block. She kissed her father.

'Thanks for dinner, Dad.'

'Thank you,' said Mariani, and shook Ladoga's vast hand. 'And for your help.'

'I'll call you tomorrow. I'll be in Dubai for the day. Sweet dreams.'

Later, Mariani lay awake in the deep blue quiet of Keira's bedroom. His hand rested on her hip, index finger lightly rubbing the ridge of the bone. He looked over: three-twenty on her digital clock. The text he'd sent to Serge Hamptons that morning was still unreturned. Gazin-Ségur PMP's *directeur sportif* had left a message that talked of difficult decisions he did not want to make, but would probably have to. Mariani glanced at the slim, delicate shape lying next to him and tried to imagine Keira in filthy patched jeans, work boots and rain hat and carrying a pailful of slops to pens where fat pink bodies writhed and blubbery mouths screamed. He rubbed his eyes and exhaled through his nose. His leg ached and his head hurt.

Fear filled him like a bad gas. Fear that his life as a rider was already over. Fear of meeting men in white coats in airless rooms who would see him as just another animal on which to experiment. And some other more vague sense of unease, to do with making choices and living with the consequences.

Why had he worried about Banquo on that descent, paid attention to him and not the road? Because Banquo had just offered him everything he had ever wanted. It was stupid to deny it. The team, the money, the chance to become the kind of rider they wrote books about. Not just another name, casually mentioned, usually prefixed by 'Hey, whatever happened to...' But the sweet perfume of this future had made him dizzy. He had made the wrong decisions.

Three-twenty-one. Life disappearing.

*

At eight, he made coffee and found croissants in the fridge. He put the breakfast on a tray and brought it into the bedroom, placing it on the table on his – the left – side of the bed. Keira was awake. He kissed her and brushed the hair off her face.

'I've been thinking,' she said.

'Bit early, isn't it?'

'You could move here. I mean in here. With me.'

He handed her a brimming white mug and a croissant. He ran through responses in his head but none seemed right.

As Keira ate, pastry flakes fell on to the duvet's white cover. 'You've always wanted to get away,' she continued. 'We're only twenty minutes from the mountains. Plenty of cyclists have homes here. Hans Banquo does, I think. If Dad's contacts prove any good and you start treatment, you'll have to be based here.' She sipped her coffee.

'Yes. And if they don't?'

'We'll work something out.'

Mariani nodded. He looked at his feet. His inability to think of anything other than the fact that his toenails needed cutting began to make him angry.

'Hey,' said Keira. 'Don't knock me down in the rush to get your socks in my cupboard.' She put the remaining third of the croissant into her mouth.

Speak, he thought, but the words seemed to run away from him.

Keira sipped more coffee and then reached down and put the mug on the floor. She looked out of the window and across the morning glitter-scapes of the city. 'I'm meeting friends in twenty minutes.' Her voice cold.

'Can we talk later? Please?'

'You know where everything is.'

She threw off the duvet and the ivory cashmere blanket that lay on top of it and walked past him towards the bathroom. The muscles in her calves flexed and released. She shut the bathroom door and locked it. He heard loud voices from the radio and the hiss of the shower but they could not disguise the sound of retching.

*

He was sitting on the black modular sofa, drinking his fourth and strongest coffee and watching a chef on the flat-screen TV prepare a raclette, when his phone rang.

'It's Gastein Ladoga.'

'Oh. Yes. Good morning.'

'I don't know what your plans are, but my contacts are willing to see you this coming week.'

'This week?' Mariani blinked twice, sat up and held the phone more tightly. His throat went dry. 'That's perfect. Yes. Thank you.'

'They'll call you. Let me know how things go.'

'Of course.'

'Is Keira there?'

'No, she had to go out.'

'All right. 'Bye for now. We're taking off. '

''Bye. And thank you again.'

He dropped the phone to the sofa and thought about the bright, sterile world of pharmaceuticals, a world which to him appeared as dark and shadowy as a prison.

In the cube of black glass and gold-painted steel that housed Meruntan Technologies, Mariani was introduced to Franck Rostaing, a bearded fat man, head of Research and Development, Psychosomatic Inhibitors.

'I don't think my problem is psychosomatic,' he said when Rostaing had explained the term.

'Neither do I,' said Rostaing. 'I didn't when I was told about it.'

'So why am I here?'

'Because men in suits like to keep other men in suits happy.'

'I see.'

'Nice to meet you.'

'Yes. Goodbye.'

In a silent room at a syringe-shaped building in the far reaches of the city, he met Kornelius Purps, Vice-president, Zinck HealthCare. Slim, languid, in white jeans, a gold-buttoned blue blazer and ochre suede loafers, Purps had eyes the colour of swimming pools and a handshake that wasn't quite firm enough. His eau-de-cologne was floral with undertones of putresence. He opened a laptop and pressed a key every time Mariani answered a question. Purps seemed somehow disappointed in his interviewee.

'You have full use of all your motor functions?'

'Yes.'

'OK. No speech impediments? No erectile dysfunction?'

'No. I mean, hardly at all.'

'Any problems walking? Do you ever find yourself staring at nothing with your mouth open? Or drooling? Or masturbating?'

'No.'

'Hmm. Any uncontrollable rages? Sudden desires for sexual violence?'

'No.'

Purps sighed. 'Any longing to commit crime? Burglary? Armed robbery? Arson?'

'No.'

'What is my name?'

'Kornelius Purps.'

'Do you dream of death?'

'How do you mean?'

'Your own? Those of familes, friends, lovers? Prostitutes? High-ranking politicians?'

Mariani hesitated for a second. 'If so, not often.'

'Any hunger for your own faecal matter?'

'Sorry?' asked Mariani, taken aback.

'Your own excreta. Shit? Do you ever want to eat it?'

'No.'

'Do you ever believe you are a Messiah and that everyone else is here to do your bidding?'

'No. Definitely not.'

'What colour is my hair?'

'Blond?'

'Do you believe, Romain, that children are evil and must be destroyed?'

'No.'

Purps closed the lid on his laptop. 'Well, thank you so much for coming in. I'm not sure we can help, but if we can, well, we have your number. Enjoy the rest of your day.'

Finally, he had coffee with Janine Venn, chief executive of Aginanal. Fortyish, firm-jawed, with cropped black hair and, she said, a cyclist herself. She appeared tired but also fidgety, as if there were some other issue she should be dealing with. In perfect English and with quick, clipped tones, she told Mariani that his problem was untreatable by any officially recognised drug.

'Meaning?'

'Well, I presume you can't take anabolic steroids, which as I'm sure you know do work to increase aggression and the urge for combat. Also to reduce sperm count, enlarge the prostate and produce breast tissue, of course.'

Mariani shifted in his chair. 'Steroids? No, I can't take anything like that.'

'The thing is, you want something that restores what you had. That doesn't exist. There is no medical treatment for traumatic brain injury.'

'Nothing?' asked Mariani, though he already knew this.

'Oh, someone's getting lobotomised mice to eat amino acids and claiming success, but that's all puff.'

Janine Venn steepled her fingers. She moved her dry, chapped lips across each other very gently.

'I'm sorry.' She stood up. 'Very nice to meet you.'

'And you.'

'Give my best to Gastein.'

'I will.'

*

For the rest of the warm heavy afternoon, Mariani wandered through the city centre. There was an air of genteel, moneyed perversity. Outside a shop that sold bespoke clothes for trans-sexuals stood a smiling male security guard wearing a fitted tweed skirt and jacket, a BlueTooth winking in his ear. For a three inch-high gold sculpture of a laughing surgeon whose hand held a decapitated woman's smiling head, an art gallery wanted more than Mariani earned in a year. He looked into one of the cafés that seemed to be on every corner. On a table nearest the window, a teenage girl in diamante-framed sunglasses was feeding forkfuls of a cream cake to a small dog. Only the animal's rear end had not been shaved: it was if it were topless, clad only in low-slung fur trousers.

He began to get a headache. There were a lot of pharmacies and Mariani went into one for pills. The automatic doors parted soundlessly. The pale wood shelves were lined with products in white boxes whose silver lettering spelled out phrases from a dystopian future: cellular regeneration and dermatalogical plumping. There were many drugs on sale for complaints that Mariani didn't realise were complaints. The air conditioning wafted over his face cool air that smelled vaguely of mint. The girl behind the counter gave him three recommendations and smiled when he made his choice. Her teeth were sleek and straight and somehow plump. The tanned silver-haired man who seemed to be in charge was sitting at an iMac and talking into yet another of Gastein Ladoga's gold mobile phones.

As Mariani turned to go, he saw a straw-blonde slim woman in a sleeve-less black dress looking blankly at the rows of face creams. He knew her, but couldn't attach a name. She turned her head slowly towards him. Only when he saw her tight, vague eyes did he recognise Claudia Banquo. Her hair was shorter than before and brushed across her head. She pushed a stray lock behind her ear with the middle finger of her left hand and Mariani saw the glitter of a diamond stud. He felt refrigerated air drift across the hairs on the back of his neck.

'How are you?' As if she bumped into him twice a week.

'Hello. I'm fine, thank you.'

She smoothed her dress down one thigh.

'Are you fine?' he asked. 'And Hans?'

She didn't seem to hear the question. 'You're visiting your girlfriend?'

'Yes.'

'How do you like the city?'

'Um. It seems very— '

'Yes.' She brushed at something on her arm and her tricep twitched. Her lipstick was the same raspberry pink he remembered.

Mariani cleared his throat. 'Are you going to…to the Giro?'

She shook her head. She inhaled, her breasts pushing gently at the matt fabric of her dress. 'Well. It's nice to see you.'

'And you.'

Claudia put out her hand and Mariani took it. He remembered their meeting in the square after the Essence, when he had felt she belonged to him. Now she was just a beautiful blonde woman, another man's wife, unattainable.

She gently released her grasp and smiled with one side of her mouth. 'Enjoy the rest of your stay. Take care.'

Without looking at the shelf, she picked a small white pot from it and walked past him to the counter. Mariani opened the door, paused for an instant and then stepped out onto the immaculate street.

Walking, he watched the city as if it were a foreign film he could not understand.

He found himself in a park. He walked straight paths and followed legible and easily visible signage. Couples rowed yellow boats on the still waters of the perfectly round lake. Two men in late middle age with brightly coloured pullovers across their shoulders, sat on a bench, sharing an éclair and thumbing BlackBerries. A line of schoolboys, in terracotta-coloured shorts, oatmeal V-necks and socks and brown sandals, walked smartly and silently behind a female teacher. Though pleasant, the images had no meaning for Mariani and he imagined that livestock must feel this way when they looked at the world.

He found a bench and sat. Next week, he realised, he would be twenty-seven. By thirty, most bike riders had reached their peak. On the U-Analyser in Keira's bathroom that morning (she'd bought the same model as him), he'd seen eighty-four point one on the readout. Even his hands felt fat. He hadn't ridden a bike for nearly three weeks. That night, his *directeur sportif* was meant to call him: Mariani knew what he was going to say. There had been no contact from Serge Hamptons.

As he watched a small girl in a pinafore dress and a pink sun hat feed cubes of bread to a politely quacking teal, Mariani thought how quickly one kind of life could be replaced by another, and how difficult it was to stop that happening.

*

He was quiet that night at dinner with Keira. Told her that Aginanal had been as useless as all the others. She too had little to say. There was an air of regret and unfocused frustration, generated, Mariani knew, mostly by himself.

She had picked up some salads from the local delicatessen and he became more interested in arranging them on his plate than eating them. He placed an artichoke alongside a small pile of bulgur wheat and then formed a rectangle around it with asparagus spears. It was healthy, low-calorie and pretty. He looked at it and longed for *guhtruzi*. It would be nice to sit at Svarik's and drink a Vighü and feel dense meat fibres between his teeth.

Soak up rich ram's juices with thick hard bread. Then, in the morning, ride to Lake Rig. And after that, spend the afternoon in the hammock, watching the trees dance in the wind.

He took an asparagus spear between thumb and middle finger and stabbed it into the bulgur wheat. He did it a number of times.

'What's going on in that thick skull of yours?' asked Keira.

'The usual. Stupid stuff.'

'Do you hate me?'

He blinked and put down his fork.

'Hate you? No. Why ask such a thing?'

'You've hardly spoken to me all day. We've had sex once since you've been here. You can't even look at me now.'

'I'm sorry.'

'I'm trying to help you. Dad's trying to help you. Do you not want to be helped?'

'Of course.'

'I'm sorry about the team. Really. But you knew it was coming.'

'Yes.' He pushed back his chair. He must not let himself be dragged down. He stood and walked around to the back of her chair. Put his arms around her neck.

'You know where I'm from. That country. We are sometimes just like this.'

'Dumb assholes.' She smiled up at him.

'Yes. Dumb assholes.'

He leant over and turned her face to his, removed a stray eyelash from her cheek and then kissed her. Softly bit the giving flesh of her lips. Ran his hands along the front of her jeans. Firm meat of her thighs.

She got up and walked towards the bedroom, pulling her T-shirt over her head as she did so. Mariani followed. In there, he flicked the lights off, closed the curtains and gently turned Keira on to her front. He felt conscious of his softening body. And he did not want her to see his face.

SiXTEEN

An hour later, he lay in the bath. It was too hot. Sweat leaked from his forehead and ran into his eyes. It made him think of the final climb of the Essence and he remembered de Vilde, face smeared with road dust, nose burnt and glowing, believing for one afternoon that he wasn't just a two-legged dog, servile and grateful, that he was in fact a champion, a prince of the road, a true king of the mountains. Mariani wondered if de Vilde had died still clinging to that belief.

He sank below the scorching water. Slowly let bubbles of air out through his nose. He began to feel as if everything he was doing was built on fantasy.

When his lungs were empty he stayed under, feeling the pressure build on his diaphragm, hoping to squeeze the sense of delusion from his body. He felt the inside of his head start to turn black. He urged himself not to falter, to purge the temptation to give up. There was a knock on the door.

He surfaced, the hair on his head like dark paint.

'Dad – on the phone!'

Jeszu.

His mind began to work. Perhaps Ladoga had another contact he'd forgotten about. Or news of a breakthrough.

He pulled himself out of the bath and wrapped a towel round his soft middle and put another across his shoulders.

He opened the door. Keira, still naked, though he hardly noticed, handed him her mobile. He put it to his ear.

'Hello?'

'Romain. How've your meetings been going?'

'Everybody is sympathetic, but…there doesn't seem to be much hope. Do you know anyone else?'

Keira stood watching him, with her head to one side, arms folded under her breasts. Half an hour ago, lying silently against her, his semen had trickled out of her on to his leg and she'd murmured, 'Bye bye, hope to see you again soon,' and he'd felt so much love for her.

'Keira's told me you're getting very down,' said Ladoga. 'I think she is too. Perhaps you could come to my house and we could talk. Just us boys.'

'Of course,' said Mariani, hoping he wasn't going to be given a reprimand about Keira or some kind of motivational speech.

'I'll send the car for you. Tomorrow at nine p.m.?'

*

The Mercedes slowed and turned right into a tree-lined private road. In the car's headlights, the tarmac looked smooth and glossy as if it had just been varnished. After a hundred metres the car came to a security gate. The driver drew up ten metres from it.

From the back seat, Mariani watched as a man in a military uniform stepped forward holding an angled pole with a camera lens built in to its end. In his other hand the guard held a small screen. He nodded at the driver and then slid the pole underneath the chassis of the car and moved it from front to back while looking at the screen. He withdrew the pole, walked around to the other side of the car and performed the same procedure. Then he waved the Mercedes through. The gate opened automatically as the car approached.

He's a chief executive in one of the safest countries in the world and they check his car for bombs, thought Mariani.

The car stopped in front of a melding of white cubes, curves and glass, a house of a type that Mariani had only ever seen in films featuring art-collecting master criminals. It seemed not to have one roof, but a number of them, built in the form of cascading ski slopes. The driver got out and opened the back door of the car.

'Goodnight, sir.'

'Goodnight.'

As Mariani walked up the short gravel drive, a door-sized panel opened in the enormous cylinder that formed the right-hand side of the house. Ladoga stepped through the opening on to the gravel and watched him approach.

Mariani saw that he was gripping his PDA between his long, taut middle finger and his thumb and propelling the device round and round with the index finger of his other hand.

When Mariani stopped in front of him, Ladoga spun the PDA with increasing speed, turning it into a silver-gold blur.

'All this information,' he said. 'The more we know, the more problems we can solve. The more we can progress.' The spinning PDA stopped dead. 'Come in, Romain.'

As the two men crossed the threshold, soft yellow pools of light began to illuminate the vast pristine space inside, as if miniature suns were rising. Apart from the heel-click of Ladoga's tan Berluti lace-ups and the dull scrape of Mariani's trainers, there was not a decibel of sound. The air felt empty and smelled of nothing. The walls were white and bare. A glass table with twelve transparent chairs arranged around it stood at one end of the room. Six glass ten-centimetre thick shelves in the form of waves ran the complete length of one wall. Mariani looked up. The ceiling of the room was not flat, but flowed and swelled like skin stretched over a human body. In the centre of the room was a white metal structure, shaped like angel's wings and with a base that reminded him of a melted doughnut.

'That's a furniture installation, in case you were wondering,' said Ladoga. 'Or, seat.'

Mariani looked at it again. It had armrests curved like the blades of scythes and built-in chrome restraints at the ankle area.

'The artist called it *Electric Chair of a Perverse but Beautiful Future Race.* Fully functioning too, he told me.' Ladoga eased himself onto the seat of the installation and stretched out his long legs.

'So,' said Mariani, hesitantly. 'You wanted to see me?' He was beginning to feel confused. This was not the man he'd met in the restaurant.

'But what *do* we know?' said Ladoga, ignoring his question and picking up his own opening thread. He put his arms on the chair's rests as if preparing for imminent execution. 'What do you know, Romain? How to fix a puncture, I suppose. How to ride a bike up a hill. Shall I tell you what I know? I know what is necessary to run a company that has grown at twenty-five per cent a year for the last five years. I know what it is like to out-manoeuvre Warren Buffett. I know what it is like to work for seventy-two hours straight. How do you think I know these things?'

Ladoga's tone was neutral. As if what he called 'these things' was just information. Mariani glanced at him and the businessman seemed to be no more than a shape, just tight angles and sharp edges. Mariani was reminded of a revolver, open for loading. He felt nervous and took half a step backwards.

'I think sometimes, too, Romain, of things I don't know, but would like to. What is it like to kill a man? To undergo life-saving surgery? To fight in a war? To live through an air crash? What is it like to touch a nuclear weapon?'

Mariani began to feel that in the next moment Ladoga could either break his neck or hug him. The man seemed to be inhabiting a parallel dimension where anything was possible. Mariani shifted his weight and had an urge to put his hands in his pockets and protect his testicles.

'I love Keira,' said Ladoga. 'My God, I love that girl.' He pushed a stray question-mark-shaped lock of dark grey hair back off his forehead. 'You seem to be vital to her future happiness. So...' He stood. 'You have heard of Alann Triesmaan, no doubt?'

The air suddenly seemed to become thinner to Mariani, and he had to snatch his next breath.

'I know his name, yes.'

'And his reputation?'

Mariani nodded.

'It's not undeserved. But he is a man of remarkable ability.'

'You know him?'

'He is...how shall I put this? He is my consultant.'

Mariani had the sensation that his bodily functions had paused their activities. 'I don't understand.'

'As I said at dinner, there are people in the world of business who are enhancing their achievements illegally. I happen to be one of them. Alann Triesmaan has enabled me to perform in the way that the business world demands – in fact, beyond it. Without his work, I think I'd probably be back coaching swimmers at a Basel high school.'

To Mariani, the white, empty room seemed suddenly full of swirling shapes in clashing colours and dissonant, conflicting noises.

'Can I get this straight?' he said. 'Triesmaan supplies you with drugs?'

'A little prosaic, Romain. He has created a bespoke compound based on my genetic and metabolic profile. It has expanded my mental and physical capacities by, he estimates, seventeen per cent. It is, as he says, the future. If the world demands growth, then we too must grow.'

Ladoga stepped closer to Mariani, towering over him.

'Let me show you the rest of the place.'

Mariani, the inside of his head alternating between emptiness and chaos, followed him towards a vast sand-blasted glass plane that seemed to operate as some kind of room divider. The plane was inset into the pale grey stone floor. As they approached it parted, providing a gap exactly the correct width for them to pass.

'I'm not proud of what I've done,' said Ladoga, as they walked through. 'I never cheated as an athlete. But once I started in business, my financial aspirations got the better of me. I started late, had a lot of ground to make up. Once successful, the pressure to maintain that success became enormous. Everything else expanded, but I had reached my limits.'

In the next space, four columns two metres high supported a fifteen metre-long glass tank that was full of water. A platform connected the top edge of the tank to a gallery that ran around the space.

'Lap pool,' said Ladoga. 'Never used it.'

A staircase with glass treads spiralled upwards to the gallery. There was no handrail. Ladoga climbed two steps at a time. Mariani trailed behind him.

'I tried meditation,' continued Ladoga, 'read Eastern philosophies, turned vegetarian. I learnt mental alertness techniques from masters of martial arts. I even experimented with LSD. Waste of time, frankly.'

At the top, he turned left. At the far end of the gallery, he opened a door. 'Spare room.'

Mariani had been expecting something on the same scale as the rest of the house, but this room was half the size of his own bedroom at home. A single bed with a pale beech frame and covered with a white duvet stood alongside one wall. A toilet and sink were partitioned from it by a single sheet of shoulder-high opaque glass. The window was the size of a hardback book.

'Not a single guest in five years,' said Ladoga. The laugh was a humour-less exhalation through his nostrils. He stood at the threshold to the cell-like space. 'The business was on the edge of collapse. Too many meetings in too many places. Too many insoluble problems. I had to be more than I was. The cycling team we were about to sponsor – or rather, one or two of the riders – made me think. Several phone calls later, I met Alann Triesmaan. Two weeks after that, GL1 arrived. Personalised, even down to the label.'

Mariani rubbed his hand over his forehead to try to ease the feeling that his skull was tightening. 'Fuck. I mean, what is it? A stimulant? Amphet-amines? Cocaine of some kind?'

'He won't tell me what's in it or how it works. That was part of the deal. I hardly think it would be approved by the Medical Council.' Ladoga smiled tightly.

'Does Keira know anything?'

'No. And she mustn't. Keira is…well, she has a black-and-white view of the world. Honest, I suppose. It's difficult to be honest with honest people.'

Ladoga led Mariani slowly back along the gallery.

'I'm telling you this for her sake, not yours. She knows you won't be happy until you're riding at your previous level. I've told her to get rid of you, but that seems not to be an option. I don't know if Triesmaan can help you. I was hoping my other, more conventional, contacts could. He can do wonderful things if you're prepared to take the risks. It's up to you.'

Mariani looked down to the cavernous white spaces below him. He be-gan to feel giddy and had a sudden urge to throw himself over the gallery's railings and on to the floor below. The desire built until it seemed to him that he was already plummeting through the air.

SEVENTEEN

Mariani walked down the silent suburban street. The houses were identical. Grey weatherboard. A porch on the right side. Trim lawns all the same shade of emerald green. Hanging baskets with pink and powder blue flowers. The evening sun shone on buffed German mid-range saloons in silver and black that had been precision-parked in short drives.

A slim couple in matching white and red tracksuits were jogging towards him. They ran in step. Mariani moved to the edge of the pavement to let them past.

'*Danke*,' said the man.

'*Danke*,' said the woman.

Their faces were tanned the colour of wheatflakes.

He came to number forty-nine. The car in the drive was an Audi A5. Mariani glanced in through the driver's window. A pair of black leather gloves was draped over the gear shift.

He paused, went to the door and then pressed the brass buzzer. It sounded with a cheery, chiming ding-dong. There was no answer. He pressed it again. He checked the text on his phone's screen. He looked at the gleaming black wooden door and the two polished brass numerals bolted to it. The address was correct. He looked at his watch. Seven p.m. The time the text had told him to be here. His teeth felt unbrushed. He hadn't slept more than an hour last night. His bowels had been unstable all day. He sank his neck further into the collar of his zipped-up jacket and pulled his beanie lower on his forehead.

In the distance, a pink cloud was impaled on the sharp point of a dark mountain.

Footsteps.

'Sorry, old cock. Just had to pop to the shop.'

Mariani turned. An eyebrowless face too near his, flushed and mouth-breathing. No chin. White flecks on fat lips. Hat on its head. Little pink feather in the hat's band.

'Let's get inside, shall we?'

Bennett held a tin of powdered milk in his left hand. With his right he dug into his trouser pocket and brought out a single brass key. He put the key in the lock. The door swung open on soundless hinges.

'Welcome, old cock.'

Bennett stepped inside. Mariani hesitated. His scrotum seemed to contract and his saliva thickened.

'Please – come in,' said Bennett. 'I'll get the kettle straight on.'

Mariani made himself put one foot in front of the other. He entered. Bennett shut the door after him with a firm and exact click.

'Tea, coffee?'

'Coffee. Please.'

'Right you are. Pop yourself in there,' said Bennett and pointed a small, scrubbed index finger towards the front room visible through an open door. 'Milk...sugar?'

'Just milk.'

'Biscuit?'

'No, thank you.'

'Right you are, old cock.'

Bennett wandered off towards the back of the house. Mariani entered the spacious front room. The immaculate carpet under his feet was mid-green. Two matching leather sofas covered in protective plastic wrapping were arranged opposite each other. Between those, a coffee table, wax fruit in a bevelled glass bowl placed exactly in the centre of its highly polished dark wood surface. Mariani could smell cleaning fluids and the concentrated floral reeks of plug-in air fresheners. The room began to feel illusory, though the bolus of discomfort that had formed in his stomach was all too tangible.

He looked at the small oil paintings arranged neatly on the walls. They were bucolic mountain scenes bathed in light the colour of newly hatched chicks, biscuit-tin visions of a kind that probably decorated the walls of every other house in the street. But even Mariani's insensitive eye could see there was a wild, reckless quality to the brushwork. They were initialled A.T.

He looked away and out through the room's sealed and triple-glazed windows. The sky was pale above these homes for lawyers, headmasters, marketing directors. The scene was like a badly composed, artless photo-graph. Nothing moved.

'Hope this is all right for you?'

Bennett was behind him and holding out a china cup and saucer. Mariani blinked and took it.

'Not too strong?'

The coffee's matt surface was pocked with white specks and there was a yellowish froth around its rim.

'Fine, thank you.'

'Lovely. Well, do sit down. He'll be here in a moment.'

Bennett turned and left. The room was very quiet, the air thick and warm.

Mariani lowered himself on to the sofa nearest the window. The plastic covering rustled as he sat. He carefully guided the saucer and cup on to the pristine table in front of him.

'We nearly met before, I believe?'

Standing in the doorway was a man who seemed to be in late middle age. He wore a suit of mid-brown corduroy, a white shirt, neatly knotted tie and well-worn brown brogues.

'Yes, the Café Ristranza in Siena,' the man continued. 'Almost six years ago now. Bennett approached you.'

Mariani nodded uncertainly because he had the curious sensation that up until he had walked in the door of this house, nothing at all had happened to him.

The man came into the room. His hair was heavy, unnaturally white and cut in a pageboy bob. His eyebrows were blond, verging on gold. Despite the man's age, his hands and features were delicate, almost pretty.

'Has Bennett made you comfortable?'

'Yes. Thank you.'

'And Mr Ladoga's chauffeur dropped you at the end of the street?'

'Yes.'

'Good. I met your father once, I believe. In an establishment in Mar-seilles. Is he well?'

'Yes, I think so.'

'Good. Well, thank you for coming. I was sorry to hear of your accident. I hope our association will prove beneficial. So…An anomaly in the orbitofrontal lobe. Leading to the expected consequences: fatigue, outbursts of self-directed rage, frustration, compulsions, bizarre ideas, visions, outbursts of obscenity. And particularly for you, a diminution in competitive response.'

'Yes.'

'"For I will restore health to you and heal you of your wounds," said the Lord." Fine words. But he has not, has he?'

'No.' Mariani could speak in nothing but monosyllables.

'No. He tends not to. He's a bit of a quack, in truth. A disappointment. Particularly, for example, to the eight million people who will die of cancer this year.' The man sighed.

'I don't want to take anything illegal,' Mariani said, in a strangely childish voice.

The man stroked his chin and smiled wanly.

'I imagine you know very little of what I do. Is that correct?'

'Yes.'

Mariani took a sip from his coffee and when he had, knew he could not take another. He put the cup down.

The white-haired man cleared his throat. 'The world gets satisfaction from watching people twisting in agony. And people, for reasons yet to be fully explained to me, are happy to twist. Perhaps it is simply necessary. Perhaps they *like* twisting. Anyway. Mr Ladoga works his one-hundred-and-twenty-hour weeks, you ride a bicycle until you can't stand up…but you can't be expected to perform that way without help. One may as well ask soldiers to fight a war with popguns and catapults. In a less psychotic world, the requisite drugs would be available across the counter. Until they are, I see it as my duty, my calling to formulate and supply them. Do you understand?'

Mariani was not entirely lying when he said, 'Yes.'

The man glanced at Mariani's abandoned cup. 'Is the coffee unacceptable? If so, I apologise. Neither Bennett nor I drink it.'

'It's very hot,' said Mariani, although it wasn't.

'Don't burn your tongue.'

Mariani looked from the coffee to the wax fruit to the pictures on the wall and then smelled the chemical simulations of forest scents. He felt a lurch of fear and had an image of himself, lying in some three-star Belgian hotel room, cold and stiff as that wax banana there, his heart a fat still lump, kit strewn on the floor in the bathroom, his glassy eyes fixed on the Artex swirls on the ceiling.

'Your mother was English, correct?'

 Mariani nodded.

'Where was she born?'

'Somewhere called Guildford.'

'Ah. I was brought up not far away. Dorking.'

 Mariani tried to smile.

'Are you enjoying the city?' asked the man.

'I like it, yes,' Mariani lied.

'It's a city of opportunity. Opportunity and silence. And chocolate. What do you hope to achieve from our association, Mr Mariani?'

'I'm not sure. Just to know if you can help.'

'Well, that depends on you. A man should be estimated not only by what he is willing to do, but what he is willing to do to himself.'

 He looked straight at Mariani. 'I'm sorry. I haven't introduced myself. Alann Triesmaan. Please, follow me.'

*

Steel treads spiralled down to a large white room. The air became chill. The space was vaulted and harshly lit. Against one wall, like a future king's sarcophagus, stood an MRI scanner. An examination table was against another. In one corner, a vast silver fridge hummed softly. Beside it, a surgeon's stainless-steel wash trough. But dominating the room was an exploded sculpture of the human brain. The skull had been split in two and the halves positioned half a metre apart. Each half was supported by a thin chrome pole that rose from the floor. The brain had also been divided and its component parts revealed and displayed. They hung, connected, in mid-air between the skull halves. The sculpture was lifesize and, Mariani realised as he moved towards it, exactly the same height as himself. It was as if he was looking inside his own dissected head.

His throat became a dry slit. 'I must ask,' he said hesitantly. 'De Vilde. What happened with de Vilde?'

'That was... unfortunate,' replied Triesmaan. 'And upsetting. He had heart irregularities that were undetectable. Dennis would only have lived another two years. He called me after he won that stage: never was a man so happy. Dennis de Vilde died with a smile on his face.'

Triesmaan lifted the corners of his own mouth sadly.

Mariani turned to look at him, to ask directly what part drugs had played in de Vilde's death, but found he could not, and in fact did not truly want to know.

'Mr Mariani.' Triesmaan put a hand on his shoulder, the touch barely there, his fingers like a ghost's. 'Another reason why I like to work with members of your profession – you are not afraid.' Triesmaan moved closer and Mariani could not help but stare into his black eyes, startling when set against his bone-white hair. 'You are prepared to go where others are not, correct?'

Mariani no longer knew what he agreed or disagreed with. His mind had begun to fog. As if he were already drugged in some way.

'Let's begin,' said Triesmaan. He took his hand away, though Mariani continued to feel a chill where the fingers had rested. The Englishman stepped soundlessly to the wash trough and began briskly to soap his hands.

*

The Mercedes cruised along late-night just-washed streets as it headed back towards the city centre. On top of his solid bald neck, the chauffeur's big head was motionless. Mariani, beyond tired, gazed out of the window, his hollow-eyed face was thinly reflected in the sparkling glass.

He thought of the *trejanzk,* a pig's worthless, spineless, half-developed stillborn.

He thought of raising his yellow jersey-clad arms on the Champs-Élysées.

He thought of ideals and whether they were simply things you said because people liked to hear them.

He thought of de Vilde, dead at thirty-four.

He thought of Gastein Ladoga, his jet, his house, the polished quality of his skin.

In his basement, Triesmaan had examined the results of Mariani's scan and made notes on a laptop. He'd taken blood, urine and faecal specimens. He'd asked him to describe what he felt was the problem and then describe what it would mean to him to overcome it. Triesmaan filmed Mariani's answers to fifty questions and his one-word responses to the photographs of fifty people. He'd asked him to talk about the times he'd been angriest, and saddest, and taped those. He made Mariani write down a description of his first sexual experience. He asked him under what circumstances he would consider killing a man.

Triesmaan wanted a week, perhaps two. Mariani's case was difficult, he explained. Anything he formulated would need adjustments as Mariani was taking it. He again mentioned that he was working at a highly experimental level. Mariani should be prepared to cope with potentially disconcerting reactions. But as long as he was carefully monitored, then risks would be minimised.

Bennett had then presented Mariani with a printed estimate for the treatment. Two hundred and seven thousand euros. Mariani did not even have a tenth of it. Numb, he agreed.

Triesmaan wished him good night, and said that he was looking forward to their journey together.

Mariani had left the house and walked past its sleeping twins with loops of words spinning in his head and a slush of anxiety and hope swilling in his stomach.

He was stumbling along towards...towards what?

Now, in the glittering city-centre street, a hunched old lady in a piebald dark fur coat was about to step on to the crossing. The driver slowed the

Mercedes to a stop. The woman began to shuffle arthritically towards the other side of the street. Mariani could see her thickly made-up face contorting with pain and effort. She turned towards the car. Her painted lips formed a kindly smile, but as Mariani watched it seemed to him that the lips receded further and further. Her mouth opened wide and her teeth were huge and brilliant, far too big for her wizened face. They curved back in on themselves and looked ready to tear into flesh. Then her face sprouted grey-brown bristles. Mariani felt his intestines turn cold and his body go rigid. He watched as the woman's ears grew out from her head and become pointed. Her nose fattened and turned cylindrical and pushed outwards from her face. But her eyes did not change. They remained human and looked at him with a ghastly directness. Very slowly, she began to nod her head as if in affirmation.

Mariani blinked, and in that instant the woman's face had somehow reversed itself into its previous harmless and wrinkled appearance. She turned back towards the other side of the road.

Mariani couldn't take his gaze from her, watching her shambling progress from out of the back window as the Mercedes moved away. What did this apparition mean? What tricks was his mind playing on him and why? Was it just the result of the accident? Still icy inside his skin and shaking slightly, he slumped down into the cushioned black leather of the rear seat.

As he'd gone into the MRI scanner, he'd closed his eyes and tried to imagine himself as a lifeless shell. But he could not. Inside him was this wriggling thing that demanded to exist. No name, no face. It felt as if it worked independently of his mind. And now this vision: the centuries-old blue-eyed beast that fed on anything, driven by its need to survive.

EiGHTEEN

Seven pairs of legs rotating almost as one. Seven sets of carbon wheels, white decals blurring. Seven men in identical aerodynamic sperm-shaped helmets crouched low on seven identical time-trial machines. Seven faces all set hard with concentration. Seven hearts pumping at three beats a second.

The long baby-blue Gazin-Ségur PMP line swept through the greens and yellows of the Italian countryside at fifty km/h. Each man rode his minute on the front and then dropped to the back. They worked as smoothly as the steel parts that glinted and spun beneath them.

The sky was cloudless and the warm May sunshine dappled the shiny skinsuits on their flattened backs as they powered up the last short tree-lined ascent and took the final corner, banking effortlessly. The team were going to win the prologue.

The breath from thousands of screaming mouths pushed them onwards. Twenty more turns of the pedals and they were through the finish line. Grasch led them home. The agony left his face. He grinned and turned, raising a big German thumb to the other six. They all slowed, and, in a huddle of men and metal, backslapped and fist-bumped.

The commentator warbled excitedly. Mariani lowered the volume on the TV. He turned away from the screen. He scraped at the week-old stubble on his cheeks and exhaled slowly.

He got up from the sofa and, slippers sliding along the blond oak flooring, slouched into the kitchen. It was ten days since he'd seen Triesmaan. There had been no word from him.

He opened the fridge door. The cold air was like a polar bear's breath on his arms and neck, exposed by his rumpled vest. The fierce light shone on packages and containers that lay on what had become 'his' shelf. Two crimson rump steaks each the size of a man's foot. Half a blood sausage, its exposed purple-brown interior pocked with fat. Moist lamb's kidneys secured in a plastic bag.

'All this…*stuff*,' Keira had said at the supermarket check-out.

'Comfort food.'

'Can't you eat chocolate for once? Or a cake?'

'Urrgh.'

As they packed her salads, crispbreads and cans of tuna, his purchases moved slowly along the belt towards them.

'My God,' said Keira. 'It's like a nightmare.' She looked away as the raw lumps and slices were scanned and Mariani bagged them.

He was worried himself by his increased need for protein. For what felt like the thousandth time, he wondered what was going on inside his body. In bed last night, Keira had murmured her wants into his ear, rubbing hard nipples against his back and slowly running her hand down his torso towards his shamefully soft penis. Mariani's heart had contracted at her words and his scrotum had tightened around his balls like a fist. All he wanted was sleep. Keira had begun humping herself against his leg and he'd put his hand back around her ass and clutched her to him and, as she chafed harder and quicker, held her tighter and urged her on, hating himself for faking it. She put her nails painfully into his neck when she came, told him she loved him, and then within a minute fell asleep. He'd got up gently and gone to the bathroom. As he pissed, he looked down at the bloodless sock of tissue that lolled in his hand, just another traitorous piece of himself.

In the kitchen now, with the commentary in the front room still audible, he put a frying pan on the heat, took the lamb's kidneys from their bag, felt their plump density in his hand and dropped them into the pan.

The organs crackled and spat. He turned them and then wandered back into the front room, unable to resist the screen.

This television's technology gave the most realistic, most highly defined image, as if, claimed the adverts, you had an eagle's eyes. Mariani had certainly never seen Grasch's smile as white or his big thighs as honed or the podium girls look as ravishing or the *maglia rosa* quite so lusciously pink as when the girls helped Grasch into it. Had flowers ever looked so radiant as the ones that Grasch now waved to the crowd?

Mariani's mind tugged violently in different directions, but he could still feel pride for his friend. The tears that began to form were nothing to do with that. He watched Grasch step down and then he turned the picture off. The brilliant black screen now showed a faint reflection of a slump-shouldered man in a pair of cut-off shorts. His hair was lank and his vest was tight around his gut. In his hand he limply held a grey plastic TV remote control.

The smell of burning meat wafted into the room, but it was only after several long moments of increasing self-disgust that Mariani was able to move away from the reflection. He wiped his hand across his face and went back to the kitchen. Smoke billowed from the dry, crackling pan. The kidneys were blackened and crusty on one side, lightly greyed on the other, but he forked them on to a plate, hacked off chunks with the fork and ate.

*

His ring tone pulled him out of sleep.

He answered and listened.

'Yes,' he said and then rang off. He sat and looked at the room. Bed, table, clock: red numerals, 16:52. The glass of water he hadn't finished, the tiny air bubbles in it. The picture of Keira and her father, cheek to cheek, smiling. The pot plant on the window sill. Ordinary things of everyday life. It didn't seem possible that what he was about to do had any connection with this room.

He picked the phone up and called the estate agent who'd sold him his house.

Keira came back ten minutes later. She kissed him and asked him how his day had been.

'How was yours?' he replied. 'It was the last screen test today, wasn't it?'

'I think I'm down to the final two. It's either me or Heidi Lafarge, the swimmer who did the *Playboy* spread last year. I saw her audition. I must admit the camera loves her tits —and so does the guy we'd be presenting with.'

'I'm going to start a treatment. I had a call.'

She kissed him again, twice. Then she hugged him. 'You told Dad?'

'Not yet.'

'He'll be thrilled. What is it exactly?'

'It's something new. Untested.'

She stroked his face. 'It's new? OK. It's safe, right?'

He shrugged. 'It's new.'

'Are there side effects? Is it dangerous?'

He shrugged again.

'You don't know?'

'It's untested.'

'You've said that. Tell me what it is.'

'It's new. It's a…new thing.

'Stop saying that. You can't take something you know nothing about. If you're going to be stupid, I'll call my doctor, ask him about it. What's the name of this stuff? Who makes it?' She took her phone from her bag, but Mariani deftly snatched it from her hand.

'It's secret.'

Keira looked confused. 'What are you talking about?'

She tried to take the phone from him. His hand closed around it tightly.

'No,' he said, turning his back. 'I'm doing this stuff. That's it. OK? That's all you have to know.'

She went into the bedroom and wrenched up the handset of the fixed line phone that was on her bedside table. Mariani came in behind her.

'Don't. Don't fuck this up for me.'

She ignored him and began stabbing buttons on the handset with her index finger.

'Keira…' He tried to take the phone from her, but she moved away.

'Hello? Is Doctor Hild available?…It's Keira Ladoga.'

He slapped the phone out of her hand and it hit the rug with a dull thud and skittered away under the bed. Keira looked at her empty palm for a long moment.

Mariani's voice was thick with husk. 'Listen, I've got to do this. I am doing this. You don't understand.' He gripped her shoulders. Her eyes tightened with pain. He brought his face close to hers. 'I have to. Do you think I want to do this? I don't. I *have* to.'

She knocked his hands away, and with a closed fist, hit him hard on his left ear. He grunted. Keira shoved him in the chest.

'Who are you? I don't know you. Look at you. Who are you?'

He blinked. It suddenly seemed to him that his face would burst and his brain – the truth of his feelings and thoughts, his guilt and shame and fears – explode into the room. He felt a wind, black-red and baking hot, start to whistle around his skull. 'I'm nobody,' he said. 'A fucking nothing. Just like my fucking father.' His voice began to rise and grate as if someone else were speaking, some scared and bitter man on the verge of personal catastrophe. 'Just a fat bag of pig shit. See?' He put his hands to the sides of her face and his thumbs on her jawline. He gripped hard and made her head move up and down so she saw the full length of him. 'See the fat bag of pig shit? Hey? See the fat bag of useless pig shit you let between your legs?'

Keira's eyes began to well up and what little she could move of her face registered pain, confusion and betrayal.

He moved her closer to him. Tightened his grip. His voice was harsh and shatteringly loud, as if amplified by the PA system of a death-metal band. 'I can't help it. I want to help it, but I can't. I'll do anything. Don't you see, you stupid cunt? I know it's wrong. But I don't care. I know it's– '

She brought the heel of her shoe hard down on the toes of his right foot. He yelled and let her go. He clutched the throbbing foot with both hands. Eyes squeezed tight, top teeth forcing themselves into his bottom lip, he stood on one leg and then made a noise in the back of his throat like a drill struggling to penetrate masonry. He took his right hand away from his foot and, with an uncontrolled sweep of his arm, slapped her across the face. He felt the heel of his palm cannon into the space under her cheekbone. She fell back across the bed as if she had swooned.

Mariani's breath came in shudders. He looked at his right hand as if it were something completely new to him.

He stepped hesitantly towards Keira's prone body. He seemed unable to decide what kind of expression he should have on his face.

Fascinated for a reason he did not understand, but which seemed to be from the distant past, Mariani reached out to put his fingers to the dark red trail that ran from Keira's left nostril to her mouth. Before he touched her, she opened her eyes.

'If you're still here in thirty seconds, you bastard, I'm calling the police.'

NiNETEEN

The sun came in through the open window and made a white rectangle on the piebald carpet. The smell in the room became more sour and the air heavier. The walls were blank, faintly yellowed, like the sole of an old man's foot. The bed was thin and spongy and he sank into it, making his back ache. His ear hurt where she'd hit him. Through the wall, he could hear a man pissing strongly into a toilet bowl.

In his bank account, which he'd checked in an internet café half an hour previously, he had seventeen thousand and nine *chōp*. Enough to pay for another three weeks at this hotel and for two sandwiches on each of those twenty-one days. He had a credit card with a twenty thousand limit.

Tomorrow he had to see Triesmaan and convince him to take the house as payment for the drugs. If it sold at the asking price, he then had to find another one and a half million *chōp*. Would Triesmaan take a slice of future earnings? Could the money be borrowed? From Grasch maybe? Banquo? Christ's wounds, Banquo would hardly miss an amount like that would he? It was, what, about a week's earnings?

He imagined the money on the bed in front of him, wads of dirty notes held together with twine. One and a half million. He couldn't ask anyone for that.

Romain Mariani, top ten finisher in two one-day Classics and the third best rider in the toughest week-long tour of the season, the pin-up boy of Eastern European bike racing according to *Cykliska* magazine, began to rub his fingers into the loose flesh around his jowls, then worked his hands through the thickets of dark hair on his cheeks before pressing and moulding every part of his face, nose, eyes, ears, forehead, tensing the fingers, feeling the hard bone beneath, moving the skin and features one way and then another and wondering why he had seventeen thousand and nine *chōp* and a stinking room in a two-star hotel and a brain with a hole in it while a man who was perhaps a quarter of a per cent better at his job than he was had a private island, an heiress wife, his own brand of cycle clothing and the kind of life that seemed to be without worry or fear or sweat-soaked dreams about dog-eating pigs.

When he was back riding again, he'd see a life coach and get himself straightened out. Buy a suit. Get a serious agent, not a bluffing asshole with a forehead full of filler. For the love of Christ, you're not some milk-faced rookie, he told himself. Yes, as soon as Triesmaan's stuff got his head better, he would train rigorously and get that apartment in Spain, fill it with nice Danish furniture and put in an en suite. He'd marry Keira. He'd become a team leader. He'd weigh his food. He'd make sure his bar tape was the most aerodynamic on the market. He'd win that tour.

First things first. Get the stuff. Let Keira cool off for a day or two, then call her and apologise: do whatever it took. He loved her. She'd been so good for him. He knew he'd lost it in the flat. That was not good. At all. Unforgiveable. What had he been doing? He knew he had been angry with himself more than her, riven with self-disgust at how easily he'd agreed to become what he'd always said he never would be. But she didn't understand how important this was. She was his, he was hers, and he should be so flattered she loved him. But... She wasn't a rider. She could never understand. He thought back to the look on her face as he held it between his hands, the fear and the panic, the realisation that the man she loved had degenerate things inside him. Well, what did she expect? He didn't have a multi-millionaire father and a fancy city-centre apartment and... His self-justifications and excuses continued, thin as the room's walls, and the man next door turned on his TV and then began to laugh.

*

Fifteen minutes later, Mariani heard the lift arrive on his floor. Ten seconds after that there was a knock on the door.

He got off the bed and opened the door. Gastein Ladoga stood in the corridor. Mariani wiped his palms down the legs of his trousers. He shifted his weight a couple of times.

Ladoga's big hands swung gently on the end of his arms. His eyes were lizard-like, hard and cold. He moved forward into the room, making Mariani scuttle backwards. Mariani saw a blur and then felt Ladoga's grip tunnelling into the sides of his neck.

With a thumb and what felt to Mariani like the two pincers of a giant, angry crab, Ladoga rocked the base of Mariani's skull to left and right. 'I'd like to tear your head off, but I know someone who'd do it better than me. Understand?'

It seemed to him that at any moment he would feel his neck muscles penetrated and the top of his spinal column squeezed flat by the crushing pressure of Ladoga's fingers. He was just able to nod. Ladoga took his hand away immediately as if Mariani were something he was loath to touch.

'You're on your own,' he said. 'I was going to help you with money. But not now. Don't ever put your hands on my daughter again.'

*

That night he sat in the dark on the very edge of the room's narrow bed and phoned Tanel. His cheeks were hot and his neck sore and there was a tightness deep inside his stomach. A dim grey light from the panel of the phone illuminated half of his right eye.

'Got the wrong number?' asked his father.

'I won't keep you.'

''S'all right. I was only trying to fix the fridge.'

Mariani paused before speaking. In the next room, the occupant was walking across the floor in heavy boots. He listened to the thudding steps as they went back and forth. There was a crackle of interference on the line and then he spoke. 'Remember you used to say clean riders are traitors. You really believed that?'

He heard Tanel sniff. 'Why?' His father's voice was wary.

'I was just thinking about things. You know. The sport. What's happened.'

The line went silent. Mariani heard the snap of his father's lighter and then an exhalation of smoke.

'I did then. I dunno what I think now.' Tanel coughed, once. 'Not sure I think anything.'

Mariani pressed the phone into his ear and bent forward, curling into himself. He spoke in rapid, staccato sentences. 'You wanted me to be like you. Do things your way. That's why you used to say all that stuff. Hit me. Spit in my face. Trying to convince me to dope, right? Couldn't stand the idea I'd do it clean. Still trying to do it outside that restaurant. With that *pot belge* in the street.'

'Hey? What's this? The Inquisition?'

Mariani pictured the downward dismissive movement of the left side of his father's mouth. 'That's it, right?'

Tanel said nothing.

'Well?' demanded Mariani.

'Yeah and no.'

'Meaning?'

Tanel was silent.

'*Meaning?*'

'Meaning...fuck...yeah, you're right,' said his father. 'But I *did* want you to be the best. That too. And if it meant lighting up, then fuck it, why not? Just about everyone else did.' Tanel coughed, each hacking bark more throaty and resonant than the last. He took in two steadying breaths. 'Bet you wish you had now, hey?'

Mariani pursed his lips and frowned as if he had just tasted something bitter. 'What?'

Tanel's voice assumed an air of blasé, all-knowing superiority. 'Looks like your career's over. You didn't get nowhere really. On the sauce, you'd've won that Giro in '07. Podiumed in that Tour de France year before last. Taken a couple of classics.'

'Maybe.'

'Now you're skint and fucked. You didn't want to be like me so you rode clean. And now you're like me anyway.'

The call ended soon after that. Mariani sat in the darkness, phone still in his hand, hating his father, but feeling more like his son than he ever had.

*

Now you're like me anyway.

The words were still crashing round his head when, two days later, he was ascending in a lift to the thirty-second floor of a luxurious city-centre apartment block. He knew that what he was about to do was the result of many things which shouldn't have happened but did, and many things that didn't happen but, with the minutest adjustment in circumstance, could have. He thought he had been about to shake off the shadow of his father. But the shadow had tracked him down. Now he had one final chance to escape, but not before the shadow received what it had wanted all along – him, Mariani, with his arms wide open and a welcoming smile on his face. Whether a different shadow, a shadow of his own, would then begin to accompany him he could not tell, but for one brief moment as he got out of the lift and walked to the door of the apartment where he had been told Triesmaan was waiting, he felt somewhere – within him, around him, he could not be sure – a new and colder darkness.

*

'We have used compounds that have never been tested on anything more advanced than rats and mice. We will need to monitor you carefully.'

Triesmaan stood and, from the kitchen's big American-style red fridge, took out a plain white cardboard box, the size of a small loaf of bread. He opened it and withdrew a thick polystyrene block in which sat twenty ampoules of colourless liquid, two neat rows of ten. He put the block on the shiny black granite surface of the kitchen table.

'RM 1,' said Triesmaan.

Mariani's mouth seemed to drain of moisture.

'I remember when I was a boy.' Triesmaan's voice was suddenly dreamy. 'I had angered my father in some way and he pushed me from him. I stumbled and smacked my knee on a hard ceramic floor. I'd never known such pain. I lay there, howling. But then my mother came up to me and held me and said something kind and funny and cleaned me up and put a plaster on my knee. It was as if my heart had been wrapped in the softest cotton wool... But as we age, that kind of succour becomes unavailable. Our ambitions fill us with bile. Disappointments overrun us. We become slaves to work, to our increasingly degraded lusts. We turn jaundiced and cynical and feel the world circling us like vultures do, hoping for our death. You understand me? No one could think ill of you for this, Mr Mariani. Picture pharmacopoeia as I do, like a mother's love.'

Mariani did not want to look at the glass phials, a third the size of his little finger. But he could not stop himself. He imagined what they were going to do for him and it was as if his eyes were fixed on diamonds or the face of a beautiful woman. In his mind one of the capsules grew to an enormous size and rotated slowly, and a light shone through the liquid, causing star-shaped twinkles to pop and spin. His breathing became short, as if he was climbing hard on a steep ascent.

'Now...' Triesmaan had regained some of his authority and calm. 'This is an experimental combination of hormones, one of which even I am not sure properly exists. We are probably about twenty years ahead of the medical establishment. You are looking at the future. A bright new truth.'

Mariani knew that he should question Triesmaan. Experimental hormones – what could that mean? But he also knew he would probably not understand the answers. And did he even really want the details? He knew he was going to take the drug, and he knew why.

Triesmaan held one of the ampoules between his thumb and index finger. 'You may be wondering about the drug showing up in tests. What you see in front of you does not have a test to prove its presence. It has no reality, to all intents and purposes. A thought – can something be illegal if it doesn't exist?' Triesmaan paused. 'On the other hand, of course it's illegal. It could, in truth, hardly be less legal. Please be aware of that.'

Mariani nodded. He found he was becoming impatient. He imagined the needle penetrating his skin and involuntarily his lips moved across each other, almost as if he were about to eat.

'It is designed to counteract the effects of your accident,' continued

Triesmaan. 'You were an aggressive, competitive athlete. This treatment will return you to that state. If you find the results are excessive in any way, then we simply alter the dosage. As I said, monitoring you is vital.'

'Excessive?'

Mariani looked up into Triesmaan's face: it was blotched and had a spongy quality that had previously been absent. Was he ill? The Englishman wiped his fingers through the sweat beading above his golden eyebrows.

'The side effects are difficult to predict. That is to be expected. In fact, I would be disappointed if there were none: it would indicate we had been too conventional. The drug identifies weakness or laxity. It will analyse where your deficiencies are and work on them. It will also exaggerate certain tendencies, increase certain needs. Your desires and proclivities, even those buried in your subconscious, will become more evident and three-dimensional.'

Mariani was about to ask Triesmaan for more details, but the pharmacologist had begun an unstoppably fast flow of scientific jargon.

'Hormones don't cause aggression,' he said, 'but rather – at the genetic level – make stimulatory and inhibitory neurons more or less sensitive to specific stimuli from other neurons. When hormones affect stimulatory neurons, they make it easier for a stimulus to elicit a behaviour. Yes? Your treatment is a concentrated hormonal cocktail blended specifically to your own unique genetic, metabolic and psychological profiles. It will both enflame the stimulatory neurons and release the inhibitory neurons from their restraining influence, with the result that– '

Mariani lost his patience. He wasn't paying two hundred thousand euros for a lecture. 'As long as it works. That's all I want to know.'

'Of course it will work.' Triesmaan mopped rivulets from his cheeks and chin. He started talking again, at such a speed the words crashed into each other. 'The lesions to your brain inhibit your stress-aggression centre, so it produces less of the corticosteroid response that prepares the body for emergency action, popularly called "fight or flight". I have created a way of amplifying the signal using a loop: your response will feed back into your brain's aggression centre which will produce the same corticosteroid signal which will again feed back to the brain – a snowball effect, if you will. Attack thresholds will lower and the urge to dominate and defeat an enemy, to turn that enemy into your victim, will be facilitated. The ensuing battle for supremacy, itself a stressor, then further activates the stress response. Resulting in, for you, Mr Mariani, peace, well-being and happiness.' Triesmaan paused, took in a deep, long breath, and a terrible, sad tiredness seemed to overcome him. Then his eyes widened. 'Now – logistics. Bennett?'

The little man came hurrying in from the open-plan living area, an incongruous figure amidst the flat's modern, minimalist stylings. He looked with concern at Triesmaan, but his master appeared not to see him. Bennett produced a leather case, unzipped it and opened it flat on the kitchen table. A row of two-millilitre syringes lay inside. Mariani felt a stab in his heart as if something had already been injected there.

TWENTY

The vein was like a blue-green seam in the off-white of his arm. The needle's point just a centimetre away. The drug, ten thousand euros' worth, so empty-looking he wondered if Triesmaan had sold him water. How could something that seemed so lifeless give him back his life?

He had a final urge to bolt and run. He forced himself back down in the chair.

'All right, old cock,' said Bennett. 'No need to fret. I'll be mother until you're confident enough to do it yourself.'

Mariani's mind spasmed. Here it was, then. The shadow. He began to feel a cramp in his gut. Something that throbbed with a kind of claustrophobic warmth began to gather at the base of his skull. He tried to swallow but his mouth's functions had failed. His eagerness and sense of resolution began to fade.

'Ready?'

Mariani closed his eyes and in the dark the fear grew. All of a sudden, he felt an immense pressure weighing down on him. Fate, the future, events: *puszta*. The opponent that could never be beaten. He felt himself begin to collapse. Slowly at first, then with gathering pace. He was becoming fragments.

Then, a tiny sharp violation. He imagined the syringe's plunger slowly moving down and pushing the liquid into him, then felt this strange flow into his arm.

It was all over in three seconds. Everything changed in two heartbeats. He was almost sick as he felt the needle withdrawn, its hard cold steel sliding out of his soft warm flesh: and then, from somewhere, the terrible thrill of the unknown.

'That's it,' said Bennett, softly.

Mariani sat back. Ice and fire seemed to exist in one sensation; it was as if the temperature in the room were increasing and dropping at the same time. It started in the depths of his bowels and then spread slowly through him. It was a feeling outside his understanding.

'It'll pass, old cock. I'll get you a coffee.'

Mariani slumped in the chair, exhaling in spurts. He glanced at Triesmaan who looked on with unseeing eyes. The sweat trickled down the side of the pharmacologist's face towards his cracked lips and he was murmuring to himself, lost in a dreamland to which he was the only visitor.

*

An hour later, back amidst the spoiled-yoghurt smell of his hotel room, Mariani sat against the bedhead and tried to picture the world beneath his skin. What processes were taking place, what parts seeking out other parts, which cells were talking to which?

He felt scratches on the inside of his skull, like flies scraping their feet. There was a lightness from the neck upwards as if his head were about to float away. His blood seemed to be throbbing, his veins looked fatter, bluer.

He touched the cotton wool taped over the puncture hole in the crook of his elbow. He was hot now and had a vision of the dull meat between his ears beginning to brighten and tiny sparks starting to flash. Was this really happening or was it all just the power of hope? He tried to focus. In the morning, he'd start working on a training plan, pencil in a few races, work out a selection of meals with the ideal combination of essential foodstuffs. Slim down, lean up. Get those ribs on show again.

Yes, he'd do all that.

Money, though. How could he get some money? He'd managed to extend his credit card's limit and make a first payment to Triesmaan of five thousand euros. There was nothing more. The house might take months. What else could he sell? All he had were his bikes. He couldn't, as yet, contemplate selling those.

The light began to dim in the humid room, the shadows darkened and lengthened and Mariani's mind wanted nothing more to do with the world. His eyelids dropped. As he slept, the drug that no man had ever put into his body before began its work.

*

He was running. Where? Smells: soil and shit and stagnant water, things rotting and rutting. A forest. He was ravenous. An indefinable need in his guts. He couldn't stop. He had huge muscles in his shoulders and they drove him forward. He ripped through the forest, running on all fours. He could hear the trees growing, the insects laughing, the worms wriggling. Thick hard bristles stood all along his back. His tongue was long and greyish. Four knife-sharp tusks curled from his wet, eager mouth. Around his head, an armour of inch-thick scar tissue. Now he knew. But he didn't care. The need was growing and he grunted with anger and frustration. He pounded on and on, looking and smelling and listening. In his dark and frantic heart he knew this was wrong, that he should try to stop, but it was too late now, too late

He woke with bulging eyes and a heaving chest. Got up and went quickly to the bathroom. Checked himself. Opened his mouth, ran his hands over his body. Looked at the colour of his eyes. Made small moaning sounds. He gazed at the face in the mirror for a long moment. Then coughed and spat. Swilled water round his mouth and spat that too.

A fat black fly watched in silence from the strip light.

TWENTY
ONE

The early-evening sun was still pouring melted-gold warmth on to the city streets. Mariani stood at the entrance to Keira's building and pushed the buzzer. Her window was open and from ten floors below, he heard the buzzer as it sounded in her hallway.

A clicking sound came from the intercom panel by his ear, followed by her voice. 'I'll call the police.'

A moustached man in fawn slacks who was carrying a slim tan brief-case appeared behind Mariani. He cleared his throat and then put a security fob to the entry box that was built into the intercom panel. He glanced at Mariani.

'Good evening,' he said, his moustache twitching. Mariani ignored him. The glass front door swung open. Glancing at him once more, the man entered the building.

Mariani put his mouth to the intercom again. 'Keira. I've been calling for three days. I need you.'

'For what?'

'I think I'm sick.'

'I agree.'

'Keira. I'm…ill. Seriously. Look at my face.' He stared into the lens of the panel's security camera.

Silence.

'Christ.'

The thick glass front door swung slowly back.

'Thank you. Thank you.'

He walked in and went to the lift. On the way up, he held his hands out and watched them quiver. He'd had four injections. He'd shown Triesmaan the tense shaking that was afflicting parts of his body, making his teeth clack one minute and his legs spasm the next. His head buzzed and banged and boomed. Tics flickered through his face. He seemed to have been taken over by a kinetic, angry spirit. His body did not seem to be his own. Triesmaan had made notes and filmed Mariani and suggested reducing the dose by ten per cent. He seemed unworried.

'I've seen far worse reactions to experimental drugs.'

Mariani did not ask him to elaborate. Triesmaan then seemed to slip into a trance: his face began to glow as if sunburnt and he began talking in circles, as if his mind were a city full of dead ends and road closures. Then Bennett had come in and told Mariani it might be better if he left. He was scared and felt completely isolated. The situation seemed to be out of control. He needed to be with someone, someone he knew and who knew him, if only for a short while.

The lift doors parted and Mariani brushed his hands across his skittering face and straightened his shoulders.

He walked down the carpeted corridor to her door. He knocked softly.

After some moments, the door was cautiously opened. Mariani saw the silver links of the security chain. Inside, Keira stood back, almost against the wall. He stared at her. She'd never been so physically vivid to him; he could picture the contractions of her purple-red heart and feel the bath-like heat of her blood. He felt he was touching her just by looking at her. His testicles throbbed and there was a buzz in his groin. He stepped forward.

'I can't let you in,' she said. 'I trusted you.'

'It won't happen again. I promise.' Christ, he thought, the *smell* of her. It was rich and smoky and spicy, with a hint of something that was honeyed and sticky.

'How sick are you? Shouldn't you be in hospital?'

Mariani shrugged. He wanted to lick her face slowly and taste the bruise he could see beneath the make-up.

She exhaled. 'You stupid asshole.'

As he thought about his tongue on her skin, he felt his mouth start to open and widen and his lips curl upwards. He tried to force his face back to its normal shape but he could not.

'Why are you doing that?' asked Keira, her eyes bright with alarm. 'You look like some kind of dog.'

Mariani's breath began to come in erratic spurts, as if he were shuddering through an extended orgasm. He began to feel frightened. 'K…Keira?'

'Yes?'

'Can I have a glass of water?'

'Stay there.'

He sat down with his back against the wall and closed his eyes. His face began to relax and the trembling in his hands stopped. He didn't feel ill. He didn't feel he was about to collapse or want to vomit. There was an unpleasant vibrancy just beneath his skin and he felt acutely conscious of what was around him. There was something very wrong, but the overriding sensation was one of fearful excitement.

She came back with the water and put it down in the gap between the door and its frame. He drank it straight down. She watched him warily.

'Do you know what this stuff is?' she asked.

'Not really.'

'I can't believe you just went ahead and took it.'

'No.'

'Don't take any more.'

He was silent.

'Romain?'

'I feel weird.' He looked at her again and his entire body prickled. 'But I think it's working.'

'Oh, sure. Look at you.'

'I feel something.'

'You've lost your mind.'

Mariani turned her words over in his head and thought they were probably true. But since taking the drug, it seemed to him that unless, in a sense, you did lose your mind, unless you fought and kicked and screamed, unless you took risks and did things you hated doing and that made you hate yourself for doing them, the world would gently suffocate you. You and your pathetic hopes and dipshit ideas.

He had begun to understand why men robbed banks and became dictators and why women with nice breasts had them sliced open and filled with silicone and wrote books about their secret lives as whores or slapped other women on TV shows. If you wanted to be anything more than a funeral waiting to happen, you had to do desperate and shameless things. And once you started, you had to keep doing them: you could never stop. He had thought himself normal: all he did was ride a bike – a bicycle, for God's sake. What could be more ordinary? But it wasn't, of course. The pain, the injuries, the closed, self-serving culture, the denials, the preoccupations with body weight, the three- thousand-five-hundred-kilometre-long Grand Tours in which two hundred men had to work together for three weeks while often wishing each other nothing but harm and disaster… Desperate, shameless.

He stood. 'I'm so sorry I hit you.' He put the empty glass back just across the threshold of the door. She watched him through half-closed eyes and dug her fingers into the back of her neck as if to relax stressed muscles.

'Can you…I mean, just let me know how you are, will you?' She looked down at the floor, as if ashamed of her request.

He nodded and walked away to the lift, taking with him impressions of Keira's smell and tastes that were so vivid, it was if he wanted to eat her.

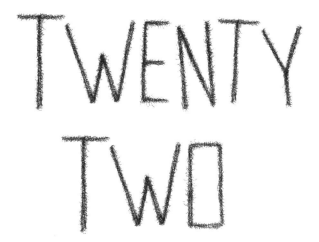

Bennett watched as Mariani clenched his fist tightly to bring out the vein. The flat light above cast hollows of doubt under his eyes. He pushed in the needle, and with his thumb, very gently pressed down on the plunger. The liquid moved silkily down the barrel. Mariani was fascinated by its purity and emptiness, by the tiny amount of it. The drug was perfection, in a way. It was the last dose, and he'd asked to inject it himself. As the plunger reached the bottom of the barrel, he sighed and slowly removed the syringe. When the needle came out a trickle of blood that briefly looked to him like the route of a stage meandered down his forearm. He wiped up the blood with his finger and put it in his mouth, tasting the blood's mineral bitterness.

'Nice technique, old cock,' said Bennett.

The burning cold, less shocking now, began to glide through Mariani's body. He closed his eyes, slowly let breath out of his mouth and pictured the serum going to work. He cajoled the chemicals, seeing them as a healing balm that was making him whole again, returning his life to him.

'Go on, go on,' he murmured softly. 'Yes.'

'All right, then?' asked Bennett.

Mariani held out his arms and the spasms were more like mild shivers than the original convulsions. He had a sense that something had been unblocked. The thrum of dark energy remained.

'Your system's lapping it up,' said Bennett. 'Clever, Dr T, isn't he?'

Mariani glanced into the living area of the flat, where Triesmaan, in a crumpled grey suit, was pacing. His lips moved continuously as if he were telling himself a string of secrets.

'There's something wrong with him, isn't there?' asked Mariani quietly.

'Dr T has an enquiring mind and likes to, shall we say, taste the fruits of his labours.'

'I thought so. Why?'

'Just to see, just to see.'

Mariani stood and moved into Triesmaan's sight line. There was no recognition in the Englishman's black eyes.

'Dr Triesmaan...'

Triesmaan's eyelids worked like the shutter of a camera, as if he were taking shots of Mariani's face.

'Yes?'

'I'm done.'

'Who are you?' asked Triesmaan.

'It's Mariani,' said Bennett. 'The cyclist. Mar-i-ani. He's finished the course.'

Triesmaan seemed to pull himself back into the here and now. 'Ah. Good. Remove your shirt please, Mr Mariani.'

He pulled his T-shirt over his head. Triesmaan began a cursory examination: feeling the pulse in Mariani's neck, looking into his eyes and checking the steadiness of his hands, palpating his stomach and kidneys.

'All absolutely fine,' he said. 'As I knew it would be. Your metabolism has accommodated the treatment extremely easily. That is the advantage of bespoke items.'

Mariani could not see the point in staying in this country a minute longer. 'I'll say goodbye then.' He held out his hand.

Triesmaan shook it. 'Perhaps we'll meet one day in Surrey. Thank you for your business.'

Bennett showed Mariani to the door.

'Good luck, old cock. Balance due in thirty days, remember. Any problems, you know where we are.'

TWENTY THREE

The plane was three-quarters full. Mariani had a window seat next to an unoccupied space. A woman with bad skin and large breasts sat in the aisle seat. When the plane took off, she clutched the wooden crucifix round her neck and muttered prayers. Her thumb stroked Jesus's face.

Mariani closed his eyes, felt the power of the jet's engines taking them seven miles away from what he could only think of as a savage and bewildering shell. He tried to blank out what was in his blood, his reactions to it, all of the last weeks. Those dumb interviews: *Any hunger for your own faecal matter?,* Triesmaan's basement, the ever-changing tone of his voice: *A man should be estimated not only by what he is willing to do, but what he is willing to do to himself,* Keira's face when he'd squeezed it between his hands: *Who are you? I don't know you,* Ladoga's rant: *What is it like to touch a nuclear weapon?*

Jeszu, what a mess. He'd got off lightly, considering. At least he was alive.

The woman in the aisle seat had finally released her crucifix and looked to be asleep. Mariani felt trapped by his seat belt and unclipped it as soon as the illuminated sign went out. At a thousand kilometres an hour, the plane speared the clouds and then headed east. Outside the window, the sky was now a pure cobalt blue and Mariani could see to what felt like the end of the universe. He'd always loved this part of a plane trip, and had, one afternoon in the middle of a particularly dismal November, caught a flight simply to experience the feeling of limitless light and space. It was like being present at the birth of the world. Eventually the brightness and the uniformity would start to depress him but for an hour or so, he liked to gaze out and try to forget what lay beneath.

The flight was short and he had only just finished his tomato juice and cheese-and-ham panino when the plane began its descent. Swirling white-grey clouds appeared, dense as Nistanjhi smoke. Rain speckled the window and Mariani turned his head away. He realised that he had no idea what to do when he landed. As the plane neared the runway, the questions crowded in. How quickly could he sell the house? How would he feel when he tried riding? Would Keira speak to him again? And somewhere, he felt that there was another question, more sinister, to do with his dreams and this drug and the way his burger had tasted last night, so good but with this strange final flavour of disappointment.

The plane lurched downwards like a man gutpunched. A groan came from its chassis as gravity and air currents pulled it in different directions. Even to Mariani, well used to the experience of landing at Airport Central, the runway seemed to be coming up too fast. He sensed other passengers shifting nervously in their seats. He glanced at the woman in the aisle seat: her right hand was tight on the crucifix, crushing the man nailed there for her sins. Her lips moved in whispered prayer and her wide eyes seemed to be asking Mariani to join her.

With a bang and then a shriek like an animal dying the wheels hit the tarmac. On the intercom, an unsteady voice welcomed them to their destination.

PART THREE

TWENTY FOUR

The customs officials were playing cards as the passengers from Mariani's flight came through. One of them had removed his shoes and socks.

In Arrivals, the three prostitutes sat in a café sharing a single cup of coffee. One of them was asleep, head thrown back. Her mouth, a tiny pink-brown cave, was wide open. The other two appeared to be counting sugar grains.

Outside, a single taxi waited. Mariani heard the folk music coming from its open windows and, as he approached, smelled meat and cheese and pastry, but did not recognise the driver until he'd got in the back. It was Stepan.

'Hey. Where you been hiding?' He turned and offered his bag of *broshkts*.

'Nowhere,' said Mariani. He half-smiled a refusal at the bag of pastries. 'No, thanks.'

'Don't blame you. They're shop bought. My bitchslut of a wife hot-footed it with a waiter at our local restaurant.'

'I'm sorry.'

'Ach! Devil take them both.' He turned the key in the ignition and the engine grated. 'Your place?'

'I guess so.'

Stepan turned up the lament on the radio and put the car into gear. He pulled away slowly from the taxi rank. Mariani neglected to put on his seat belt.

'We've all been wondering about you. Couple of guys I know did Hell of Hgruh. Pair of idiots in Crédit Haussman kit? Said they rode with you for a while.'

'Yes.'

'Said you were looking good. But then sort of blew up.'

Mariani wanted to blank that day from his mind. 'Something like that.'

'Bad day at the office, eh?'

Mariani expected a lecture, another of 'Stepan's Laws' about body weight and gear ratios. But it didn't come. The driver seemed lost in thought. He put a cigarette in his mouth but forgot to light it. The singer on the radio began a long, slow, wailing scale and Stepan exhaled mournfully. On the floor under the passenger seat, Mariani noticed what looked like the teated end of a condom.

They passed the ruin of the old petrol station. The landscape was vague, disorganised, dreary. Mariani slid down in his seat and closed his eyes. He thought about getting back on his bike again. The drug had obviously had some kind of effect, but until he began to turn the cranks, the possibility remained that he had spent two hundred thousand euros, ruined his relationship with Keira and betrayed his ideals…for nothing.

'So are you fucked then?' Stepan asked, as if reading his mind.

Mariani smiled humourlessly. 'I wouldn't put it quite that way.'

'Wounds of the Devil! We were counting on you. I mean, no pressure, but what else have we got in this dungheap? Seen the new hundred-*chõp* notes? There's nothing on the back of them. Nothing.'

'Nothing?'

'Nothing. I mean some people moaned about the *sotinko* factory on the back of the old notes, though fair enough, *sotinko's* a good drink and sells well in Moldova too. But look.'

Stepan scrabbled about in his pocket and then produced a limp bill that already looked old and worn. He handed it over his shoulder to Mariani who examined it, feeling its greasy coating. Airport Central on the front but the reverse was just a five-by-twelve centimetre grey-green rectangle, as empty as the sky. Mariani dropped it back on the front passenger seat. He almost smiled.

'We couldn't even find a decent enough song for Eurovision this year,' said Stepan. 'The football team's ranked below the Solomon Islands. Everyone's wishing Papa Jhö was still around: *Fair and True* has reported loads more sightings of him recently – but then they also said it rained frogs over the Hgruh last week. They reckon those gyppos might have put a hex on the country – what they call it, *hinji*? It's all donkey shit.'

'What about Golgotha?' asked Mariani.

'Oh yes, he's been sniffing about,' laughed Stepan. 'Rumours he took a baby over your way.'

'Really?' Mariani pictured the hog pounding through the woods, its prize limp in its savage jaws. The tingling of dark energy in his veins increased in intensity. He felt the presence of the beast more clearly than ever, as if it were now stepping out of his dreams and hallucinations. He looked out of the window, half-expecting to see Golgotha racing alongside the car.

'Ach, who knows what's real and what's not any more?' Stepan was saying. 'More to the point, who cares? The country's just one big dog fight. No rules except keep breathing, somehow, anyhow. My carpenter mate Floris is doing gay porn in Salzburg at the moment. No one's building houses, how's he supposed to earn a crust? We always joked he could knock nails in with his dick, so he might as well put it to good use. Those Austrian boys are in for a proper skewering. Pay's not bad – a third more than doing straight,' he says.

'How's business for you?'

'Ach!' Stepan changed lanes to avoid a trudging piebald horse. 'Have to let the hookers use the back seat for ten per cent – don't worry, I wipe it all down afterwards. That tides me over – nights along the road here, it's heaving like it's Half-price for Ladies Night at Dringl's…those old bags get the bus out from the airport, another lot pile over from the Hgruh, there's a pair of gyppos…and the things those girls'll do! Makes my 'tache curl, I tell you.'

The driver's shoulders slumped as he carefully increased his speed to seventy-five. The engine seemed to be tearing at itself and the smell of burning oil filled the inside of the car.

'Big end – could go any time. Fucking pile of junk. My luck's like this country – gone to shit. Just when things seem to be going along nicely… boom.' He tore the *gruhkyk's* foot from the dash and threw it savagely out of the window. 'For *Jeszu's* sake, get back on that bike and give us something, will you?' he shouted over his shoulder. 'I'm not saying podium, just top twenty. Something. Anything.'

At that moment, Mariani had a sudden urge to tell the driver exactly what had happened in the last three weeks and how far he had gone and how much he had risked. But then the sky became toneless as if someone had turned down the contrast, and the moment faded. Staring out at the grey light and the ash-coloured mountains, Mariani felt as lonely as he had ever done. As lonely as when his mother had died. As lonely as when, with his father's fist descending towards him, he would close his eyes and wait for the pain. As lonely as when he had first turned pro and sat at Formica-topped tables in roadside hotels, repeatedly answering the questions from his new team-mates, 'Who are you?' and 'What are you doing here?', his grizzled French, Spanish and Italian interlocutors talking to him as if he were an inbred cretin from the mountains.

Who... are... you?... What... are... you... doing... here?

At the junction for the village, Stepan indicated, turned off and began the long climb through the trees. The Giûrgïu seemed to have abandoned their makeshift houses. A single *dornei* sat at the roadside and chewed savagely at its rear end.

They passed Curse Corner in silence. When they arrived in the village, Mariani pulled his beanie below his eyebrows and slid further down the seat. He felt his lips tighten and his arm twinge where the needle had pierced the veins. As they passed Svarik's, he put up one hand to cover his face, peering at the empty café through the corner of his eye. If Svarik knew he had hit Keira or taken drugs, his friend would never speak to him again. Mariani thought of how, when he went to the café, Svarik would always refuse to smoke. He wondered how many cigarettes Svarik had denied himself for his sake.

When the car creaked to a stop outside the house, the skies were a dark, liverish colour.

Stepan turned to Mariani. 'Remember what I said last time?'

'You told me to win a big one.'

'No need to repeat it then. I'll just add "please".'

Mariani paid, tipping with his last five *chõp*. Gripping the handle of his bag tightly, he opened the gate and walked slowly towards the front door.

*

The newspapers were full of doom. The main domestic issue was the continuing decrease in the male life expectancy: the average age was now fifty-nine, just above Haiti. The country's roads were now officially the most dangerous in Europe.

He took sips from his coffee and sat drumming his fingers on the table, concentrating on the vibrancy beneath his skin. After a few minutes, he picked up his phone and dialled.

'Hi.'

'Hi.'

She was silent for several moments before she continued.

'Where are you?'

'Home,' said Mariani.

'Oh.'

'How are you?'

'All right.'

'You don't sound it.'

'Dad's not well.'

'Oh.' Mariani felt a pinprick of anxiety at the base of his skull. 'What is it?'

'He's just sick. Ill.'

''Flu? Food poisoning?'

'He's in hospital. Can't get out of bed. He talks very slowly and doesn't make any sense. He sleeps almost all the time.'

With a cramping sensation in his stomach, Mariani heard Ladoga explaining his deal with Triesmaan; *'He won't tell me what's in it or how it works.'*

'They're doing tests,' said Keira. 'Maybe it's some kind of ME or virus thing.' She sounded lonely and afraid. 'Acute stress maybe. Thought it would catch up with him eventually. What about you?'

'I'm OK.'

'Did that treatment work?'

'I'm not sure yet,' he said offhandedly, trying to cover his rising concern. All of a sudden, he felt weak and small. 'Keira?'

'Yes?'

'I'm sorry for everything. I love you. I don't want us to… I mean, I'd like to…somehow…if possible…'

'I don't know if it is.' There was a silence on the line. 'I miss you, though.'

'I want you. More than ever. You feel very...' The next word came out inadvertently, but somehow seemed entirely true. '...*Delicious* to me.'

'Delicious?' She almost laughed.

'That's the nearest I can get,' said Mariani. He remembered, when he'd gone to her flat, the overwhelming way she'd aroused his appetites. He shut his eyes, not knowing if the sensation was healthy or otherwise.

'Right. Well.'

'Can I call you again?'

She hesitantly agreed. He guessed he had been, if not forgiven, then in some way allowed back. He hoped they could start again. He hoped everything could now start again.

TWENTY FIVE

Mariani had never fully imagined what had been injected into his blood-stream. Or how it might work. He knew nothing of the way drugs create positive sensations that, depending on their potency, can become irrepress-ible desires. So he did not associate the odd pangs of gut-twisting hunger that began to bother him with anything other than a change of diet and the stress of expectation.

Bennett had advised him to wait a week after the final injection before testing the effects, but after just four days Mariani found the mounting need to assess his future had become too strong.

His kit felt fresh and new against his skin. As he wheeled a bike down the hall towards the front door, the tick-click-tick from the chain and rear cassette sounded reassuringly purposeful. Outside, he put his left shoe on first, as he always had, and then clipped it into the pedal, the mechanism making a satisfying thunk. He swung his other leg over the top tube. His backside seemed to meld with the saddle.

The trees were still. The road empty. His intestines tightened, not un-pleasantly, with nerves. He raised himself on the pedals, pushed slowly down, the bike eased effortlessly forward, and despite not having ridden for months and being ten kilos overweight, he knew as the power was transferred from his legs into the cranks that, whatever it was Triesmaan had given him, it had worked. For a moment he wondered if it was a trick of his mind, pure hope providing the sensation. Ten more pedal strokes. No. It was there. The thing he had lost.

Tears came to his eyes. But instead of crying, he smiled. He laughed, louder and louder.

*

He rode thirty kilometres, thinking all the way, setting targets, listing pos-sible teams and where he might fit in. There was still time to get into shape for next season. When should he ring Serge Hamptons? Except he wasn't going to ring Serge Hamptons, he was going to get a decent agent; that was one of the promises he'd made himself. Well, show form in some races and the agents would come flocking. And as soon as he got back, he'd order some digital weighing scales for his food, check the prices of flats in the three Hans Banquo-approved French villages, scan the net for information on the drag co-efficients of various brands of bar tape.

The air was warm and the road surface felt as smooth as black ivory. Birds sang. The chain moved instantly and silently across the sprockets. The bike changed position on the road at the merest nudge and seemed to want to go faster than he could ever remember. At a short, steep incline, he closed his eyes for a second and pictured Trent Mitchell: dyed gold hair flowing out of his helmet and down his back, legs waxed by his mother, yellow diamond glinting in one ear, emerald in the other. The Australian *trejanzk* was twenty metres ahead and pedalling smugly towards the top of the incline. He thought he'd left Mariani way back, he'd not see that miserable little grey-faced commie jerk-off again today...

Mariani felt the urge build. He was ten metres behind Mitchell now and could see the punk kangaroo tattoos that coloured both of the Australian's stringy calves. Mariani pushed harder, to nearly forty-five km/h, and the effort was really hurting but it was all going to be worth it because he went past Mitchell like a blazing comet and when he glanced over his shoulder, he clearly saw Mitchell's face, and on it the look which Mariani had thought he'd never provoke on a rival's face again. Yes, that's right, you motherfucking smear of dickcheese: Romain Mariani has scorched your soul.

He was ravenous by the time he got home. There was nothing in the fridge, just a year-old bag of oats in the cupboard, so after a quick shower, and dressed in a long-sleeved shirt, he walked down the path towards the café.

Svarik was smoking and watching infra-red footage of a night hunt on TV. When he saw Mariani come in, he hastily ground the cigarette out in a saucer and flapped at the grey haze drifting across the counter.

Mariani put out his hand. Svarik shook it.

'Coffee?' he asked.

'If I must.'

Mariani sat at his usual place and waited. When it came, the coffee was as bad as it had ever been and the roll Svarik brought with it was heavy and dry. Svarik sat down opposite him.

'Where's Varta?' asked Mariani.

'Campaigning.' Svarik scratched at his stubble. 'She's got yellow hair.'

'What?'

'Dyed it. To look like Hillary Clinton. Bought a trouser suit.'

'Think she'll win?'

Svarik moved his bottom lip backwards and forwards, a gesture that seemed to communicate not only his uncertainty about the result but also about the whole concept of winning and losing.

Mariani sipped his coffee. 'I've been riding.'

Svarik sniffed and nodded.

'Coming back next season.'

'Thought you were finished.' Svarik half-closed one eye as he looked at Mariani.

'Seems not.'

Svarik looked around the yellowing walls of the café and then at Mariani, as if to check that it really was his friend sitting there.

'Well...good.' He breathed in and his frown became slightly deeper. 'How's that then?'

Mariani shrugged. 'Luck.'

'Luck?' Svarik repeated the word as if he didn't understand that either. He sniffed and stood up and went back behind the counter. He turned off the TV and began to slice a blood sausage on to a plate. 'I bought the Bang & Olufsen stereo from that Giûrgii,' he said. 'The volume knob don't work.'

TWENTY SIX

Consumed

The next morning Mariani woke early and rode out to Lake Rig. It was cool, and the pedals turned easily. When he had completed ten circuits he dismounted and sat on the thick grass at the lakeside. He watched a grebe as it snapped angrily at a submissive rival. He took his phone from his back pocket and dialled.

A robotic female voice answered. 'Serge Hamptons Sports Management.'

'This is Romain Mariani. Can I speak to Serge, please?'

'Please hold.'

Mariani held.

A minute passed. He imagined Hamptons patting away at his stiff forehead and selecting a voice tone. Then the agent was on the line.

'Romain. Long time. Good to hear.' The tonal option he'd gone for was non-committal.

'Yes. Hello.'

'I was thinking about calling you.'

'Were you?'

'Just to see if…well, you know.' Hamptons cleared his throat. 'Anyway, how are– '

'Can you get me on to a team, any team, it doesn't matter which, for a race in about a month?'

'Whoah! Tough ask. Super tough. You've not been seen for some time, Romain. I don't have to tell you how quick people forget…'

'How much?'

'Excuse me?'

Mariani didn't think before he spoke again. 'Half my salary for the next five years?'

'What?'

'Sixty per cent?'

'Well, I…there *might* be something…let me make some calls. Don't go anywhere.'

Hamptons rang off. Mariani lay back on the grass, his mind whirring. In a month he could lose five kilos and get back to about seventy-five per cent of his peak fitness. That would see him through a one-day race with a

185

second-string team. He could get in a breakaway, show some strength and get the sponsor TV time. If the course were flat, he'd work for the team's sprinter. If it was hilly, he could attack on the climbs, cause some panic and pain. It didn't matter, he'd do whatever the team asked him to. All he wanted was to re-establish himself.

The sun warming his face reminded him of the heat he'd felt standing next to Banquo in the square after the Essence. That glimpse of a life in which not a fragment of potential had been wasted. The response a man provoked by making flesh the dreams of millions. Hamptons could have all his salary if he wanted. Mariani knew he had a maximum of ten more years in the sport. He wanted to feel that heat on his face as soon as possible, be the rider he knew he should have been.

A quarter of an hour went by. He began to worry. Perhaps no one would have him, not for any race. Would he have to get on the phone, ring round, beg? Did he have the balls to call Banquo, ask him to pull some strings? Thirty minutes passed. Forty-five.

Then his phone bleeped and Hamptons was in his ear again.

'You're in luck. New one-dayer this year in jolly old Great Britain: you'll like it, lots of rain and drunk people. Maybe you could visit family, watch some cricket. Little team's just started, Godet-RMG, one of their guys lost a fight with a double-decker coach last week: his pelvis is like crazy paving. Tishland Speyer's the head honch. Says he knew you when you were a rookie. It took some jaw but he's willing to take a punt. Now, ringers ain't strictly kosher, but 'cos this is first time out and 'cos it's Great Britain the rules are — well, let's say they're open to interpretation. But they've got some good guys on the start line, basically anyone who's not doing the Tour. They want you at a training week in Bulgaria...'

'Bulgaria?'

'They're new, Romain, and their main sponsor sells compost, so you'll be lucky if you're not camping and hand-killing your own food.' Hamptons laughed.

'It's fine. I used to go to Bulgaria on holiday as a kid.'

'Nice. Anyway, you get there — it's a fortnight from today — and they'll check you out. Do OK and you're in. Do OK in the race and…well, who knows? What's your weight?'

'Eighty-four,' said Mariani, taking off two kilos.

'I told them eighty. Try my blueberry soup diet for a week. I'll e-mail it to you. Listen, Romain, arm round shoulder moment – are you sure you're, you know, ready for this?'

'I'm ready.'

'OK.' An exhalation of breath came down the phone. 'Arm removed. So – you said sixty per cent, right?'

*

He texted Keira in the afternoon, asking after her father. *Same* came the reply. *Please let me know anything that happens* he texted back and added an '*x*' and then another before pressing Send.

He ate dinner at Svarik's and went to bed feeling fine, but woke just after two with a slick of hot sweat on his face. He got up and rubbed the crook of his arm, looking at the purple-red dots there. He pictured the needle slipping into one of them, heard from somewhere the very faintest pop as the skin was broken and the infinitesimal hiss and swish of liquid as it travelled along the barrel of the syringe. The sequence replayed itself. The sounds were louder, the images sharper, the sensation more demanding.

His skin was tacky and his scalp oily. He felt soiled and got up to shower, washing his hair roughly, wishing he could get the cold water inside his skull. He went back to bed and half-slept until the sun rose just after six.

After a breakfast of *cudhi* porridge that he made with water, he sat down with a piece of paper and a pen and tried to put his life into some kind of order. In the left half of the page, he wrote down facts. In the other, possibilities. He had to keep stopping to massage his arm as the veins and muscles seemed possessed by an itching fire. When he'd written down all he knew and all he could foresee, he tried to connect the two halves. But the page quickly became a mass of winding lines and question marks. He got up and went to the fridge, but its harsh light shone on empty space. The *cudhi* had done little to satisfy him. He checked the freezer compartment. Nothing but old ice.

He had no food and no money to buy any with. There were many other issues, but that seemed the most pressing.

He swore and the word seemed to bounce off the blank plaster walls and thud back into his ears. He couldn't keep running up credit at Svarik's: he still owed him several thousand from earlier in the year.

He picked up the phone and dialled.

Flôntina, Herzy's wife, answered and immediately began asking Mariani why they hadn't seen him for so long. She told him that Herzy was cycling everywhere now and losing his paunch, and then asked Mariani to hang on.

He heard her gravelly voice call her husband's name. He waited for several minutes and then heard the shuffle-scrape of Herzy's wrecked laceless boots.

'Lazy shithead,' said his brother. 'Where you been?'

Behind Herzy's gruff tone, Marini sensed concern. Perhaps, at some time in the future, he would tell him. But not now. 'I'm your only brother, right?'

'Ach, what you want?'

'Listen. Can you lend me some money? Say five thousand?'

'Shit of the Devil! You want to tup some cheaper nannies.' Herzy dropped his voice to a stage whisper. 'Marghjini Hrij is offering lick, suck and coffee for two hundred.'

'Marghjini Hrij is seventy-five, a hunchback witch and one-fifty kilos.'

'Coffee's good, though.'

'How much can you spare, then?'

'Gimme a bike and I'll let you have four.'

'Those bikes cost a hundred thousand.'

'You can only ride one at a time. I'm getting quick. I'm gonna enter the Olympics.'

'All right. You lend me the money, I'll lend you the bike.'

Herzy was quiet for a moment. 'You got a problem?'

'Me? No,' Mariani said quickly.

'You've been on TV. I got a magazine with your lazy dumb face on the front. Why don't you have any loot, hey?'

Mariani looked down at the floor before answering. 'It's complicated.'

'OK.' Herzy sniffed. 'Listen, there's another thing.' His voice sounded suddenly tired.

*

The smaller pigs were in the pen. As he approached, they began to squeal and snort, jostling along the fence, their pale can-shaped snouts wriggling and twitching. He stared at them and listened to their pleas for food. After a minute, he looked left towards the house and the pigs knew he was leaving them and their begging became desperate.

As Mariani approached, he saw Tanel come to the door and stand there, smoking indifferently and clearing his throat.

He waited until his youngest son was less than a metre away.

'You're fat,' he said, then turned and shuffled back inside the house, coughing. Mariani followed. The front room was over-lit, the windows were closed and Tanel had a fire burning dully in the grate.

'Make yourself something if you want it.' He nodded towards the kitchen.

'I'm all right.'

'Good for you.'

Tanel collapsed slowly into his chair. The room smelled of hot old leather, mildew and wood dust. Mariani noticed that his father had put more pictures up on the mantel: Tanel with a boyish Jan Ullrich, with Bjarne Riis, with a young Richard Virenque. Upright, smiling men, skin lustrous with health.

The burning coal and wood shifted. A flame licked upwards and then sank back. Tanel stared at the chicken's feet he now had for hands.

'How long?' asked Mariani, watching the fire's glow. There was a mound of ash underneath the grate. Tanel's face was a similar dirty white.

'Three, four, maybe six.'

'Right. Months?'

'No.'

Mariani moved his mouth around and felt sweat start to run down from his hairline. Inside his right arm, fiery worms convulsed and insects were breeding in his head. His stomach turned over heavily. After his early ride, he'd eaten a rabbit leg and some cold ham for breakfast, but now he was skittish with hunger again.

'Maybe I will have something,' he said, and went into the kitchen. It felt damp. Crusted plates filled the sink at all angles. On the mottled wooden work surface, a fly clung to a smear of red on a carving knife. According to the calendar on the wall it was still April. He sensed with a dark-edged clarity the dismal full stop that his father's life was about to come to. He felt more convinced than ever that seeing Triesmaan and taking the drug had been the right – the only – thing to do, even if in so many ways it had also been wrong. Strange too, he thought, that Tanel's illness should appear so quickly after his traits had begun to show in his son; it was as if passing on the deep flaws that had ruined him and those closest to him had been his life's work, and now he could go, job done, to his grave.

But as the ache in his guts intensified, he began to wonder if whatever Tanel had passed on had become infected in some way and was now beginning to mutate.

In the fridge, light flickered over a half-eaten bowl of cereal and a slice of old bread with something black scraped across it. Behind that there was an object wrapped in foil. Mariani tore at the foil.

'You want this chop?' he called.

'My lunch.'

Mariani took a knife from a drawer and carefully cut inside the edge of the stringy meat piece, reducing its size by about a quarter but leaving its shape the same. He put his booty in his mouth and, tough though it was, he savoured it. He folded the tin foil around the remains and replaced it in the fridge.

When he'd run the cold tap over his arm and got himself a glass of water, he went back to the front room. Tanel's eyes were closed. His mouth hardly moved as he spoke.

'Herzy'll get the farm. You want any of the junk in here, take it.'

'Don't think so.'

'Going to try for a contract?'

Mariani nodded. 'Soon.'

'Yeah. You're the size of a sow. What team'll look at you?'

'Weight'll come off.'

'What about your head?'

'Getting there.'

'They say it was the knock-off Varitestone, the stuff Mr Sixty used to get for us, that's done for me,' said Tanel, and coughed. 'Fucking joke. Took that twenty years ago. Worked, too. Got me a fourth up Huez in 'ninety-one. More likely the chimneys, eh? Fucking quacks. Never listen to a man in a white coat, hey?'

'I'm taking something,' said Mariani. 'Thought you'd like to know.'

Tanel appeared not to hear. 'Wouldn't mind seeing Mr Sixty again before I disappear,' he said with a small smile. 'Maybe I'll call him up. Probably in prison.' He laughed and coughed.

After slowly taking a breath that Mariani worried might he his last, Tanel focused on his son.

'Take as much as you can fucking get away with.' His head lolled to one side. 'Should've done it years ago.'

'Aren't you ashamed of me?'

'Ashamed?' asked Tanel. 'Ashamed? Grow up.'

Mariani said nothing more. He had hoped his father would be disappointed, as if all these years he had been secretly holding his son up as a moral bulwark, a man of defiance and independence who would not give in, no matter how strong the temptation, how fierce the pressure. But now he realised that though Tanel was many hateful things, he was not a hypocrite. Strangely, he felt a fractured respect for the shrinking, bitter figure huddled in front of him.

When, ten minutes later, Tanel had fallen asleep, Mariani watched a thin line of drool begin to leak out of his father's mouth. As it reached the bottom of his chin, Mariani took a tissue from his pocket and wiped it away.

His eyes drifted to the photos on the mantel. He asked himself in which of them Tanel looked happiest. He decided, and took that memory away with him.

Halfway down the path, just as he was approaching the pig pen, a hot furious wave passed through him and in his head a bellow sounded for something that had no name. He clutched the pen's fencing, groaned and shook. The pigs shrieked. He clutched the meat of his thigh and dug his fingers in. Every time, it was getting worse.

*

He had forgotten that the house was up for sale. When the agent phoned to tell him an offer had been put in, he didn't know what to say. He was nearly two million *chõp* in debt, with no immediate source of income. Triesmaan would need his money in three weeks. After paying off Svarik, he had just over half of Herzy's four thousand left. There was an unopened utility bill on the kitchen table.

'This the only interest you've had?' he asked the agent.

'The market's very slow. I'm advising anyone with a decent offer to take it.'

'It's a hundred and twenty thousand less than I paid for it.'

'Times are indeed hard. I have had to take an evening job myself.'

'Can I think about it?'

'The buyer is asking for a quick decision.'

'Can you ring me at the end of the day?'

'I would really take this offer.'

'Call me at five, could you?'

He put the phone down and got up and went to find the piece of paper on which he'd tried to organise his life. It was in a drawer in the kitchen. He looked at it for a minute and then tore it into a number of tiny pieces and and washed them down the waste.

Then he called Herzy again and asked if he had a spare room.

After that, Slirik Fingh rang and asked him if he wanted to go for dinner.

TWENTY SEVEN

Hoxtia's meaty fug smelled to him like perfume. He watched the flush-faced old man spit-roasting ducks just inside the doorway and his eyes focused on the man's hand as he spooned golden liquid goose fat over the ducks' breasts.

He had never known hunger like this. His stomach felt like a caldera.

The leather-aproned owner, himself built like a side of the ox for which Hoxtia was both famous and named, showed Mariani and Slirik Fingh to their table and then brought menus. Mariani was on the verge of handing it back and simply saying, 'Good, thanks.'

'I called you a few times. How you been?' asked Fingh. He had sutures in a three-centimetre wound over the top of one eyebrow. He wore a lilac-coloured suede jacket with silver skulls for buttons and had grown a pubescent moustache.

Mariani nodded.

'Sure?' asked Fingh, eyes on his dampening face.

'Uh. Bit hot. You?'

'Ach. Business,' he said, and fingered the wound. 'As dangerous as cycling these days.'

'I won't ask.'

'What you having?'

'Hare livers, ox-heart pâté, game bird *mixhta*, flank steak, side order of crispy pig ears.'

Fingh thought for a moment. 'And for main course?'

Mariani *lijzk*-ied without enthusiasm.

'Two *renas* to start and then a bottle of Lake Rig *tgreszv*?' said Fingh.

'You're on your own. I'm in training.'

'For what? World Meat Eating Championships?'

A broad-bottomed waiter, his face almost completely thatched with a dense beard, brought a jug of water and with it a stuffed squirrel, its reddish back slotted and thick coins of the animal's dried meat placed in the slots. Mariani ate two of them while he ordered. His arm felt like it was roasting in one of the restaurant's ovens. With his napkin, he dabbed at the burning sweat on his forehead and then gulped a glass of water, wishing it were colder.

The waiter went away and then returned with Fingh's *rena*. He sipped the greenish liquid and with a look of deepening concern watched Mariani as he fidgeted in his seat, wiped sweat from his forehead and made small gasps.

'You don't have to say anything,' said Fingh.

'What?'

'It's none of my business.' He leant closer to Mariani. 'But, look, if you want some stuff, let me know, OK? Don't go to the Giûrgïu or some shithead with a few bags of baby laxative.'

Mariani almost started laughing. 'You think I'm taking drugs?'

Fingh clicked his tongue and raised his eyebrows in a gesture that asked Mariani not to take him for a fool. He put his *rena* down. 'Pills. Smokes. *Hdervij* if you want, but only the black. It'll be good and it'll be clean.'

'I just need some fucking food,' said Mariani, and picked up his fork, holding it in his fist like a club.

'All right, all right,' said Fingh. He sniffed and smoothed his moustache. 'So...Tour de France podium, next year? Then you can run for President, hey?'

'Uh. Going to work my way up with a nice little team, take it race by race. Idea is to get back into best shape by Christmas.'

'Want someone to ride with while you're here? Can't say I'm fit – knee's a bit shot – but I'll keep you company. Hey, I saw Rihli yesterday.'

'Rihli?' Mariani's eyes kept flicking to the kitchen door, hoping to see the waiter come through it with laden plates. The hunger was everywhere, from his toes to his ears.

'Beard. Earrings. Mad. Gave you a little trouble on the Hgruh?'

'Oh. Him.'

'Running for Area Governor. Gonna win, too.'

'Amnesty for wife-beaters!'

'What? That's a crime? She hit me first, officer.'

'You still seeing that girl?' Mariani glanced ravenously across to the diners on the next table, a small bald man with a prosthetic hand and a beautiful Giûrgïu woman whose hair was peroxide blonde on one side and raven black on the other. The woman was pushing a piece of liver around her plate and at any moment Mariani felt he would reach over and snatch it away with his fork.

Fingh looked sheepish. 'Natalia? Uh. Probably get married next year. If she hasn't stoved my head in by then. You gonna get spliced?'

'I hope.'

'What's her point of view?'

'I'd like to know that.'

'I'd get that *franzyxk* tucked up. Bet she doesn't slap you around.'

'No,' said Mariani, thinking momentarily of the heavy way Keira's body had fallen to the bed when he'd hit her. 'What's keeping this food?' He slapped the table three times with increasing force and noise, making the cutlery jump and Fingh's glass of *rena* judder unsteadily.

'Hey! Look, Romain,' said Fingh, lifting his glass protectively into the air. 'Come on now. What the fuck've you been taking? You look like you're about to kill someone.'

Mariani wasn't listening. 'I could eat a– '

'You said that already. It's not that shit they give the dogs before a fight, is it? Not *Krusha*?'

'Shut *up*. I'm not doing any fucking drugs. Idiot!' Mariani picked another piece of squirrel from out of the stuffed beast's back and pushed it into his mouth. He'd now eaten them all.

'Hey. No need to be rude. I'm only trying – '

'Thank Christ,' said Mariani as he saw the waiter approaching.

Upon arrival, he put the plates and meat-laden serving dish down on the table. He pulled a bottle of *tgreszv* from his pocket and opened it. Mariani stabbed a pig's ear with his fork, feverishly cut it in half and put the top part into his mouth. But as he chewed, feeling the fibres and tendons with his tongue, he did not get the relief he was so desperate for.

'This food's no good,' he said. The second half of the ear followed the first and he began gnashing his teeth as if beneath the table someone were squeezing his testicles. 'This food's no *fucking* good!' he shouted at the waiter through a mouth full of mushed pig skin.

The waiter, bottle of wine in one hand and corkscrew in the other, stared at him. 'I'm sorry, sir?'

Mariani snatched at a roasted woodcock and tore the bird apart. He began chewing on a leg, his eyes half-closed. A drop of sweat hung from the point of his chin. It fell into the bird's carcass.

'Romain?' Fingh squinted at him. 'Jesus Christ.'

Mariani felt as if his brain was going to combust and grey lava pour out of his ears. His shirt was a wet steaming rag but his hands were cold. A searingly bright light was flashing in his head. Everything inside his chest was itching and he had an immediate urge to put his hand all the way down his throat and scratch long and hard at his own internal organs. He took a drink of water and swilled it round the pulp of pork and game bird that coated his tongue and palate. He swallowed, gulping hard.

He stood up.

'This food's no fucking good!' he shouted to the entire room.

He picked up his flank steak from the plate and, clutching it to him, stumbled out of the restaurant.

*

Three twenty-four.

Mariani got out of bed. He hadn't slept a minute. Slumped in the taxi on his way home, he'd waited for death. He felt sure it was imminent. Once he was inside the house he'd been fervently, bitterly sick. He then sat on the vomit-splattered toilet and, with his whole body shuddering, unleashed a torrent of semi-liquid matter that scorched his rectal lining as it cascaded out of him.

His mind had churned and his body had itched and given off waves of heat. He felt the walls closing in, the air thicken in his nose and mouth. He was trapped. In his body, his room, his house. He gripped his pillow in fear. Somewhere outside a cockerel screamed.

He got dressed in old kit and filled two bidons with cold water. The bike was by the front door. He pushed the bidons into the holders and then wheeled the bike outside. The night was a dense blue-black and the breeze was picking up. As he stood there, he heard the first spits of rain hit the path.

Bare-headed, he wheeled the bike towards the road, the clack of his shoes and ticking of the rear hub loud in the air. He had no lights, never rode in the dark.

He pushed off and felt the rain wet his forehead and cheeks. The moon disappeared behind a cloud and gave out a smudged and faltering glow. Out of the village and towards Lake Rig, the trees and fields and the road all unfamiliar and strange in the cavelike dark, only half-there as if in some deep dream. A pulse of wind pushed him from behind and he picked up speed. The rain thickened and the tyres hissed. Mariani wiped water off his face and tried to put his life, whatever was left of it, into turning the pedals, keeping the speed high, moving forward, reducing himself to constituent parts, becoming nothing but an engine making power. It was very dark.

The branches bowed and the raindrops grew harder and bigger. Mariani's heart worked and he rode towards the lake as fast as he ever had. He thought he could sweat out this sickness, and then the rain and wind would sluice it away and he would be free and clean.

He rolled on into endless night.

The dark seemed to close around him, the only light pinpricks from farmhouses where people slept in quiet beds until it was time to begin their quiet lives again. He was drenched now and hardly able to see, navigating on memory and hope. When the lake appeared, he began to ride as if death were chasing him, his mouth open and his back parallel to the road. He tasted rain, the drops splashing against his bared teeth. The wind slapped his face, and then pushed at his back, bullying him along. On and on. Two laps, three, five. His face sopping. His teeth gritted. Going and going, waiting to be saved, until the light started to come up and he realised no one was coming, not now and not ever, and he returned without knowing how, bedraggled and spent, purblind, little more than cold bones, to the dark cell of his room where he sat and knew he had to see Triesmaan again.

TWENTY EiGHT

'Should I wait, sir?' asked the taxi driver.

'Yes.'

Mariani got out and walked to the door of number forty-nine. The Audi was in the drive. He pressed the buzzer. There was no answer, so he knocked loudly. He took out his phone and dialled, but as Bennett hadn't picked up the previous seven times Mariani did not expect him to do so now.

He was about to knock again when the air went hazy. The numerals on the door blurred. Sweat leached on to his forehead. A scorching silent roar passed through him. They were coming four or five times a day now and lasting longer each time. He clutched his stomach and groaned and shook. His heart boomed.

'Are you all right, sir?' the taxi driver called through the car's open window.

Mariani raised a hand and nodded. The spasm passed. He took deep breaths and looked around the soundless street. Not a single sign of humanity.

Then the door slowly began to open. Mariani watched as Bennett's pale face appeared in the gap. He was hatless, revealing tufts of hair like white grass on the sides of his head.

'Is he in there?' asked Mariani.

'He can't see you now.'

Mariani wrenched open the door. Bennett tried to stand in his way, but Mariani pushed the little man to one side.

He went in. The house no longer smelled of toilet cleaner and room freshener. Now there was a tang of things gone old and rotten: dishrags and vegetables. The light was grey and in the front room the paintings on the walls look drab and flat and sad.

Bennett came up beside him. He pulled at Mariani's sleeve. His putty-coloured bald face was crumpled with worry. 'What am I going to do?'

'Where is he?'

'Downstairs. Been there for days.'

Mariani's footsteps were hard on the steel treads as he descended into the basement. Bennett followed, mewling.

On the examination table, wearing a white shift, lay Triesmaan. His skin had yellowed and his features seemed to have thinned: his mouth was just a slit below his nose. He looked like an old man, days dead. The room was lit only by a semi-circle of large candles that had been placed on a small table close to his head.

'*Jeszu,*' said Mariani.

Bennett's mouth twisted like a small, landed fish.

Mariani stepped closer to the prone, motionless figure. 'Dr Triesmaan...'

The lines of his lips were bluish, like a vein.

'Dr Triesmaan, I have to...'

Triesmaan's eyes stayed shut as words came out of the caved-in mouth in a cracked whisper. 'I'm sorry for you.'

'Why isn't he in hospital?' Mariani asked.

'Won't go,' snivelled Bennett.

'It was a mistake,' said Triesmaan.

'What?' Mariani's breathing began to deepen and something squeezed his heart. 'I need more. I feel like I'm burning and I have this terrible hunger...'

'All the work on it has been destroyed. It was too unstable.'

'What was in it?' He was shouting now. 'Why do I feel like this?'

The tip of Triesmaan's greyish tongue appeared and tried to moisten his barely visible lips. Candlelight dappled his face. Mariani had to lean closer to hear him. 'The potency...was too much. That's why you've become dependent. Your body and mind have become dependent.'

'Dependent?'

Triesmaan said nothing. A hint of some distant happiness floated across his features. Life seemed to be leaking away through his pores. His skin began taking on the same thickened, plastic quality that Mariani had seen when his mother was in her last minutes.

When Triesmaan did talk, his words were whispers from a bad dream. 'To do what needed to be done, I could not synthesise the hormones. They had to the harvested...from source.'

'From source?' repeated Mariani.

'From the brain. The human brain.'

Mariani flinched. He heard the words but still did not understand.

Triesmaan was taking small hurried breaths. Bennett tried to put a glass of water to his mouth, but he turned his head away.

'I told you it was experimental. I told you I wasn't even sure if some... of the hormones existed. It was always a... risk.'

Mariani saw again the colourless liquid, so pure in the syringe, and then pictured the insertion of strange sucking instruments into a grey, ridged, jelly-like mass that gently quivered. He almost gagged. He glanced for a moment at the sculpture of the deconstructed human brain that stood in the basement and a terrible furious disappointment began to descend on him.

'I'm sorry for you,' said Triesmaan. 'But go away now. I want nothing more to do... with any of you.'

Bennett put one hand on his pate and with his other began pulling at the clump of hair above his ear. 'Oh,' he said. 'Oh.'

Triesmann exhaled. He did not take a breath in. One of the candles flared.

'Don't,' said Mariani. He put both hands on Triesmaan's shoulders and began to shake him, gently at first, but when there was no response, he pulled Triesmaan upright and then slammed him back down on the examination table.

Silence. The pharmacologist's head slowly turned to the side. His lips began to part. Mariani could not take his eyes away as the mouth widened and the darkness inside it seemed to deepen.

*

'Keira, if you're there, pick up. Please pick– '

'Romain? What is it? Stop shouting.'

'Don't go anywhere. I'll be there in forty-five minutes.'

'Romain– '

'Just don't go anywhere.' He rang off. 'Can you speed up?' he said to the taxi driver.

'I'm sorry, sir, the limit here is– '

'Speed the *fuck* up.'

*

She let him in without a word and he followed her into the front room. The TV was on, the sound muted. On the screen, a man was judging another man who wore a sparkly suit and stood on a brightly lit stage. The judge looked somehow disillusioned.

'I'm late,' she said. 'I should be at the hospital.'

'Oh. Yes.' Mariani clawed at his face. 'How is he?'

'Slightly worse.'

'Oh. Keira, look– '

'I should go.'

He felt the empty fire lurking. He tried to think in a straight line.

'Can you just listen to me for…'

He doubled up as the spasms began to twist and stretch his insides. He folded his arms across his chest as if trying to hold himself together.

'Are you sick? What is it?'

Keira helped him to the sofa. He lay back.

Mariani groaned and clutched at her hand. 'That stuff. It's… I don't know what it is. But I'm…I've got to get more.'

'Then get some.' Her head was shaking slightly from side to side.

'There isn't any.'

'Isn't any? Why not?'

'Keira. Look, this…it's all just a terrible mistake.' Mariani started to lose himself. He became nothing but the words that spewed out of his throat. 'Everything's gone wrong and Triesmaan's fucking dead and I need to be in Bulgaria in two weeks…'

He raved and kept on raving, punctuating his raving with sobs, throwing his life out into the air in shattered, jagged pieces, raving on and on about his father's yellowing fingers and Triesmaan's mouth as he died and Golgotha's wide blue eyes and the taste of the pigs' ears in Hoxtia...until she hit him hard twice in the face with her open hand.

'Shut up. Stop. Just stop now. Yes?'

He looked up at her, blinking.

'OK? You're OK now?'

He nodded quickly.

She looked at him through half-closed eyes, as if he emitted a light that was too harsh. 'I wish I'd never met you,' she said quietly.

He sniffed and took a deep breath. 'Do you want me to leave?'

She flicked her bottom lip on her top teeth and slowly looked away from him towards the TV. On the shining stage the show's losing contestants were smiling and waving goodbye to a wildly clapping audience.

*

The stunted young woman in the hospital bed made animal noises. Her arm kept swiping at some invisible annoyance. The camera closed in on her mouth and the odd shapes it made. Mariani paused the clip. He sat back in the chair, looked away from the laptop's screen and wiped his hand across his face. According to the dry medical text accompanying the clip, the girl had been diagnosed with Creutzfeldt-Jakob disease only two weeks before the film had been shot: she had died a week later. Fifteen years previously, she had been treated with Human Growth Hormone – 'cadaver-derived' according to the text. Mariani read as much as he could understand of the last two sentences: *Based on the assumption that infectious prions causing the disease were transferred along with the cadaver-derived HGH, it was removed from the market. In 1985, biosynthetic human growth hormone replaced pituitary-derived human growth hormone for therapeutic use.*

'Anything?' Keira stood in the doorway.

Mariani shrugged. 'Do you know what...prions....are?'

She shook her head.

He searched again. *The word prion is derived from the words protein and infection. Prions are responsible for the transmissible spongiform encephalopathies in a variety of mammals, including bovine spongiform encephalopathy (BSE, also known as 'mad cow disease') in cattle and Creutzfeldt-Jakob disease (CJD) in humans. All known prion diseases affect the structure of the brain and all are untreatable and universally fatal.*

Thoughts clattered through his mind: hormones, if taken direct from people, could contain diseases. Did he have a disease? Impossible to answer: it had taken fifteen years before that woman showed symptoms. His immediate problem was the addiction. But to what precisely was he addicted? He didn't know even what hormones he'd been taking. Would he ever know? And how would he find a substitute?

'There's nothing,' he said.

'We've – you've – got to try and see someone. There must be another doctor who knows as much as this Triesmaan did, worked the same way.'

'It's an addiction. I know that. I need whatever he was giving me. Or a substitute.'

'He's a bastard. *Was* a bastard. And you're an asshole. The whole thing stinks. I'd go to the police if…if…Christ, Romain. As if it's not bad enough that Dad's ill.'

Her eyes dampened and she turned to face the wall, then glanced back at him. Mariani could sense that her mind was turning over.

'You never told me what you talked about the night you went to see him,' she said.

'You, mostly.'

He got up and touched her shoulder, the first contact since he had arrived. He circled the end of his finger on the ridge of bone, and then with his hand gently squeezed the muscle below. He could feel his breathing start to quicken, but the cause, he knew, was not simply lust. This was something bigger and not right. His stomach made an odd croaking sound.

He felt her shoulders tense. 'I should be at the hospital,' she said.

*

They lay awake. A warm breeze came in through the window and a high clear moon lent a pale patina to the dark. Mariani had been ready to sleep on the sofa, but she had told him not to be so childish. They had talked and got nowhere.

Under the sheet his thigh touched hers and Keira didn't flinch. Carefully, he put his hand on her arm. Something, a dog or fox, barked in the street below. The breeze came in stronger and warmer and as it did he felt his heart begin to thud. He bit down on his lip and tried to force back whatever was coming. Her hand covered his and she turned on to her side. Her fingers began to trail though his hair. She sighed. He felt his intestines tighten. He could not hold down a groan and Keira imagined the wrong cause. She sat up and took off her shirt. Mariani saw her, pale and naked, in the bluish light. The thing that had barked began to howl. Some other beast joined in and the two laments seemed to float in the moving air.

He could smell the city. Dust and food and fumes. He could smell so many things, his olfactory neurons suddenly denser – as dense, he realised in a split-second flashback, as those of Golgotha when it had run amok in his dreams. Sweat began to form on his skin.

'You OK?' asked Keira.

He murmured assent, but inside him a force was stirring, more grotesque than any that had previously assailed him. He heard its bellowing, but along with its anger he could feel its growing sense of excitement. As Keira held his head and brought it against her breasts, his internal organs seemed to be grinding against each other in some brutal but increasingly carnal way. Mariani listened to her heart's deep fast thump and felt the rush of a dark and primeval need. The two night animals wailed with despondent fury. His breath began to come in random exhalations. He felt his stomach open up and the flood of urgent juices. He tasted Keira's skin with his tongue, salty, slightly bitter, and he felt the tongue's receptors transmit their satisfaction. The foulness convulsing inside him began to shapeshift.

Mariani's mouth travelled down Keira's firm torso and she moved her legs apart. Her smell was heady, almost overpowering, and he realised that an urge was building in him that was beyond sexual. It seemed to him as he breathed in the tang from her and his mouth filled with saliva that her smell and taste was the secret to life's continuum, the guarantee of his heart's next beat. He positioned his face between her thighs, saw the flesh semi-illuminated there by the light from the window. It glistened and looked beautiful. He heard both her wordless encouragement and also a sigh of pleasure and expectation from what seemed to be himself, although he made no sound. The hot breeze brought in a waft of food smells, cloying and sweet. Irresistible. Whatever had been spastic and contorted inside him seemed to smooth and straighten. He opened his mouth wide.

Mariani put the tip of his tongue to her and ran the taste round his mouth. The secretions of a human body, mucus, plasma: they were ambrosial. Pyridine, squalene, urea, acetic and lactic acids, ketones, aldehydes. Hints of blood. Nothing had ever tasted quite so vivid to him.

He closed his eyes. Then, in the blackness, a blacker vision. Nightmarish, revolting, depraved. A trespass into the inhuman. It was also, he realised to his horror, completely satisfying. He wanted to do it. He was going to do it. His eyes sprang open. He stared at the moist flesh. The muscles in his neck locked as he fought against the impulse that was willing him to do the vile thing, the only thing that could possibly give him true relief.

He cried out. Keira sat up quickly.

'What is it?'

Mariani pushed himself away from her. He was hyperventilating, clutching at his head with one hand and scraping at his mouth with the other.

He scrabbled away from her. Naked, he staggered to the bathroom, spewed hot and acrid bile, and then ran out of the flat.

TWENTY NINE

Mariani, grub-white in the light from the fluorescent tubes in the corridor's ceiling, held up his hands as Keira moved towards him. 'Keep away!'

'Come back inside. Please.'

He shook his head. 'No. Go in. Lock the door. Do it!'

The lift doors opened. From between them, still wearing the same fawn slacks, came the moustached resident that Mariani had seen on his previous visit. The man held an unlit rubber torch in his left hand. A small elderly dog in a gingham coat trotted beside him. Both of them slowed and gazed upon the scene: an unclothed, grimacing Mariani, and Keira wearing only a blue shirt.

'Hey,' shouted Mariani. He ran, penis jiggling, towards the man and his dog. The man gripped the lead tighter. 'Tell her,' begged Mariani. He got hold of the man's arm. 'She *has* to get away from me.'

The man's face creased with fear and bewilderment. The dog growled.

'What's your name?' Mariani began slowly but firmly to shake the man. 'What's your name?' he repeated.

'Dorph. I have asthma.'

'Listen, Dorph. Something dreadful's going to happen. To her. Listen to me! You take her inside and– '

'Romain, stop it.' Keira tried to pull him away from the rapidly blinking Dorph.

The dog yapped once feebly and bared its broken teeth. Mariani shook Dorph harder. His moustache danced. The dog stood on its hind legs and looked quizzical. Keira released Mariani and stepped away with her hands held open.

'All right, I'm going. I'm going inside. Look.' She moved away. 'Look. All right?'

'Lock the door. Don't let me in. Just throw out my clothes.'

Mariani watched her go back inside the flat. The door closed and he heard the click of the lock. The corridor was quiet again. Then he realised he was still gripping Dorph's shoulders. He let go.

Dorph's little dog looked up at Mariani and cocked its head to one side.

'Well,' said the neighbour, with a faltering half-smile, 'good night.' He led the dog away.

The door to Keira's flat opened and Mariani's clothes, along with his phone, flew out into the corridor. The door shut again.

He had just zipped his trousers when his phone rang. He answered it.

'Are you coming back in now?'

'No. Keira...'

'Either come back in or go away. If you do that I'll never see you again. I know it was my idea for you to come here and see someone in the first place, and I feel bad about that and what's happened, but I just...'

Mariani could hear her voice break as she held back a loud sob. He could hear it in his other ear as it came through the door. The light above him flickered for a moment.

'It's...I don't understand what's in my head...I had these thoughts about you...disgusting...I can't trust myself...'

'What thoughts?' Another sob cracked the question in two.

'I wanted... I wanted to... I can't say...'

'Romain...look...'

'It's best I go. Don't give up on me. That's all I ask.'

'Just come inside.'

'Don't give up on me. Please?'

A long moment passed.

'All right.'

He took the phone away from his ear and cut the line. Then, with tears runneling down his face, he walked away. In the street he flagged down a taxi and told the driver to take him to the airport.

*

He was home by ten-thirty. In twelve days' time, he had to be in Bulgaria. The details, along with a pointed note from Serge Hamptons about the vital importance of his attendance, and which just as clearly set out the terms for their revised contract, were waiting for him in his email.

Over the next two days the spasms came more quickly. Every four hours, every three. He slept in between them. All he could do on the bike was thirty minutes five times a day. He gulped Paracetamol, antacid medicine, tablets for flatulence. He clutched hot water bottles to his stomach. He took laxatives until his shuddering movements were just stringy dribbles. Nothing stopped the searing waves, the thudding pulse in his ears and teeth and stomach, the increasingly outraged demands that seemed to come from every cell. Huge meals left him unsatisfied. He could sense something ghastly and unavoidable coming towards him, some kind of piecing together of all the uneasiness he'd felt ever since the collapse on the last climb of the Essence, but he couldn't imagine the shape it might take. He would simply have to wait and see what was standing at the door when he opened it. That was the worst thing. The options disappearing. The realisation that he could do nothing but see this through to the end.

He walked in the forest one afternoon. The rain was light and cool on his face. Under a huge oak, he sat down on dryish earth, listening to the patpatpat of the drips on the leaves above him. He closed his eyes. When he opened them, a woman was standing a metre away, watching him. A Giûrgïi. Her age impossible to tell. A battered beaded hat askew on her head.

'Yuh?' Her voice was guttural, and for a second Mariani though that the *dornei* she had with her had spoken. One of the dog's ears was just a nub of scar tissue.

'Sorry?'

'What 'tis you whan?'

Mariani shook his head.

'You don't whan noffin, hey? Sure? 'Lectricals? Chimneys? Got best *riki*. Ever'one whan somffin.'

The woman turned her face to the forest and scanned the treetops as if might be something there she could offer him.

'Summer's gone,' she said. 'Weather's been all jumble.'

'Yes.'

'You whan anyffin, we get it,' she said.

She trundled past him, deeper into the forest. The dog went with her, head down.

He sat for a few more minutes, watching the evening sky begin to yellow then redden. When he got back to the house, he lay down on the sofa but could not get comfortable. An idea formed in his head.

He rose and went to the training room, testing the locks on the doors to the garden. Then he walked quickly to the café.

Varta was sitting down at a table with a pen and a notebook in front of her. She had a scarf tied around her peroxided hair.

'He's hunting,' she said. 'Don't disturb me. I'm writing a speech.'

Mariani bent forward at the waist, rubbed his hands together as if he were slowly washing them and then cleared his throat. He looked like a guilt-plagued man about to confess to a serious crime.

Varta sighed and put down her pen. 'What's the matter? The state of you.'

'Listen, if you don't… if you don't see me for five days, come up to the house.'

'And do what?'

'Whatever you need to.'

'What does that mean?'

Mariani shrugged.

Varta frowned and tapped her thumb and third finger alternately on the table as if playing two notes on a piano. 'All right. Do you want something? Coffee?'

He shook his head. 'Five days.'

Mariani walked away from the café and up the road to the house. He ran his hands across his scalp. The sky was nearly dark. He opened the front door and went inside.

THIRTY

He glanced around. A mattress on the floor. A tureen of grey, congealing *cudhi*. A spoon. Both chamber pots. A bucket in case he was sick. The TV. A flannel and a towel. His toothbrush. The bike and stationary trainer pushed up against the wall. He held his mobile phone in his hand and thought for a moment. Then he turned the key in the lock, removed it, bent down and slid both the key and his phone through the gap between the floor and the door, making sure they were out of reach.

You'll never be able to overcome the addiction, Triesmaan had said.

He had to.

He thought about the feeling he'd had in Keira's bedroom, the awful compulsion when he'd inhaled her wonderful scents. He thought about the fact that the hormones he had taken were not synthesised and how they had been formulated to lower his attack thresholds, to make him think of other people as victims. He thought about his metabolic yearnings for red meat.

He stopped thinking.

This sickness, whatever it was, had to leave his body.

He reasoned he was used to suffering. All cyclists were. That, supposedly, was what had enabled Armstrong to endure the harshest chemotherapy. It would have been nice to know if that capacity had also helped someone get through cold turkey. Well, he would see. Perhaps he too could go on to write an autobiography and guest on chat shows and earn a fortune as an after-dinner speaker. Perhaps he too would date rock stars and collect modern art.

In this room, he'd endured many hours of pain. He switched on the TV and settled back on the mattress to wait for more.

*

Rain fell, leaves fell. A nickel-grey storm quickly began. White-hot wires of electricity fissured the boiling sky. He ate three small spoonsful every two hours. The wind made frightened cries. He lay on the mattress staring at the colours on the screen, the crazed characters eagerly striking each other with a succession of increasingly large weapons, to no effect.

The spasms came and went, each one slightly longer and more intense. In the marrow of his bones and the lining of his heart he ached for relief. He twisted and curled like a dying snake. His hands gripped the blanket. An impending bowel movement wracked him. He sat on the pot and for a moment thought he was going to pass his entire stomach, but what came out was just reeking swampish water.

By nightfall, the storm had faded. A dark and heavy silence descended. He did not want to sleep, envisioning the dreams he knew would come. He kept the television on and stared hard at the smirking, fighting animals, plotting each other's destruction to the accompaniment of chaotic music.

The past repeatedly broke into the room, appearing in numb, thinly realised hallucinations. One day Tanel was there and began flaying his back with an inner tube, though he felt nothing. On another, his mother sat beside him and stroked his brow and talked of England's green fields. On a third, the black-haired girl he'd so miserably lost his virginity to stood in the corner, playing with the chain on her right ankle with the toes of her bare left foot and smoking a cigarette, the filter of which was ringed with her orange lipstick.

But then a very real, very present scenario took hold of him. The light was dark grey and misty and mud was splashing against his legs. He was chasing something down, something he very much wanted. Black birds screamed in a threatening sky. The wind was sharp in the wet tunnels of his nostrils. His quarry ran ahead of him, but he knew it could not escape. He increased his pace, his heart hammering at the thought of the capture and aftermath, and his flesh was pumped with hot blood. The path became steep but it didn't matter to him. He pounded on and there it was, close now, about to reach the top of the climb. He knew it, recognised its shape and its actions, but didn't understand its existence. It was just meat. Something that lived but had to die. The saliva frothed in his mouth and his tongue buzzed and he ground his teeth and readied himself. Muscles tensed and he could already feel the delicious softness in his mouth, the hot thick juices flowing down his throat. The feeling of peace as he ate. He put on a final spurt of speed and then, in a frenzy of appetites, launched himself into the air.

He came awake with a shout.

And that was how it was for what felt like for ever. No escape.

Time passed. Winds blew. Rain came.

Grey light faded to black. Black faded back to grey.

If he were the beast, he thought, then he would behave like the beast.

He shat muck.

He crawled on all fours.

He let his teeth yellow.

He snuffled and snorted and made pinched and snarling faces. He cried out for what every moral law told him he could not have.

He lay on the mattress and writhed in a slurry of his own sweat and skin. He rubbed his face along the cold glass panels of the garden doors. In his underwear, he sat on the bike with his head on the handlebars, slowly turning the pedals with bare feet as the inferno engulfed his viscera.

For forty-eight hours he did not eat but let the flames consume him. The agony just a fact, unchanging and unpacifiable. He ground the ends of his fingers against the concrete floor. He bit into his knee. He lay on his back, spread-eagled, and asked the house to fall in and bury him.

And when after five days the key turned in the lock and the door was carefully pushed open, a delusional Mariani raised himself weakly on to his elbows. The air seemed to warp and shimmer as Varta came into the room, her hand to her mouth. Her figure blurred and her voice distorted. Svarik's face appeared from out of the dark, crumpled with disgust at the stinking, splattered room and creased with fear at the sight of the wretched, groaning Mariani stretched across its floor. Seeing Svarik's reactions to him, Mariani felt they were right because now he had no choice but to accept what he had become. A thing from some shrieking world of perpetual night where all you did was survive. To do so, it was necessary to commit vile acts without an instant's thought. He knew what he was.

A slim figure waited at the oversized luggage carousel. He wore a beanie and a grey hooded jacket and carried a holdall in his left hand. After some minutes a beep sounded and then a large black case appeared on the carousel's rubber slats. He reached down, grabbed the handle and swung the case smoothly off the carousel.

He wheeled it towards Customs. One of the officers glanced at the man as he went past, noting his gaunt unshaven face and troubled eyes, but then, probably reminding himself that it was never the obvious ones, let him go.

It had been a hot summer in Bulgaria. Outside Sofia airport it was over thirty degrees but the man did not remove his beanie. He slid a pair of dark glasses over his eyes and looked for the taxi rank. He found it and joined a queue. It moved quickly. In less than five minutes, he was handing over an address written on a piece of paper.

The taxi driver, a crinkle-haired man with gold rings on every finger, got out and lifted the big black case on to the roof rack. It was heavy and, thanks to forty years of driving taxis, his back was bad: the case gave him difficulty. He began to strap it down. His passenger watched him carefully, testing the tightness of the straps when the driver had finished.

'Bik? Bik?' The driver made a pedalling action with his hands.

The man nodded. He got into the back of the taxi. The leatherette seat was hot and the car's interior smelt of oil and fish paste. The diamond-bright early-July sun cast white highlights of exploding stars on the car's pitted chrome bumpers. The driver got in, started the engine and drove away from the airport.

Using what little English he had, the driver made several attempts at conversation during the thirty-minute journey to the hotel. His passenger either did not reply or shrugged as if he didn't understand. The driver gave up.

The hotel was on the outskirts of a small town, opposite a supermarket. A green sign advertised its name, which translated roughly as 'Hotel with Everything'. Along the bottom of the sign, an illuminated word announced Vacancies.

The taxi pulled up outside the front entrance. The slim man got out. He watched as a teenager in a green uniform and a bellboy's hat helped the driver remove the case from the roof rack.

'Welcome, sir,' said the teenager, speaking English. 'You join the team?'

The man nodded. The teenager made to take the black case, but the man got there ahead of him.

'Sure, sir?' said the teenager, and the man nodded again. Then he paid the driver, thanked him and wheeled his big black case into reception.

The room was overlit and warm. Bright thin Bulgarian pop music played. In detachable white capital letters on a signboard were the words 'Welocme to cyling team Godet-RMG. We wish you success'.

Behind the reception desk, a shyly smiling pretty young woman with dark roots showing in her custard-coloured hair watched the slim man as he came towards her. He took off his dark glasses and rubbed a knuckle across his left eyelid.

'Good afternoon, sir, and welcome,' she said.

'Thank you.'

'May I have your passport, please?'

The man took the document from the pocket of his jacket and passed it across. She checked the name inside and shifted the register towards him.

'Please sign and we will escort you to your room.'

The man picked up the pen and paused as if unsure who he was. Then he signed. The words were illegible.

'Thank you,' said the receptionist, returning his passport. 'I hope, Mr Mariani, that you will enjoy your stay.'

*

The room was functional and the bed clean. There was a small en suite bathroom, which surprised him. Mariani sat down and looked around the room, thinking about what, apart from his bike, was inside his unopened case. Then there was a knock at the door. His heart jumped and his shoulders tensed with alarm.

He inhaled deeply. Then he cleared his throat. 'Come in.'

The door opened and Tishland Speyer appeared. He wore a baggy purple tracksuit top, knee-length camouflage shorts and matching flip-flops. He had a pair of wraparound sunglasses on top of his greying head. He was tanned the colour of molasses.

'Romain Mariani,' he said.

'Hello, Tishland.'

'Nice of you to come.'

'Nice to be invited.'

'Was kinda wondering what happened to you. Seemed to get over that little scrape and then disappear. Heard a few things on the jungle drums...'

'Yes?' Mariani tried to keep his eyes steady on Speyer's face.

'Retirement,' he said. 'Turned to crime. Going to marry into money and live the life of the idle rich.'

'Just a few issues. You know?'

Speyer nodded. 'How you liking the Ritz-Carlton?'

'There's a bed.' Mariani shrugged. 'Two beds.'

'You're on your ownsome. Sakov's a no-show.'

'Sakov?'

'Kazakh boy with a helluva engine but an even bigger capacity for booze. Fell off a yak yesterday.'

Mariani nodded, as if he was not surprised.

'You look older,' said Speyer.

'I am.'

'What's it been – six years? Your first Giro, my last.'

'I think so.'

'Lotta water,' said Speyer. 'I remember - hah! – you didn't say a word that whole tour until that day Triesmaan's laughing boy came up to you.'

'I don't recall.'

'Whatever happened to him?'

'Who?'

'Triesmaan. I heard rumours about de Vilde?'

Mariani shrugged. 'When do we ride? Tomorrow?'

'Yeah. Bring any kit?'

'Yes.'

'Our new strip was supposed to be here, but…' Speyer shook his thick grey curls and sighed. 'Money. Hate the stuff.'

'It's kit. It doesn't matter.'

'I'm a *directeur sportif* now, boy, everything matters. Oh – massage. You either get my soothing hands or the sweet girl on reception: she's six months into physio training. She's not a talker, so you might prefer her. OK?'

Mariani nodded.

'Listen, I'll leave you to get your shit assembled and we'll see you at six for a sentimental but heartfelt motivational speech by yours truly and then some fine Bulgarian cooking: that's some real heavy lifting – hope you're hungry.'

'I look forward to it.'

'Oh, and sorry to hear about your old man. Surprised you didn't can us.'

'We weren't close. Always arguing.'

'Shame,' said Speyer. 'Make your peace before he went?'

'Kind of.'

Speyer nodded slowly. With his left thumb, he began to rub the scar on the inside of his right wrist, a gesture Mariani knew signified deep thought. Speyer lowered his head slightly and looked at him from under his eyebrows. 'See you at six.'

'Yes. And, thanks, Tishland.'

When Speyer had gone, Mariani went up to the door, put his hand on the slim brass bolt and slowly slid it across. Then he began to unpack.

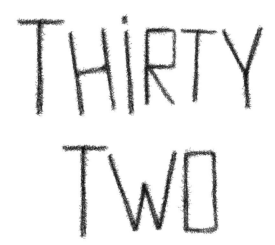

At ten the next morning, eight men in a variety of cycling kit, grey, pink, orange, green, rode slowly away from the hotel. They were followed by Tishland Speyer in a hired brown Seat estate, soft-paced R&B drifting from its stereo.

He had explained the previous night that the first day was a leg-stretcher. No one would be wired up. This was a chance to put some easy kilometres in the muscles and enjoy the delightful Bulgarian countryside. And no shows of testosterone, boys, please.

The team had been a going concern for a year. The riders were young, willing and crucially, cheap. None of them had ridden a Grand Tour. They all knew Mariani's name, but none knew him personally. They kept a respectful distance, and any questions they might have had about his whereabouts for the past year they kept to themselves.

On a deserted single carriageway with endless views of wheat fields, Mariani cruised along in the back several, trying to re-imagine himself as a rider. He knew Speyer would be watching him, seeing how he looked on the bike, how he fitted with the others. Speyer had never been the most talented, but always the sharpest: in the one season that Mariani had ridden with him, Speyer's tactical calls and insights into the behaviour of opposing teams had never been wrong. He understood better than anyone the obsessions and despairs of young men trying to do something with their lives by winning bike races.

Mariani forced himself to concentrate on the rotation of the pedals and find a rhythm. Anything else that came to mind he batted away, but like the pedals his thoughts travelled in circles and returned again and again to what he had been forced to do.

'*Ca va?*' asked Feuilleton, a boyish big-eared climber.

'*Bien.*'

'You like English better?'

'Sure.'

'My father, he rode on the same team with your father.'

'Yes?'

'In three Grand Tours. They shared rooms. My father said he had spirit for the team, never rode for himself. I'm sorry for his death.'

'Thank you.'

'He was young, still?'

Mariani nodded.

'You'd prefer not to talk about it?' asked Feuilleton, warily.

Mariani shrugged and moved his head from one side to the other.

'I understand. Still. A terrible thing.'

Speyer came alongside in the car. He turned off the music. 'Romain, can you come to the front? Take it on for ten kilometres or so? Just above tempo?'

Mariani nodded. He'd expected this. He hadn't believed Speyer's easy-going 'no testosterone' talk for a second. He pushed down hard on the cranks and after half a dozen hard turns the other seven riders were behind him. Speyer then accelerated past. Mariani knew the American wasn't simply showing the way.

Mariani increased the pace and the team quickly stopped bunching and formed a long whip-like line. His computer showed forty-five km/h: after the past few months, he wondered how long he would be able to maintain it. The days locked in the training room had brought his weight down: at least he looked the part. But he knew he would be relying on muscle memory and the hundreds of thousands of kilometres ridden in the past. He tried to visualise times in races when he'd felt almost as if he had no legs at all, such was the effortlessness of his riding. Images of the time trial he'd won, *Jeszu*, less than a year ago, flicked though his mind. Concentrate on that, he lectured himself. The day you were better than everyone. Remember how it felt: the tarmac flying past beneath you, the roar of the parting air blending with the bellows from the crowd.

He glanced over his shoulder, saw the line stretching back, following him. The riders' features were like stone.

He knew Speyer would be constantly looking at him in the rear view, checking what was in his face, the way his legs moved, the set of his shoulders, whether he was at one with the bike or fighting it. Speyer would be searching for clues, tics, tells: somewhere in that car he'd have a camera running for later analysis. Mariani was under surveillance.

After four kilometres, he began to feel the effort. He struggled to keep his face untroubled and his legs turning. It began to seem pointless. All he had been through, all he had lost – was it for this, to be sweating his guts out leading a bunch of kids in mismatching kit on a Bulgarian country road while being scrutinised by Tishland 'The Shrink' Speyer? It began to appear like the darkest, funniest joke to him. A smile crossed his features. Then laughter began to bubble. He could not hold it back. It was so fucking funny. If these boys behind him knew, if Speyer knew…where he had been…what he had done…what was in his case…Despite the searing sensations in his atrophied muscles and the rasping in his throat and the sickness in his heart, Mariani found himself shouting laughter to the sky.

THIRTY THREE

The next morning Speyer ordered them to ride easy until he told them to stop. Mariani tried to meld with the others and stay out of Speyer's eyeline. After two hours, Speyer pulled up by a river and the team rolled in, dismounted and then listened as in his deep, quiet voice, he read a poem. 'Our belief is that when men keep near/ They can disassemble the things they fear…' Mariani understood its theme was brotherhood, and when the others clapped, he forced himself to clap as well.

Speyer then made them take off their shoes and socks and give each other piggybacks across the cold flowing water. After that, he got them to change partners and dance the tango to a CD he played on the Seat's stereo. Mariani was paired with Dewbury, a halitotic Welshman with the rhythmic sense of a log. Speyer awarded them the wooden spoon, which they then had to use as a microphone in part two of their humiliation. Speyer insisted they put on miniskirts and wigs and then he held up lyric boards while Mariani and Dewbury duetted on a version of 'I Will Survive'.

The applause was tumultuous and Mariani bowed and Dewbury blew kisses and the sense of camaraderie hung brightly in the warm air. Mariani stood smirking and wanting to smash himself in the head with a rock.

Speyer announced that lunch was served and handed out foil-wrapped chicken legs, plain rolls, and kids' sweets for dessert. He poured them coffee from a thermos. Then he grinned at them, told them all they were great guys with a great future, and said he was sorry but there was now to be three hours of through and off on a nice flat circuit, each rider to take a minute at the front of the line.

'How hard we go?' asked Jaderenhio, a Colombian twenty year-old with eyes like chocolate pools and a missing front tooth.

'How hard can you go?' asked Speyer. 'Find out.'

Jaderenhio whooped and told the others that he was the man and that they were pussies and the next three hours would confirm this fact, and then tonight they could all suck his sweet Colombian dick and kiss his sweet Colombian ass, but only if they asked nice.

By his third turn at the front, riding at fifty-five km/h, Mariani was not feeling well. By his tenth, he fully believed his chest cavity was going to explode. He dropped to the back with his head numb and the rest of him wrapped in tendrils of a dreadful, will-sapping pain. He knew he could not take another turn at that effort level. The inexperience of the others saved him. They had all worked too hard too early, particularly Jaderenhio, and the pace at the front now dropped quickly. Mariani was able to freewheel in the line, saving energy, and by his eleventh turn the team's speed was under forty-five. He still found that shockingly hard and could not keep the exhaustion from his face. His tongue lolled from his mouth and his skin was turning grey. An industrial machine was pounding in his head. Bile kept spurting into his throat and his hamstrings felt like they were dissolving in lactic acid. When they got back to the hotel, almost his whole body had gone into spasm, his limbs as rigid as the bike's carbon-fibre tubing. He came to a stop in the entrance area, found that he could not move at all, not even to unclip from a pedal, and was on the point of simply dropping sideways to the ground when the bellboy rushed forward and put out a supporting hand. There he stayed, hunched, trembling, sweating streams.

The next morning was free time, which, though he heard the others tumble raucously downstairs well before eight, Mariani spent in bed, immobile. The girl from reception brought him up his breakfast. When she had gone, he locked the door and went to his bike case. Back in bed, he ate a roll and some cereal, sipped orange juice, and then closed his eyes and washed down what was not on the tray with coffee.

Just before eleven and with his legs still as brittle as kindling, he phoned reception again. The girl answered and Mariani asked if it would be possible to have a massage.

She came up ten minutes later carrying her table. Mariani, in underwear and T-shirt, climbed on to it creakily.

'You are in trouble?' she said as she warmed oil between her palms.

'Yes.'

'Where?'

'Everywhere.'

He watched her hands as she began stroking her thumbs along the tense ridges of his quadriceps and the inflamed tissue around his knees.

'Nasty,' she said. 'You are in bad condition.'

He gazed at her strong fingers making firm circles. The white skin covering the flesh beneath. He ground his teeth together.

How could he live with what he'd done?

'Why?' asked the receptionist.

Mariani shrugged.

'Men,' she said. 'They must always be proving themselves. Climb this, eat that, drink this, hit that. What does it do? Gets you nasty legs.'

She began to work harder, pushing her knuckles deep into the clumps and twists of muscle and fascia. Mariani groaned and made himself stop watching her hands. He lay back and for a while thought of nothing: then the unknotting and loosening took over his mind and he began gently, emptily to wish that lives could be restored in the same way and wondered then how long he would need to be on the table for that to happen and he pictured the scene as a burly tattooed man got to work and dug in his elbows and then another bigger man joined in and a woman too and they were all pummelling and kneading and squeezing and the strain was showing on their faces and then they all began to get sick of him and his stubbornly perverted and appalling existence and they began to mash him and smash him and...

'OK? I finish,' the girl was saying, and nudging him awake.

'Oh. Yes.'

She went to the basin and turned on the tap. Mariani sat up and climbed down. He watched her wash and then dry her hands.

'Better now?' she said.

'Thank you.'

She smiled at him. 'Lunchtime.'

*

In the afternoon, they rode twenty kilometres out to a steep climb that snaked up through a deep forest

'Nine repeats,' said Speyer. 'This little sweetie is about the same length as the one you'll be doing in a few weeks. Keep that figure in mind, gentle-men. Nine. So don't bust your load on the first one. Winner gets a ride back in the car. Last man gets to wash the kit tonight – by hand. Ready? Bang.'

The road ran straight for five hundred metres and then became a series of ever-tightening bends, a miniaturised Alpe d'Huez. Feuilleton was the best climber and the others tried to hang on behind him. But by the end of the second lap, he was twenty metres ahead.

Mariani wondered what he'd have to do to convince Speyer to give him a place. He might have bluffed through the first day, but he had been very visibly the most tired after day two. Tomorrow was a long easy ride. These climbs were probably his last chance to show Speyer what he wanted to see.

He let the others chase Feuilleton and sat at the back with Sciacci, the time-trial specialist, watching the Italian-American grind the pedals as if he were riding through quicksand.

'Mountains prove God is a shit,' said Sciacci. 'I'll have rubber gloves on tonight.'

'Try a higher gear,' said Mariani. 'Two if you want. Don't muscle it.'

Sciacci shifted the chain across two sprockets to the nineteen.

'OK?' asked Mariani.

Sciacci nodded.

'Move back in the saddle. Any cramp?'

'Soon.'

'Get out of the saddle. With me. OK?'

They both stood for ten pedal strokes and then sat again.

'Drink. Now shake the legs. There's the top. We'll make some ground up on the descent. Come on. Only eight left.'

Half an hour later Feuilleton sat in the car. Jaderenhio spent his evening scrubbing shorts.

*

Before breakfast on the fourth day there was a knock on Mariani's door. He opened it. Speyer. Mariani swallowed.

'Got a minute?'

He opened the door wide and Speyer walked in, his flip-flops slapping on the room's thin carpet.

'Tidy boy,' he said, looking round.

'I lose things otherwise,' said Mariani.

'Mmm.'

Speyer went to the window and looked out. Mariani watched him rub the white scar on his dark wrist.

'Listen,' said Speyer.

'OK.'

'You've obviously let things go a little. You're not quite where I hoped you'd be.'

Mariani sniffed.

'But I'm not too concerned about that,' Speyer continued. 'Three more weeks' good work and you can do a job for us. Kinda cross between a nursemaid and a cowpuncher. Interested?'

'Of course. I'm glad.'

'OK. There's something else.'

'Yes?'

Speyer said nothing. For several long moments he looked out of the window towards the entrance area. 'That bellboy's a nice kid, isn't he? He's all over the bikes too.'

'Something else?'

'Yeah. You going to tell me what it is?'

'What?' Mariani's eyes flicked to his bike case.

'Well?'

'What?'

'Come on, Romain. Let's have it.'

'It? What it?'

'*The* it.'

'There is no it.'

'I think there is an it. I think there is. You're twitchy. You can't look me in the face. Not only do you laugh but you laugh too loudly – you *yell* with laughter – and at things that aren't funny. Roman Mariani doesn't laugh, let alone yell. You're hiding something.'

'No. Tishland. I'm...' Mariani squeezed his eyes shut, saw the deep blackness and the spots of fizzing static and in there, much too clearly, red flesh and moonlight on a blade. He gradually lifted his eyelids. Speyer, head cocked to one side, was staring at him as if were some kind of zoo exhibit. 'Look,' said Mariani, 'my head's not quite...My father's just died. Plus, look, I'll tell you, I split up with my girlfriend. I ran out of money – I had to sell my house. Everything's gone wrong. I've...I've...not been eating properly. Or sleeping – bad dreams. The worry. I have to live with my brother now. On his pig farm. I wasn't going to tell you. I didn't want ...I didn't want to bring it here. Tishland– '

Mariani's words had come out in a mad skittering rush. Speyer's eyes ranged around the room as if to follow their random path.

'You used to be a nice, simple boy.'

'I just need to start again. I know where I am now.'

'Look me in the eye and say there's no *it*.'

'Tishland, I just told you...'

'And I heard you. Tell me there's no *other* it. Go on, Romain. Tell me. Tell me and you'll be on the start line.'

Mariani blinked twice and then looked into the American's brown eyes. Holding down everything inside him, he told Speyer what he wanted ed to hear.

THIRTY FOUR

He went back to what, for only another eight days, was his home. The house sale had gone through quickly, the papers were signed and there was a ten per cent deposit of fifty thousand *chōp* already sitting in his account. He emptied his holdall on to the bedroom floor and kicked his clothes into a corner. He went to the kitchen for a glass of water. When he came back, he opened the bike case and did what needed to be done: he'd put the bike together later. He went back to the kitchen, paused over the sink, gagged and then brushed his teeth twice and swilled and gargled a super-strength mouthwash.

In two days he would have to go out again. Where to, he wasn't yet sure. Maybe the same place. He lay back on the bed and tried to think through his options.

The phone interrupted him just as he came to a decision. He went out to the hall and listened to its one-beat jangle for a few moments, imagining who was waiting for him to pick up. He pictured Keira in her bedroom, phone held between her ear and her shoulder. Then it was no longer her but another woman, the one he'd used the knife on, the one he'd damaged; though she could not know who he was, and even if she had somehow found out, what reason could she have to call him? Blackmail? He blinked three or four times and then cautiously drew the phone to his ear.

'Hello.'

'Lazy brother. You coming to the funeral tomorrow?'

'I'll be there.'

'Hey, I made your room nice. Got one of those air fresheners you plug in. Summer Meadows. Taken that manure smell right away. All cosy now.'

'Thanks.'

'You get on that team thing?'

'I think so.'

'Then what you got to worry about, hey? See you at the church at ten. They done a good job on him. Looks better than I seen him for years.'

Mariani was quiet for a moment, imagining his father's lifeless face, shaved and primped, his moustache neatly trimmed. Free at last from fury. 'Maybe I shouldn't come. He hated me.'

'Nah. He wasn't as good as you. That's what he hated. You were better, and no rocket fuel either.'

In the hospital, Mariani had stood looking at his dead father. When the others had left he'd told him everything in a fervent tearful whisper, used the cooling body as his confessor. The whole sorry, filthy story along with reasons and excuses and questions about what he was supposed to do now. He'd stupidly kept looking at Tanel's empty face for a response, and for a quarter of a second thought he'd seen a hint of a smile. When he'd finished, he'd taken his father's limp and wretched hand and held it and then stared at it and then looked at the door, but the thought backed away, turned and ran.

'I'll see you at the church,' he said now.

'Yuh, all right. And cheer *up*, will you?'

*

In the afternoon he rode a hundred kilometres and then came back and showered. He wanted to call Keira and tell her about his place on the team, thinking pathetically that this might be the first step to a reconciliation. But then he thought that through with more rigour. The phone stayed undisturbed.

He emailed Tishland Speyer with the details of his ride and outlined his training schedule for the rest of the week. Speyer replied with thoughts about the schedule and to tell him that the team's bike sponsorship had fallen through – 'a significant bummer' – so could Mariani be prepared to bring his bike with him to England?

On his laptop, Mariani tapped out 'It's not about the bike' and sent it to Speyer.

There was nothing for him to do now, so he wandered around the house, picking things up and putting things down, deciding what he could get rid of before the move. Almost everything, he realised.

In the kitchen, a darkening window showed him his own face. Though he had rarely looked into a mirror recently, he stared at the reflection. He was shocked by how ordinary, how familiar it appeared. The features hardly seemed to have changed over the years. He searched the eyes for some new gleam of loathsomeness or mania, but found none. The forehead and chin were not bulging or pitted. He opened his mouth wide and put out his tongue. It was pink and moist. Why not foul and covered with rotting slime?

He turned away, his head filled with a dense block of confusion. He tried to imagine himself in his mother's womb, and in detail examined the image of the curled foetus for some indication of its future. Was it always inevitable that he would turn into what he had become?

The thought made his knees weak and he had to sit at the table, gripping its legs with whitening knuckles as if for his own personal stability. How was this going to end? Scenarios spun through his mind like stills from cheap horror films but none seemed plausible. The truth was blander and more awful. He would simply carry on until something stopped him.

So at seven, when he was hungry, he walked down the path to the café for dinner. He felt the wind on his face. His footsteps were steady and even. There was the café door. He opened it. Svarik nodded at him. He nodded back, sat down.

After Svarik had unlocked the door of the training room and picked him off the floor and cleaned him up, there had been a two-minute conversation in which his friend told Mariani that whatever he was doing was his own business, though he understood all men had their demons and their bad ideas that led them to make wrong choices. But anyway, as he'd said, it was none of his business. Mariani had admitted that indeed he'd got one of those bad ideas in his head, but hopefully it was all over now. It had not been referred to since.

Svarik came over now, muttered condolences for Tanel's death. Then the dwarfboy came in and sat at his usual table in the corner. He waved solemnly at Mariani who waved back.

The café's other regulars began to arrive and the evening progressed as so many had in the past. The counterfeit stereo played a Sibelius symphony and Varta forced a bowl of *franzyxk* on Mariani and then outlined more of her policies, with all of which he agreed.

Later, flat on his back in the darkness, he listened to the night noises and eventually the pictures in his head faded to nothing and he slept.

THIRTY FIVE

There were eight darkly dressed people in the church the next morning. The service celebrating the short, unhappy life of Tanel Mariani was conducted by one of them and lasted under half an hour. Fifteen minutes after that, the seven others were walking slowly away from the graveyard and back towards the house of the dead man's younger son.

Tanel's brother Novtik, a neat-faced shopkeeper in a town on the other side of the country, who Mariani hadn't seen for over three years, had cried helplessly since the first word of the service and was still dabbing at his eyes with a purple handkerchief when Mariani welcomed him inside and handed him a glass of *sotinko*.

'Don't know why I'm in such floods,' he said, and took a sip of his drink. 'We were hardly the closest of brothers, he always thought I was a dullard: he could be harsh. I hadn't spoken to him for many months. I suppose it's just… the waste. I mean, he had all that talent.' Novtik brought the handkerchief to his reddened eyes again and then gave out a shuddering sigh. 'Ach! Herzy told me that all those drugs Tanel took might have brought on the illness. D'you think that's true, Romain?'

He looked down at the floor. 'I don't think it's… easy to say.'

'Why would he do that to himself, though? I'll never understand it. Do you?'

'Not really,' said Mariani, shifting his weight.

'All right, I can see it's a hard sport and all that, but…oh, I don't know, I'm just a simple shopkeeper. I never had all that energy Tanel had. And now – I climb upstairs to bed, I'm out of breath. But I'm glad in a way, if that's what talent does to you…I mean, I'm still on this earth, while he's…' Novtik turned his head, closed his eyes and bit hard on his bottom lip.

Mariani topped up his uncle's *sotinko*.

Novtik recovered himself. 'I know you're far too sensible ever to get involved in all that nonsense. I can see that from your nice house – yes, I know you're selling, but still – and the way you talk and hold yourself. And I bet that accident made you value life, hey? Something like that makes a person look at himself and …oh, I'm sorry, Romain, I'm upsetting you with my stupid talk.'

'No, it's…I'm fine,' said Mariani, who'd found his mouth beginning to tremble at his uncle's words.

'You've had it hard the last year or so.' Novtik put a consoling hand on his nephew's arm. 'But I'm proud of the way you've come through it. You've shown real character. And you'll get your reward, I'm sure. Oh, anyway, let's talk about happier things. I hear you're going to England to race. Your mother's country. Been there before?'

'No.'

'No, nor me. I don't know much about it. It seems quite decadent: a lot of money and scandals.'

'It's only a one-day race. I won't be there long.'

'Think you'll win?'

'We work as a team. I'm there to help others, really.'

'Ach, come now, Romain. Forget all that old communist spirit. Look where it's got us. Look at those farms at Grihji – just ruins now. Look where it got Tanel.' He sniffed and his eyes began to leak again. 'It's all about the individual now. You go over there and win, Romain. For *yourself.*'

'What's that, Uncle?' Herzy had joined them. He had a tumbler two-thirds full of *rena* clutched in his thick left paw.

'I was telling Romain to go and achieve some personal glory.'

'And make some damn loot. He owes me thousands…ooof!'

'Shut up, you,' said Flôntina, who had come up behind her husband and knuckle-jabbed him in the kidneys. 'Romain shouldn't even think about money. Not him. His job is to show the world we've changed. Clear all these crazies out of the papers for good. That's all foreigners know us for. Sex-mad monks and rapacious hogs. Seen those tours they're offering now? "The Search for Golgotha". They take you round in a beat-up Gourovsko van looking for a hairy pig. Very twenty-first century. I've always said Romain could be the new face of the nation, haven't I, Herz?'

'It would be a damn lazy face…'

'I went on a Dracula Tour in Transylvania,' said Novtik. 'They do a short break, just three days. It was very good, they re-enacted the Ritual Kill-ing of the Living Dead. Listen, I respect your viewpoint, Flôntina, but I can't agree. Romain must think only about himself. That is how success is achieved these days. He should think like an American. Go on a…what do they call it?…personal journey. Win this race – and next stop Hollywood!'

'*The Impoverished Cyclist* – oh, yes, that would have them queuing round the block, hey!' Herzy laughed and drained his glass.

'He's young and nice-looking and well-behaved,' said Flôntina. 'He doesn't smoke. He's slim. He's quite tall. He's been to many countries and he knows famous people. He could be an ambassador or present travel shows for export.'

'The Search for Golgotha, hey?' said Novtik thoughtfully. 'I might look into that.'

'He's going to back my campaign as well, aren't you Romain?' said Varta, as she handed round some biscuits spread with *gruhkyk* pâté. 'Hey, I found a cookbook in your kitchen…you starting to grow up at last?'

As his friends and relatives continued to discuss his future, Mariani made gestures of agreement and forced his smile muscles to work. It was almost instinctive now. He did what was required of him. When the house had emptied, he cleared away bottles and wiped ashtrays and washed glasses and plates. He felt both less and more than human. Sordid and soulless, but with an imperviousness, a carapace, that kept his abysmal reality from destroying him: he presumed he was glad of it but still wished it would dissolve and allow him to be obliterated.

For a moment he thought of his father, cold and still in the cold still mud. The loneliness of it. He went to the front room and knelt and opened the last of the drawers in the small chest there. Tanel's face looked back at him, the joy almost lifting out of the framed photograph. It was not an expression Mariani had ever witnessed in him in life and this was not the man he knew. But, perhaps for that reason, he looked at the picture for a good while.

THIRTY SIX

He used a different taxi company this time. A brown Yinczü appeared at nine. With five thousand *chŏp* in his pocket, and over his shoulder a small rucksack packed with a beanie, scarf and plastic sealable food bag amongst other items, Mariani left the house and walked down the path towards the car. He heard the phone in the house begin to ring as he got into the Yinczü, but could not think of anyone he would want to speak to and told the driver to take him to the airport.

When he got there, he put on the beanie and wound the scarf around the lower part of his face. He waited for a bus that would take him back along Road C. When it came, a number of other people got on. Mariani found a pair of empty seats about two-thirds of the way down and stretched across both of them. He kept his face close to the window and did not look at his reflection. As the bus neared Grihji, he saw the eight or nine prostitutes who worked this stretch of the road. Its proximity to the airport, and the cover and privacy the farm's buildings gave to passing trade had made it popular. On Friday nights there was more activity at the farm than there had ever been in its time as an agro-social experiment.

With several others, Mariani got off about a kilometre past Grihji, close to a small town. He dawdled behind a young couple walking towards the lights and then doubled back towards the main road. The sky was grey, streaked with ink-like black smears. A big moon blazed a yellowish light.

Ten minutes later, he was standing about fifty metres from the Giûrgïu woman. Five metres to the left of a flickering streetlamp, she was wearing the same plastic-looking coat and, as before, had a cigarette between her thickly painted lips. Her left hand was deep in one pocket.

He walked slowly towards her.

A rattling lorry came hurtling down the carriageway and its headlights beamed into Mariani's face, illuminating his squinting, panicked eyes. He turned away and waited for the lorry to pass. Its backdraft sprayed him with road grit. He brushed away several shards that had stuck to his forehead and stepped closer to the prostitute.

When he was ten metres away, she saw him.

'You,' she said.

'Yes. Are you all right?'

'You whan same thin'?'

'I have more money.'

'Yuh?'

Mariani nodded. She peered at him more closely. He pulled the beanie down below his eyebrows.

'Why you whan this?'

'I can't say.'

'How much you have then?'

'Three thousand.'

She dropped her cigarette on the ground and trod on it. 'One more. Got a car now?'

'No.'

'*Jeszu.*'

Mariani looked around. A taxi passed slowly, the driver peering out – was it Stepan? Mariani half-turned away and stared at the ground. As he did, he remembered how he had concluded what it was necessary to do to have any kind of presence, register as anything other than random markings inside a mainframe, be more than just a slowly corroding shell that paid taxes and bought products until it was time to rot or burn. Well, here he was, doing it: on this road again, with his rucksack over his shoulder again, with her again.

'I'm sorry,' he said.

'You a jumble. I get van for 'nother thousand.'

'All right.' They had nearly been seen last time. He couldn't take that chance again.

'Five minutes.' She took a phone out of the pocket of her coat and dialled. After several moments she spoke using words Mariani didn't understand, then put the phone back in her pocket. 'Van comin',' she said.

He nodded.

The prostitute shrugged. She lit another cigarette and let smoke out of the side of her mouth. 'You gunna whan more 'fter this?'

'Why?'

'Maybe we do a deal.'

'What?'

'We Giûrgïu. You whan anyffin, we get it. Speak to Drielxuc when he come.'

'Drielxuc?'

'He drive the van.'

'Right.'

'You whan anyffin else? 'Lectricals? Chimneys? Got best *riki*.'

Mariani shook his head.

'Baby?'

'A baby?'

'Uh.'

'You sell babies?'

She nodded. 'Gotta live.'

A dirty green transit van pulled up. Its windows were opaque with grime and the spare wheel was bolted to its rear-left axle. The prostitute pulled at the passenger door and it opened with a squeal.

'Yuh?' she said to Mariani, motioning him inside.

Breathing in deeply, then slowly out, he climbed into the van. In the driver's seat was a dark-faced boy of around nineteen. He wore a black velvet cap. The arms of his T-shirt were neatly folded past his shoulders. His biceps were smooth and hard and his hands heavily ringed. He did not look at Mariani. The van smelt of diesel and wet wood and cold fat. The prostitute got in beside Mariani and closed the door with a loud smack. The youth put the van into gear and set off down Road C towards Grihji. He did not look at either passenger, but Mariani could feel his eyes.

'Drielxuc,' said the prostitute, pushing her chin towards the youth. Mariani tightened his lips in acknowledgement.

Drielxuc drove the van like he was administering an efficient beating. He shifted gears with fierce but smooth jabs and turned the wheel as if coolly wrenching a man's ear from his head. There was silence until they got to the main complex of the farm. In the courtyard they passed two darkened saloons in which bobbing silhouettes could just be seen through misted windows. Drielxuc stopped the van behind a roofless hangar that housed the metal skeleton of a Gourovsko combine harvester.

'Money,' he said, his voice softer than Mariani had expected.

He dug into his trouser pocket and pulled out the five notes. He counted four and gave them to Drielxuc.

'Knife.'

With damp fingers, Mariani unzipped his rucksack, took out the knife and handed it over. Drielxuc brushed his thumb across the blade's edge. His fingers closed around the black handle.

The moonlight glinted on the ten centimetres of hard steel. The Giûrgïi gently shook his head and then looked at Mariani with accusing eyes.

So this is it, he thought. This is where it ends. In a dirty stinking van with a prostitute and a thug. He felt very tired and his shoulders slumped. He looked away, ready to feel the skin across his throat sliced open. He didn't want to die, not this way, not any way, but he wondered if, after all, it might not be for the best.

He heard Drielxuc click his tongue and sigh. 'This thing shit,' he said. 'Cut noffin with this.' He handed the knife back to Mariani.

'What?'

'Lemme see what I got in the back,' said the Giûrgïi and started to open his door. 'Cleaver or somffin.'

The prostitute whispered to Drielxuc and he looked at Mariani and nodded.

'You whan deal?' he said.

'I...I don't know.'

'Up to you.'

For a reason he couldn't understand, Mariani had an urgent need to explain himself. He wanted them to know that he was not just some sick freak getting his twisted thrills by cutting pieces off prostitutes.

'Listen,' he said. 'I'm not what you think.'

'Don' think noffin,' said Drielxuc. 'No' here to think. Here to trade. S'all 'tis. You whan somffin, we get somffin.'

'It's just... I had an accident, hurt my head and took a drug, but it all went wrong,' blurted Mariani. 'And now I can't get any more of the drug but I'm addicted to what it was made from, which was human hormones, and this is the only way I can— '

Drielxuc was looking at him with searching eyes. 'You from Çigi?'

'What?'

In an instant, Drielxuc's hand had pulled the scarf from his face. 'You the bike man.'

Mariani tried to cover his features with his hand.

'The bike man. You know Pitû?'

'Pitû?'

Drielxuc slitted his eyes and waved, using his entire forearm. 'Pitû. My little brother.'

'Oh. The boy. Yes. He comes to the café.'

'He talks 'bout you. Whans to ride a bike like you.'

'Does he?'

' "Wheee," he goes, "wheee...bike man!"' Drielxuc laughed, showing chipped teeth. 'It's bike man,' he said to the prostitute, who nodded disinterestedly. 'So, bike man, you in a supershitpile of trouble, hey? Crazy drug stuff, hey?'

Mariani nodded.

'Where you geddit, bike man? Kazakhstan, I guess. We got stuff for other bike men there.'

'Kazakhstan? No.'

'Albania? We get new dance juice there, sell it at Dringl's.'

'No. I had it... it's a special— '

'Is special, sure — superspecial! Hak hak!' He laughed with a harsh seal-like bark.

'It was a mistake.'

'OK. Lissen. I call now, I get somffin by end tomorrow. Somffin big. You whan, bike man?'

'Big?' Mariani's voice was small and faint.

'From Macedonia. They got noffin there, have to sell anyffin to live. Anyffin. Wha' you whan, bike man? Jus' tell me. Put in an order! Hak hak!'

Mariani inhaled and bowed his head. Something, the smell in the van perhaps, was making him feel queasy and vile.

'Hey, bike man, lissen,' said Drielxuc in a more reflective tone. 'Thas wan't funny, yuh? You got a shitpile there, sure. Some shitpiles funny – yours not.'

Mariani didn't say anything.

'So, you whan? Special prices for bike man...'

Drielxuc ran through his list of what he could make available. It was short, a mere five items. When he'd finished Mariani looked out of the black windscreen and across the broken-down buildings of a utopian dream, as to his left the prostitute pulled her packet of cigarettes out of her coat pocket, the middle finger of the hand holding it nothing but a bandaged stump.

THIRTY SEVEN

'Hi…Romain…it's me…Keira. I'm calling…well, to find out how you are and…stuff…and to tell you that Dad's starting to come round. I mean, he's not talking or anything, but there's definitely something there…and the doctors are hopeful. Look, just…I don't know…just give me a call if you can. 'Bye.'

Mariani replayed the message again as he took off his jacket. At the end of it he reached for the phone and began to dial her number. But at the last digit, he paused. The thought of talking to her after what, just half an hour ago, he had agreed with Drielxuc, was dreadful. What if he broke down and told her everything? He resolved to text her instead, to tell her he'd got the message and…and…what else could he say? Just something consoling about her father and maybe mention he was on a team, make her feel he was in a better place, returning to normality. He took his mobile and thumbed out the message, thinking of her face as she read it. If he could hold that face in his mind, he would not lose everything, he would be more than just a nightmare creature: this was his hope.

*

At eleven the next night, Mariani took delivery from Drielxuc.

The Giûrgïi sauntered into the house with a small brown cardboard box under his arm. Behind each ear he had a half-smoked cigarette. Mud from his boots dropped on to the floor as he walked.

'Here 'tis, bike man. From good strong boy, too, not some old crumble. Where you whan it?'

Mariani indicated that Drielxuc should put the box on the kitchen table.

'Is it packed in ice or something?' he asked, after a few moments.

Drielxuc nodded. 'Otherwise it spoil quick, yuh? Like fish.' He held his nose and then made his hak-hak laugh while lifting the brim of his cap up and down.

Mariani looked at the box. It was nearly square and almost exactly the same size as the ones his Jelly Babies arrived from England in. He began to pick at the skin on his lower lip with a fingernail.

'You whan check the goods?' asked Drielxuc. 'Don' like disappointed customers.'

Mariani wiped his palms on his trousers. He thought about a scal-
pel slicing through pale young skin. 'Look...no one was...this didn't
cause anyone's...'

Drielxuc put a filthy hand on Mariani's shoulder. 'Boy got 'nother. Is
like balls, yuh?' he said, patting his groin. 'You can do OK even if you lose
one. Boy alive and he got fifty thousand.' Drielxuc made an encouraging
face as if to assure Mariani that the donor had actually done pretty well
from the deal.

Drielxuc opened the box. He lifted out a plastic sealable bag. The ice
inside it surrounded another plastic bag in which was a kidney the size of a
man's fist. Mariani took in a deep breath.

'Happy, bike man?' asked Drielxuc.

He nodded. After the initial shock of its presence in his kitchen, the
organ began to look anonymous; it was just a larger version of something
he'd seen in a butcher's window. It wasn't like the prostitute's finger – that
had somehow been imbued with her personality. When he'd put the finger down on the kitchen surface, he'd gazed at the long, purple-painted,
slightly ragged nail and it was if she was in the room, smoking and looking
at him disdainfully.

Drielxuc replaced the bag in the box.

'So, anytime you whan more, you call, yuh? I deal if you whan, three
for price of two maybe. Times is hard. I get you anyffin. You whan woman,
stereo, BMW? *Dornei*? Dance juice?' He pulled a paper bag from the patch
pocket on the thigh of his loose, pond slime-coloured canvas trousers, and
opened it up for Mariani to look into. Inside were a dozen or so large purple pills. 'Best *Krusha* in the country. You pedal fuck'n fast on one of these,
bike man. Hak-hak! You whan?'

Mariani shook his head. 'I'm fine.'

'Here my number,' said Drielxuc. 'Write it down, yuh?'

Mariani found a pen and a piece of paper.

'Ready? Is long. Three, nine, nine...' When he'd finished, the Giûrgïi had dictated a total of twenty-one digits.

'What kind of network's that?' asked Mariani.

'Giûrgïuphone!' Drielxuc half-closed one eye and pointed, then waggled his index finger at Mariani, as if to say 'no more of your naughty questions, young man'.

'I'll get the money,' said Mariani. He went into his bedroom and from his underwear drawer took out a bulging manila envelope. He tried not to think about the amount inside or what it was buying or what Keira might say if she happened to walk in just at this moment. In the kitchen, Drielxuc began to whistle a strange and lilting tune, and then in a falsetto voice sang, in his own language, words that seemed to express a deep and abiding sadness. Mariani held the envelope in both hands and stood still, listening.

After a short while he filled his lungs slowly with air and exhaled. His pulse was drumming in his ears. He felt the blood running through his veins. His life was continuing. For how much longer he could not guess, but at odd and unexpected moments, sometimes in the dark as he waited for sleep but more often in the clear light of day, he had the sense that a kind of conclusion, one he would recognise and know to be inevitable, was being pieced together.

*

He trained in the mornings, rested in the afternoons, and in the evenings, put things he no longer needed into black plastic rubbish sacks. There were over ten full bags by the time he'd finished. Apart from his bed, bikes and the furniture, all he owned now fitted into two medium-sized suitcases.

He moved out the day before he flew to England. He woke early that morning and lay in bed looking out of the window. It was very quiet. The sun quickly brightened and warmed the room. He wished he didn't have to leave this bed. Making a big effort, he threw back the sheets and got up. The U-Analyser was by the bed and he stepped on to it. The red numerals read seventy-three point four. Body fat five point seven per cent. He was ready, physically at least, to race.

THIRTY EIGHT

Just after ten, Herzy pulled up outside the house in a hired van. Mariani heard the scrape of boots as his brother came down the path. Oddly, they'd become closer in the last few months. Perhaps, he thought, it was simply because of his own worsened circumstances; but then again, Herzy had never been jealous of his life as an athlete. And why should he be? Herzy loved farming, he loved Flôntina, he loved his camping holidays on the Black Sea with his farmer friends: he reckoned he'd got a sweet deal and he didn't want anything to spoil it.

'Kettle on?' said Herzy, banging on the front door and then letting himself in. 'I won't shift a stick before I've had coffee. Hey, what's in this?' He lightly kicked a blue coldbox that was standing on the hall floor. On top of it rested the two suitcases.

Mariani came out of the bedroom. 'Few things I made last night. Trying to learn how to cook. Haven't tasted them yet. Black, three sugars, right?'

'Two and a half. Flôntina's on at me to lose some lard before the holiday. "Look at your lovely slim brother," she keeps saying. "Now *him* I wouldn't mind seeing on Kavarna beach in some Speedos… bet *he* doesn't fry his eggs in butter and sprinkle crisps on his *franzyxk*." Maybe you can give me some diet tips.'

Herzy followed him into the empty kitchen. The kettle, two mugs, a jar of coffee , a spoon and a packet of sugar stood on the otherwise bare surface. Mariani filled the kettle and switched it on. There was silence for a few moments. Then the kettle slowly began to tick.

'Sad to go?' asked Herzy, wiping his index finger across his nose.

Mariani shrugged. 'Got to.'

'It'd kill me to leave the farm.'

'That's your life, Herz. This is bricks and mortar.'

'Still.' His brother looked away, his eyes searching the room.

'Uh. Anyway, it doesn't seem right to be here anymore.'

'Don't it?'

'No. I shouldn't stay here.' Over the last few days, Mariani had experienced a general sense of impending departure, provoked by more than the house move. He felt as if he were in a kind of airlock.

Herzy nodded. 'P'raps you can buy it back later…when…when your face is on the cover of a magazine again.'

'Maybe.'

The kettle began to shriek. Mariani made the coffees. Herzy resumed whistling, more softly than before.

'Hey, a fridge was delivered for you this morning.'

'Uh. I'm not taking this one.'

'Why not use ours?'

'I wake up hungry at funny times. It's easier.'

Herzy frowned, but then nodded. 'Want a lift to the airport tomorrow?'

'Flight's at nine. I can get a taxi.'

'I'm up at five. Save your loot.'

'Great. Thanks.'

'Let's get this stuff loaded then.'

Thirty minutes later, Mariani placed his keys on the stairs and had a final gaze around the bedroom, front room, training room and kitchen. Then he stood in the hall. His teeth were clamped together and his eyelids trembling as he thought of the years that had disappeared.

He swallowed hard and inhaled. Herzy had already taken the suitcases. Grasping his coldbox, he left the house, closing the door behind him.

*

In the van, he picked up the day's copy of *Fair and True* that was resting on the front seat. He finished the twelve pages of sport, indifferent to the national football team's 3-0 defeat by Albania and noting blankly that Trent Mitchell had been suspended from the upcoming Tour de France after an A-sample tested positive for use of the appetite suppressant ephedrine. Mitchell claimed his mother might have given it to him without his knowledge: they'd had rows about his weight. The B-sample test might clear him, but the results would not be known until after the start of the Tour. Feraz-Hi:Gen had kept his contract and he was free to race in other events. The piece ended by asking if anyone had seen Romain Mariani recently.

He flicked quickly through the rest of the paper. On page four was a tiny blurred photograph of a distant black shape in front of a copse of trees: the headline claimed this was Golgotha running across a field, but the story seemed half-hearted. Mariani looked closely at the picture, but could make out nothing. He realised that he had not dreamt or speculated about the beast for some time. He'd sensed its absence after the accident, but this time it was different. Mariani felt that its meaning for him, the reason for his connection with the animal, had in many ways become apparent. It represented so much of what he wanted to be – remorseless, dominant, unstoppable – and so much of what he feared he would become – savage, unfeeling, inhuman. Now that was understood, perhaps there was no longer a need for Golgotha. But his tie with the creature had been so strong, he couldn't believe that they would simply drift apart. There was, he suspected, a final scene to be played out between them.

As he wondered what that might be, he turned to page two of the newspaper. There, he saw a half-page article that made his stomach squeeze itself into a tiny hard ball: 'MAN DEMANDS FLESH FROM PROSTITUTES'. The picture accompanying the piece was of a carving knife suspended above a female foot.

The streets of our country grow ever more sinister. To the gibbering ghost of Papa Jhö, crazed porcine carnivore Golgotha, sexual predator Nannįckh the Mad Monk and adolescent stalker The Listening Girl, we must now add a new and even more frightening spectre, a night creature with inhuman desires.

In two separate incidents on Road C, close to the old abandoned collective farm of Grihgji, a male pervert described as 'young and dark' approached two prostitutes and offered money in exchange, not for a sexual act, but, revoltingly, a body part. 'He wanted a finger or a toe,' said blonde Hegheruc X, who plies her trade there nightly. 'He offered a thousand chŏp. There are some real weirdos out there, but I've never been asked anything like this.' Ranughihi J, a Giûrgïi, the second streetwalker approached by the maniac, wept as she said, 'He had a knife and a syringe of what he said was morphine. He told me what he wanted, I said no and then he went away. He was quite polite.'

Police have urged prostitutes in the area to take extra care and immediately to report anyone acting suspiciously.

Mariani closed the paper and put it back on the front seat. Was that him? Was this the man he'd have to tell Keira about? Yes, he'd approached those women. He'd had no relief from the withdrawal symptoms for several days; his mind was cracking with the realisation of what he'd become: when he'd crawled out of that training room it was the only idea that seemed half-way feasible. He presumed Ranughihi – if that was her name, which he doubted – must have kept her hand in her coat pocket while being interviewed: it was not a nice thing to admit to, no matter who you were. He thought for a moment, listening to Herzy's tuneless humming and the grind of the van's engine. Should he call Drielxuc? Ask him to make sure the prostitute didn't talk to the paper again? Obviously, if Mariani was exposed – and the woman did now know who he was – there would be no 'repeat purchase': but then he assumed Drielxuc was only in it for the money, and how much money would Mariani's future 'orders' really make the Giûrgïu trader? As much as *Fair and True* would pay for the story? Then, of course, his own activities would be exposed and he'd probably go to jail. Drielxuc could always blackmail Mariani; there was nothing he could do about that.

In fact, he thought, there was nothing he could do about any of it. He had the sense of moving towards a snare of his own making.

*

The dense smell of Summer Meadows was making his head swim. It reminded him of Triesmaan's living room. He went to the point on the wall and unplugged the white plastic scent holder and tossed it under the bed.

He opened the paper and read the story for the fourth time. Some of the words seemed to thicken and enlarge.

Sinister…pervert…spectre…inhuman…creature…

He opened his laptop and with two fingers began hesitantly tapping out an email to Keira.

I wanted to let you know what I am before you find out from some other source. The drug I took has given me back my life, but also destroyed me. In a way I don't really understand, it has created an insatiable need in me for — there is no other way to say this, but I can hardly type the words — human flesh.

I know you'll think I have gone mad. I have wondered about that myself sometimes. Someone cleverer than me can piece it all together, but it seems to make a kind of sense. The human hormones I took. My food cravings. My aggressive instincts as a rider, which the drug brought back and exaggerated.

I only need very small amounts. Perhaps that's one of the reasons I haven't simply turned myself in. Plus there's the dreadful, disgusting shame of it all. And, I'll admit, sick though it sounds — and perhaps this is the real sickness — I want to get back to riding, though I have a feeling that may not be for long.

After you've read this, I expect you'll never want to see me again. I hope your father recovers. Good luck for your future. I wish our times together could have been happier. I love you.

He looked at what he'd written. It wasn't exactly what he wanted to say, but at least, he felt, it was the work of a human being. No matter what happened, no matter how much longer he was allowed to go on, he must not allow himself to become anything else. He put the email into the Drafts folder and got up to see if Herzy needed any help feeding the pigs.

THIRTY NINE

Tishland Speyer was driving the team bus over from France and had arranged to pick up Mariani at Gatwick airport and take him to the hotel. Speyer had been delayed in traffic and Mariani faced a three-hour wait. He found a seat in the main concourse.

So this was England. The great nation of his maternal forebears. The airport was huge and busy but also slightly dilapidated and there were a lot of notices half-apologising for things not working: toilets, mostly. From what he could tell, the people here liked to make phone calls, drink vast milky coffees, eat sandwiches from packets, wear football kit in public and show off their paunches.

He put an arm across his bike box, and watched passengers and staff as they walked and talked, sat and waited, read, worked, looked at their mobiles, yawned, drank, ate, queued. He wondered what secrets they were keeping, what they had in their bags and in their heads that they didn't want anyone else to know about. What about that man there, in his shorts, sandals and sombrero? Planning a bank robbery? That large woman wearing the expensive jeans and spitting foul words into her iPhone – did she beat the beautifully dressed children who were trailing along so miserably behind her? And were all these people looking at him and thinking along the same lines? Skinny guy there with the darting, dark eyes…definitely up to no good… looks like he's running from something…what's he trying to get away with, what's he got in his past or in his future? What's in that big weird case of his?

He took out the race profile Speyer had sent him. The course began on a road in central London called The Mall and then went out west through the city, over the Thames, through some kind of park, called Richmond, where deer were kept and then looped through the countryside. After that, the central feature: nine ascents of a two-kilometre climb, Box Hill. He traced the climb and its descent with his finger: this would be where the race was decided. The majority of the course looked narrow and twisting and there would be a lot of flesh left on tarmac if the weather were wet.

To pass the time, he bought a small-sized newspaper called the *Sun* and an unwieldy one, the *Guardian*. He opened that and quickly turned the pages.

Downfall...dead...madness...huge...crime...battle... panic...row....revolt.

He sighed and turned to Sport: there was a quarter-page piece about the upcoming race. Mariani skimmed it and managed to work out that Feraz-Hi:Gen Pro-Racing would be on the start line and that race favourite Trent Mitchell would be the team's leader. He pictured Mitchell's face: sour eyes, expression like a weasel that had just pissed on its boots. Mariani slowly scratched at the stubble on his chin and listened to the rasping noise it made.

His phone bleeped. *There in 5* read the text. He put both papers in his bag, thinking he would take them home to show Varta, then stood up and headed for the exit. With narrowed eyes, a thin woman wearing a tracksuit and eating a crayfish sandwich watched him go.

When it arrived several minutes later, the yellow-and-orange vehicle that Speyer was driving reminded Mariani of the buses that took the children from his area to school. It was a very long way from the refitted Volvo 9700 that Gazin-Ségur PMP had used: that had been more akin to a Club Class air cabin, with psychiatrist-approved mood lighting and fully adjustable leather seats complete with electric calf supports, Bose headphones, and integrated storage units to house the riders› team-issue MacBook Pros. Some of the riders preferred the bus to their hotel rooms.

'Welcome aboard,' said Speyer as the main door slowly opened. 'Put your bike in one of those storage areas underneath. Not the first one – the handle's broken.'

Mariani did that and then got on.

'I took the interior from the RV that we were using and then me and my old man kind of persuaded it into a coach I bought from this French third-division soccer team,' said Speyer.

Mariani stood next to him and looked down the aisle of the bus. Ten seats covered in shiny red leatherette. At the back, a tiny kitchen and a door on which brass letters spelled out the words 'Poop House'.

'It ain't the QE2,' said Speyer, 'but it's all we've got. Ever thought this was what your career would come to?'

'It's not about the bus.'

Speyer smiled and pinched Mariani's left buttock. 'Feels good, excellent density – you're in much better shape.'

'Where are the others?'

'On their way. Gotta come back here three times today. Take a pew and we'll get to the hotel.'

Mariani dropped into the front seat. He put his hand on the seat's material, as slippery as if it had been greased. Speyer gunned the engine, found an R&B station on the radio and set off.

*

By ten p.m. all the riders were sitting close together in the lounge area of the hotel, one of a chain, and definitely, as Speyer had warned, not its flagship.

Dressed in camouflage shorts, he was addressing the team.

'Listen. I'm not going to give you any of that Al Pacino *Any Given Sunday* bullshit about inches and dying for the guy alongside you. That's for meat-heads on football teams who wear shoulder pads and think they're butch. Day after tomorrow *is* the biggest day in this team's short existence, but I don't want you to obsess about that. You do, you'll freak. What I want you to think about is why you're in this sport. You're in it because you like riding bikes fast. That's when you feel at your best, that's when this ass-backwards world begins to make a bit of sense. Now, we'll need to do that Sunday: trust me, this'll be the fastest, hardest day in the saddle you've ever had. But what we'll also need to do if this team's going to get anywhere is to show something you can't measure in watts. That isn't the size of your balls or the badness of your attitude. What we need to show is *respect*. OK? Respect.'

Speyer handed each of them a piece of paper and a pen.

'Write this. R, E, S, P, E, C, T. Now I'm gonna tell you what it means. It means that this two-bit team of ours with our heap-of-shit bus and our plant-food sponsor, acts like one of the big boys. We respect the riders, we respect the race and we respect this sport. We don't go in there like a pit-bull with a boner. We show class and we show dignity. We don't trash talk and we don't try and ride anyone into the bushes... and if we want to pee, we get off the bike first. We act like we belong. Two things about that. First, it'll settle you in. Second, it'll mean the race won't think about you much, and when the race isn't thinking about you, then maybe, just maybe, you can take it by surprise. OK, ladies, beddy-byes. Put those pieces of paper under your pillows. See you in the morning.'

The seven riders rose. As Mariani was walking past Speyer, the American touched his arm. 'Got a minute?'

When the others had disappeared into the lifts, Speyer sat down with him.

'Think you can work with that?'

Mariani nodded. He thought Speyer had said the correct things, though most likely they would prove irrelevant come the race.

'OK,' said Speyer. ''Cos I know I'm not paying you shit, but I need you to look after 'em.'

'Me?'

'You know how hard this'll be. There are some good boys there, very good boys – but they *are* boys. Just hold 'em together; and if they get into any trouble, pull 'em out of it.'

'What if *I'm* in trouble?'

'Hell, Romain – ask Trent Mitchell to pull you out of it.'

Mariani looked at Speyer and Speyer looked back at him.

'I just want us not to die here, Romain. We show something…anything… and it'll really help us.'

Mariani ran his hands over the back of his head. He'd shorn his hair down to stubble before he came. He could feel the bones of his skull.

'Anyway,' said Speyer, 'good news. I got a local shop to get us three spare bikes and a bunch of wheels. All they wanted was a mention in the interview when we win.'

'Funny.'

'Yeah, they love a joke round here – felt the water pressure?'

'Who's in the car on Sunday?'

'I'm driving, but we got a surprise mechanic.'

'Who?'

'As I said, surprise.'

FORTY

Mariani was sharing with Dewbury and the Welshman's snoring was operatic. By five-thirty, as light was beginning to filter through the skin-thin orange curtains, he could stand no more.

He got up, beginning to sweat now. Under his feet, the carpet felt like a pan scourer. He glanced at Dewbury. Then he padded over to his bike case, silently unlocked it, and from a zipped compartment inside took an opaque re-sealable plastic bag. He went into the bathroom and closed the door. He slid the bolt, put the toilet seat down, sat. Harsh light flooded from the ceiling, glaring down on his hands and what he had in them, which by all visible evidence was a meat and cheese *broshkt*.

He ate.

The immediate relief. His mind's revulsion, his body's redress.

He wiped pastry crumbs from his lips and re-sealed the bag. At the sink, he brushed his teeth hard twice, flossed, gargled with a blue mouthwash and then repeated the procedure. He took in deep, steadying breaths of air. He splashed his face and then shaved. A drop of blood, berry-bright, fell from his chin and into the sink, exploding in the water.

Taking the bag, he unlocked and then opened the door.

'Mornin',' said Dewbury, sitting up in bed. His eyes went from Mariani's face to the bag in his hand and then back to his face.

'Morning,' said Mariani. He put the bag back in his bike case, his mind working. 'Food from home. Stinks.'

Dewbury nodded thoughtfully. 'No problem, mate. No problem at all.'

There was a short silence.

'Want to watch telly?' asked Dewbury.

'Sure.'

Dewbury took the remote from the cabinet that divided the two single beds and pointed it at the small grey box attached by a bracket to the wall. There were only five channels and he went through them all six or seven times before settling on a kids' show called *CBeebies*. Then he got out his laptop and his mobile. From the corner of his eye, Mariani watched Dewbury as the Welshman's attention darted from one screen to another.

'Got a blog?' asked Dewbury.

Mariani shook his head.

'Website? Facebook?'

'No.'

'Twitter?'

Mariani shook his head again.

'Nothing? People have got to know what you're up to, mate.'

'Not much.'

'That don't matter. Punt out any old shit. Just keeps you in their heads.'

Mariani nodded. 'You're doing something now?'

'Few tweets.' Dewbury showed him: *Tmrw gonna be war totally up for it lets see whos got the big guns.*

'You sound confident.'

'Mate, I'm fucking bricking it. But I ain't gonna tweet that, am I?'

*

Mariani didn't like *CBeebies*. By seven he was sitting in the hotel's Breakfast Bar and upending a carton of UHT milk into a small cup of coffee. He looked at the ranks of Variety Pack cereals on the sideboard and gave some time over to considering what might be the best combination. He was thinking Cornflakes and Special K with an Alpen topping when he looked up to see a vaguely familiar fresh-faced boy of about seventeen wander into the reception area. He had a rucksack on his shoulder. Mariani couldn't place him until he imagined a jaunty green bellboy's hat on his head.

The boy caught Mariani's eye and after a moment grinned shyly at him. He raised his hand and the boy sloped into the Breakfast Bar.

'Good morning, sir.'

'Good morning.'

'You remember me? Marko...from the hotel?'

'Yes.'

They looked at each other for a moment, the boy shifting gently from foot to foot.

'I am very happy to be here, sir,' he said.

'Good.' Mariani nodded.

'It is a good job for me. I came overnight on a coach.'

'You're working here?'

Marko grinned. 'I am very thankful to Mr Speyer.'

Mariani blinked. 'You're... the mechanic?'

Marko grinned again. 'I am very thankful to Mr Speyer.'

'Right,' said Mariani, and inhaled. 'Some breakfast?'

'If that is possible, sir.'

Mariani got up and led the way to the food counters and began to empty Variety Packs of cereal into white plastic bowls.

FORTY
ONE

On the night before the race, the team napped, ate an early dinner – half a chicken, a small mountain of pasta, pureed fruit, no coffee in case it brought on diarrhoea – and then played cards until nine-thirty when Speyer demanded they get to bed.

Dewbury was restless and his tongue-clicking and throat-clearing meant Mariani found it difficult to get off to sleep. The streetlamps threw dull orange light into the room. Distant sirens rose and fell. A security alarm began ringing. Just after one a.m. he came to realise that he was now actively listening out for sounds that would keep him awake. Air brakes sighed and spat. Diesel engines rumbled. A man yelled, sorrowfully, 'Oh, you wanker'. It occurred to Mariani that he did not want the next day, or the race, to come. It seemed to him that its start, the comeback he had so feverishly wanted, would somehow actually be a kind of finish, or at least the start of the end. His stomach tightened with apprehension, but after a while he felt oddly calm and drifted between a benign floating half-sleep and sudden spasms of wide-eyed panic. The sheets were cool and light one moment and heavy with hot sweat the next.

At around six, through semi-conscious eyes, he saw Dewbury climb out of bed and then get down on his knees. Mariani initially thought he might be praying. He watched as the Welshman put an arm under the bed's wooden frame. There was a patting sound and a few seconds later Dewbury stood up. In his hand, a small blue package.

'Hey,' said Mariani.

'All right?' Dewbury began to unwrap the plastic covering on the package. Within seconds he'd revealed a small medical bag. He unzipped it and took out a syringe and a small ampoule of pale yellow liquid.

'You don't have to do that,' said Mariani.

Dewbury broke the end off the ampoule. 'I do if I'm gonna get through this.'

'It'll be OK.'

'Why are *you* then?'

'What?'

'Doing stuff?'

'I don't do anything.'

'Come on. In the bathroom?'

'As I said. Food.'

'Yeah, sure. Lots of guys who don't like needles will put stuff in their food. Kid I knew used to bury pills in his energy bars. What's in those snacks of yours?'

Mariani shook his head. 'Nothing.'

'You don't want me to do this?' asked Dewbury, brandishing the syringe like a tiny épée. 'You want me to ride clean?'

'You'll be OK.'

'You're totally anti? Take nothing?'

'Nothing.'

'Then let me have some of it.'

'What?'

'Your "food". Then I'll know you're clean too.'

Mariani sniffed. 'You won't like it.'

'Mate, I'm Welsh. We eat anything.'

'Not this.'

'Try me.'

'Look. I know you're nervous. You want to do well, show something. I understand.'

'What's the problem? If you ride clean, I'll ride clean. Come on. I like foreign grub. Curry, Thai…'

'It can upset your stomach… if you're not used to the seasoning…'

'All right.' Dewbury pushed the plunger of the syringe down to expel air and then put the tip of the needle into the ampoule.

Mariani tried to stay logical. What would do Dewbury the most damage? If he injected the syringe's contents, the Welshman might fail a test, get suspended, his promising career be ruined before he was even twenty-one; and if he didn't get caught now, then what? More and more drugs as he struggled with his fears and paranoia?

And the alternative? Two bites of something that, as long as he didn't know what it was, would do him no harm at all.

'OK,' said Mariani. 'But you puke, don't blame me.'

Dewbury blew air out of the side of his mouth. 'Cheers, mate. Phew. Never done this stuff before…it's just…well, you know.' He put the syringe down and went into the bathroom with the ampoule. Mariani heard the toilet flush. Dewbury came back into the bedroom.

Mariani went to the bike case and took out his re-sealable bag. He opened it. He had three of the slightly overcooked *broshkts* left. He gave one to Dewbury.

The Welshman broke the *broshkt* almost in half and brought it up to his pointed nose. 'Yeah, see what you mean. Strong, innit?'

He moistened his lips and brought one of the two pieces to his mouth. Mariani looked away.

*

Under a darkening sky, the Godet RMG bus pulled up into its allotted parking space in Horse Guards Parade. Speyer had no sooner turned off the engine than a six-wheeled vehicle that looked as if it was transporting grunts to an interplanetary war throbbed to a stop alongside. It was painted a deep midnight blue and decaled on its back panel was the pink logo of the team breathing the oxygen-enriched air inside: Feraz-Hi:Gen Pro-Racing.

'*Merde…*' murmured Feuilleton.

Mariani watched the other riders turn to stare as the machine's smoked-glass doors parted soundlessly.

Sipping espresso from small white paper cups, the Feraz-Hi:Gen team members descended from the mothership. Two mechanics quickly set up an awning and another clipped three glittering bikes into stationary trainers. Mariani watched Trent Mitchell closely. He seemed absent-minded and stood apart. He picked at the neck of his jersey as if it were restraining him. His buttocks had a pronounced swell: he was definitely carrying extra pounds. His mother was nowhere to be seen. He looked as if he'd rather be anywhere but here.

Mariani stood and left the bus. Mitchell saw him coming but his head flicked to the side as if Mariani was someone he didn't need to recognise.

Mariani walked past and down to the start line. Rain had begun to fall, more like a light sweat. He put the hood of his waterproof jacket over his head. The Mall was still almost empty of people, just a few fans and officials, milling. A man with a little boy pointed his camera at Mariani and flashed off a picture. A blonde woman wearing an orange fleece with the name of an energy drink on it handed him one of their products. A three-metre high bidon skipped and jigged. On the PA a male voice spoke very quickly as if running out of time.

Mariani stood in front of the ICA, looking along the reddish tarmac, imagining himself and one hundred and twenty-seven other riders, lined up and pointing west, waiting nervously to start six hours of pain, panic and suspicion. He wondered if the Queen of England had ever ridden a bicycle. He walked slowly towards Buckingham Palace and tried to picture the lives of the people inside, but could not. He thought they probably lived as Lihgrinjhi had with flocks of fearful flunkeys, nine phones, a personal interrogation chamber and a room dedicated to bread. They'd have problems though, just as Lihgrinjhi suffered from migraines and dysphagia, gout, and, it was rumoured, a hole in the heart. They'd be obsessive too: when the dictator's private apartments were ransacked, there were stacks of comic books and foreign telephone directories, hundreds of tins of fruitcake, cupboards full of unworn hats. Yes, they would live like that, those people in the bland building, its stone the same colour as the sky. They'd live like Lihgrinjhi, like everyone, like Mariani himself, each clinging to their absurd constructed world because anything outside it choked them with fear.

The rain pat-patted on the hood of his jacket. He tried to clear his mind. He had a job to do and he would see it through to the end. He breathed in soft damp air and walked back to the team bus.

FORTY TWO

The second-from-last actor to play Dr Who fired a gun at the sky. Two hundred and seventy-eight people clapped wet hands. The peloton rolled slowly past Buckingham Palace. Mariani had nodded at several riders, but talked to no one. He wanted to feel clean and empty, with no thoughts of the past and no hopes for the future. He had a number on his back, his feet in the pedals, and speed and cadence showing on his computer. For the next two hundred and fifty kilometres, he wanted to be nothing but the race.

Jaderenhio sat to his left, Sciacci to his right. He could feel them trying to match his position, match his cadence. It made him uncomfortable and he wanted to tell them to stop.

The peloton gathered itself and rolled forward. Thirty, thirty-five, forty km/h. The great centre of London flashed past. Bronze men on pedestals, plastic women in shop windows. Hotels. Embassies. Museums. EAT, read Mariani. SIMPLY FOOD. PRET A MANGER.

As they turned into the Kings Road, a rider at the front accelerated and another two went with him. The first break of the day. Rumbles and murmurs from inside the peloton like the burbles of an acid stomach.

'What we do?' asked Jaderenhio.

'Nothing,' said Mariani.

The speed increased as the river neared. Already the road was slick and shiny with water. Riders flitted by like prettily coloured fish, tyres whooshing and hissing, pushing to get to the front.

'What we do?' asked Jaderenhio again.

Mariani could tell the Colombian was already starting to panic. He looked over his shoulder. They were about twenty from the back.

'Move up,' he said. 'But easy. You go.'

He knew Jaderenhio needed to burn off the unstable energy bubbling through him. He sat behind the Colombian as Jaderinhio found a gap and kicked hard, dirty spray spinning off his back wheel. The others followed, and as the peloton swept over the river, they were slotted in the front third. Jaderenhio turned and grinned, wet-faced, eyes shining in the gloom.

This was where Mariani wanted to stay for the next two hundred and forty kilometres. Out of the way, out of trouble. But this was a bike race.

Trouble was always close. They whipped past supermarkets and coffee outlets, took a hard right, and then behind him Mariani heard clatters and grunts as riders collided on the corner and went down. He didn't look back.

He kept his legs and eyes moving. The rest of him was still. Unnecessary movement used energy. He knew he would need everything he had and have to find more.

Ahead, he could see the deep pink of Feraz-Hi:Gen, already at the front and in control, beginning to grind the other teams down, establishing dominance. Their message: We are Feraz-Hi:Gen Pro-Racing and we are here to push our fists up your assholes.

A left. A long lane. Speed bumps. Then they were in the park. The speed on Mariani's computer clicked up to forty-five km/h.

The deer warily watched this vast, strange multi-coloured animal, moving almost as fast as they could. They heard its hissing roar, felt its power. They twitched and stepped back.

Clouds shifted irascibly. Within five minutes, the peloton had left the park and was speeding through deserted suburban streets. Takeaways. Neat ugly houses. Cars in drives.

South and west. Quickly through a smaller park where drenched boys astride mini racers clapped and squeaked and an ice-cream van chimed 'Eye of the Tiger'. Right and further south.

Mariani had Jaderenhio to his left and Dewbury to his right. He sensed empty space behind him. He glanced over his shoulder. Five metres back, four riders in silver grey, two abreast, riding hard. But just as he was about to turn his head to face front, it was as if an invisible hand had come down from the skies and swatted the front two to the ground.

The sounds of metal and flesh smacking onto tarmac and the panicked and distressed shouts of grown men filled the quiet streets. The horns of team cars sounded like the cries of troubled animals.

'Cunt almighty,' said Dewbury, glancing back.

Riders and bikes were scattered all over the road surface. Men kneeling, crouching, trying to stand, clutching at ripped and bleeding knees, peering at grazed buttocks, gingerly pressing necks and shoulders.

'Forget it,' said Mariani, thin-lipped.

He took a drink and adjusted his glasses. He was in this race, right in the middle of it, caught up in its rhythm and forward motion.

Forty riders remained in the front group. They veered left and the carnage vanished. Feraz-Hi:Gen accelerated hard, keen to make the most of the crash and kill off the chances of those wounded or held up. Fractures, dislocations, lacerations: gifts to the men who had not sustained them. Mariani's computer read fifty km/h, then fifty-two. They were on open roads now and the group began to stretch out. With race radios banned, Mariani had no idea of the time gap to the crash group: at this speed probably several minutes already.

The race became part celebration and part frenzy, endorphins released by the euphoria of escaping the crash masking the pain of the effort the group was making to capitalise on it. They were moving at a kilometre a minute as if already preparing for the final sprint.

'Fuck,' panted Dewbury. Behind the light-enhancing lenses on his glasses, his eyes were narrow with effort.

Sixty-five km/h. Sixty-eight. Seventy. Mariani checked his computer in disbelief. He had forgotten the difference between training and competing. In a race you were urged on by old, indelible forces: fear, shame, guilt, anger, the need to survive, the power of the pack. It was easy to lose a sense of yourself. At moments like these riders were nothing but cavemen pounding rocks into the heads of already-dead enemies. Mariani was not unhappy to do that.

The group reached the southernmost point of the route and turned towards the start of the Box Hill climb. The pace calmed. Mariani could feel the group rethinking its approach, preparing for a different kind of effort. They all knew that the race would be decided here, that the dreams of most of them would die on one of the nine circuits.

The raindrops seemed bigger and colder now and Mariani had an icy stream running down his back. Riders began looking around, checking others for signs of nerves and tiredness. Suspicion replaced euphoria.

He lifted his bidon from its cage. It was nearly empty. He raised his arm for the team car to come up to him. Where was Speyer? He must have made it through the crash by now. A motorbike roared past, the wing mirror just grazing his shoulder.

The road narrowed. Trees reached over from both verges and blocked the sky. The climb started. Feraz-Hi:Gen attacked immediately and a gap opened. Three pink shirts led two riders in green from Crédit Haussman and two dirty greys from Grimaldi Electric. The other Feraz-Hi:Gen riders fell back. Godet RMG led the chase group. Mariani could sense Jaderenhio and Dewbury looking at him with questions in their eyes.

'They're going away,' said Dewbury.

Mariani wiped sweat and rain off his face.

'We should go too,' said Jaderenhio, and stood on the pedals.

'Hey,' said Mariani and shook his head. But Jaderenhio ignored him and his bike shot forward into the gap.

Mariani let him go.

'He'll die,' said Dewbury.

'Yes.' Mariani glanced back to see who might want to work with him and Dewbury. Two more from Grimaldi – they would do nothing: why chase your own riders? Three from ComNorg…Gobder, Volvulus and Vek, was it? A Deflin-Exo; from the ugly riding style, most likely Scling. In the past, Mariani had been on many breakaways with Scling: not one had survived to the finish.

The other fifteen were indistinguishable. It didn't matter. His only orders had been to look after his teammates and, with the exception of one, that had proved impossible. The road was too narrow for cars to pass, so if he wanted to talk to Speyer, he'd need to drop right to the back. And what would Speyer have to say? The time for instructions had gone. Mariani was on a bike and he had to ride it: that was all.

They came to a feed station. He took a musette, looked inside, picked out the few bits he liked and threw the rest away. He ate and drank. The rain came down. He was in limbo, where much bike racing took place. In the past, wanting to make things happen, Mariani had not liked it here. But today it was a sanctuary. There was nothing to do but keep moving forward, from one metre to the next, one minute to the next, one lap to the next. Keep going until he couldn't. Events would either reveal themselves or they would not.

✦

FORTY THREE

Up.

Trees. Farms. Café.

Down.

Trees. Houses. Pubs.

Up.

Trees. Farms.

Down.

Trees. Houses.

Up.

Trees.

Down.

Trees.

Up.

Down.

His consciousness was narrowing. The race proceeding. He'd forgotten how often riding was simply sitting still. You had to limit your imagination – it was why many of the best riders didn't have one. Think about possibilities, picture scenarios, you might act on them and that was almost always fatal. You had to step outside yourself, become as numb as your ass. Tanel had said that racing was good practice for life and an even better one for death.

Six laps of Box Hill and nothing had changed. The motorbike pillion held up a board to Mariani. It told him his group was over three minutes behind the leaders. He almost shrugged. The result at this moment was inevitable. Feraz-Hi:Gen would break the others in the lead group and then shepherd Mitchell to victory. If Mariani and Dewbury kept going, they might make top twenty. That would be fine; Speyer would be exultant and the plant-food boys would write another cheque. But Mariani was tiring. His legs were tight and his back ached from the climbing. He badly wanted to piss. None of his gears felt right. Had the air thickened somehow? Even he was growing sick of the soapy English rain. He looked around again. The group was down to eight including him and Dewbury. He flicked his elbow at Volvulus to get him to come through and work on the front, but the Ukrainian ignored the gesture.

They rounded a bend and Mariani could see Jaderenhio at the side of the road, bent over his bike as if someone had folded him in two.

The Colombian looked up pitifully. He had taken off his glasses and was coughing and slowly shaking his head. Mariani knew it was pointless to wait for him. His day was done. He was rubbish, to be picked up and thrown in the back of a vehicle.

Lap seven. Scling rode alongside Mariani.

'Great job. Keep it going,' he said.

'Thanks,' said Mariani. With his hand, he offered the Luxembourgian the open road ahead.

'Love to…but….' Scling said, as if disappointed, and fell back.

They crested, then descended. The race would be over in less than ninety minutes. Mariani blew thin snot from his nose. If he could just keep the pedals turning for ninety minutes: less than the length of a film. But the idea of moving forward began to seem difficult to understand.

Concentrate, he told himself, stay inside the race. Push pedals, bike moves. Simple. Look at computer. Speed: 31. Trip: 191. Cadence: 88. Watts: 325. These are real. These are what matter. But even as his legs took him in one direction, his mind began to go in the other: backwards. His brain seemed to soften and fissure.

The opponent he feared more than any other joined the race.

'To do what needed to be done, I could not synthesise the hormones. They had to the gathered… from source,' the rider next to him was saying in a deathly whisper.

He looked away. To his left was Vek. 'What do you know, Romain?' asked Vek. 'How to fix a puncture, I suppose. How to ride a bike up a hill. Shall I tell you what *I* know?'

Mariani squeezed his eyes shut for a moment, trying to harden his mind. But now he was truly going backwards, dropping through the group.

'I call now, I get somffin by end tomorrow. Somffin big. You whan, bike man?' said Gobder.

'Would you care to go away now?' said a rider wearing mirrored 'Hansi' sunglasses and whose sideburns were the same length as his ears.

Mariani looked down at his hands, his arms, his legs. 'You win,' he murmured. 'I lose.'

He could hardly change gear or squeeze the brake levers. He licked lips that were bitter with salt. The tunnel of trees began to close in on him. He tried to pull in big lungfuls of the wet air but all his passages were tight. The light darkened and he thought of sleep. His head began to drop and his breathing slowed. His eyelids were like sheets of lead.

Then it was raining, raining much harder, spurting down his neck and back.

He opened his eyes. Some kid — ten, eleven maybe — in wet jeans, was running alongside, firing a red water pistol at him.

'Hey, mate!'

In his other hand the kid held up a burger for Mariani's inspection.

'Mate! Mon-jay!'

A burger. The kid was offering him a burger. Never, in his six years as a professional bike racer, had a fan offered him a burger. With cheese, by the looks of it.

'Mon-jay!'

Eat. Yes. Of course. His inefficiency. He had to eat.

He nodded at the kid and took the burger and with his teeth tore off a mouthful and then two more. It had slippery, half-raw onions and its cheese was sticky. It was cold. But it was food. Protein.

He felt a hand on his back. He looked to his right. Speyer was there in the car, leaning across Marco.

'You all right?' shouted Speyer. 'What you doing, for God's sake?'

Mariani swallowed. He wiped his lips. 'I have to eat. You understand? I have to eat.'

'Just ride,' Speyer yelled. 'Just fucking ride.'

He rode.

*

At the start of the eighth lap, the motorbike came back to Mariani's group. The board held by the pillion now indicated that the gap to the leaders had come down by thirty seconds. Mariani frowned. Had there been a crash ahead? A mechanical?

He looked at Dewbury. Then, though it was agony to do it, he pushed the cranks harder. After another five hundred metres, Mariani saw the back of a rider, a Grimaldi. He was tight-shouldered and hunched, a wet rag. Within thirty seconds, they'd caught him and gone past. Mariani realised he was now seventh. Not that it mattered. If he had learnt anything it was that where you were at any given moment was not where you were going to end up.

By the top of the climb, they'd caught and dropped a Crédit Haussman and the other Grimaldi, both destroyed by trying to keep with Mitchell and his lieutenants.

'We're fucking fifth,' said Dewbury.

'We're nowhere,' said Mariani.

But something had changed in the dynamic of the race. He could sense it. Scling could, too. He came to the front and led along the *faux plat* and then into the descent, charging into corners and refusing to brake until the last moment, his back wheel twitching and hopping.

They turned for the ninth and final ascent. And there, no more than four hundred metres away, was the leading group, three riders in pink, one in green. Mariani could not be sure, but it seemed as if they were in the middle of a raging argument.

Despite the stress and tensions of bike racing, and the close proximity of aggressive and competitive men to each other, riders rarely lost their temper: they saw it as a waste of energy and an admission of weakness. Actual fighting was almost non-existent. But as the chase group neared the leaders, Mariani saw one pink-clad arm lash out at the rider in green.

'...the fuck?' asked Scling.

Mariani shrugged. 'Who's the Haussman?'

'Dunno.'

In his head, Mariani scanned the start list he'd been given the previous night. Who was riding for Haussman? Gubb, Redondo, Primo-forte…

'Pronk,' said Mariani. The Dutch party-fiend and syphilis-chaser who'd once trash talked him out of a stage win on Mount Etna.

'*La bouche de merde,*' said Scling.

The lead group was moving at little more than walking pace and Mariani could now hear raised voices. The Feraz-Hi:Gen team car was alongside the four riders: whoever was in the passenger seat was jabbing his index finger at the man in green. The camera bike buzzed back and forth.

'Say that again. Say that again, you clog-wearing cunt…'

The words, spat out in a nasal Australian accent, came spearing down the hill.

'Shittin' hell,' said Dewberry.

Scling looked at Mariani and smirked.

Less than a minute later, they were on the back of the group. The Crédit Hausmann rider turned. It was Pronk.

'Ah, hallo, boys. Nice to see you, Romain,' he said. 'Join the party.'

'What's going on, Pronk?' asked Scling.

'Trent's lost his sense of humour.'

Mitchell turned and glared at Pronk. 'Another fuckin' word from you and…'

Pronk shrugged. 'Only saying nice things about his mother…what super suck she gives for an old fat whore…'

'I'm fuckin'…I'm fuckin'…warnin'…'

Pronk dropped back several metres to talk to Mariani and Scling. 'They were about to nail me, go for a clean sweep. I podium here and I'll get a contract for next year. Just thought I'd throw some shit and see what stuck. Thought at one stage he was gonna climb off and have a good cry.'

Scling snickered. 'Good work, Pronk.'

Mariani looked at Mitchell. The Australian's focus seemed to have gone entirely: his head was moving in random patterns, as if no part of the present situation could hold his interest. His teammates rode alongside him, whispering, touching him on the shoulder. Mariani understood. Mitchell was suffering as he had suffered. The Australian had let whatever was outside the race inside.

Thoughts tumbled through Mariani's head. He was almost sick with tiredness. But here was an opportunity to smash the race apart, to re-negotiate the inevitable. He had to take it. After the descent, it was a straight run back into the centre of London. If five or six of them could pull out a gap on the Feraz-Hi:Gen riders and work together...

Mariani, Pronk and Scling all looked at each other. Mariani gave Dewberry's arm the merest tap, an indication of an imminent attack. Then, for a moment, nothing happened at all, no one pedalled and even the rain seemed to stop. Into the moment poured all the riders' sparkling bright dreams of glory.

The moment exploded.

Scling threw himself towards the top of the hill. In his wheel, Pronk, Mariani, Dewbury, Volvulus, Gobder. There was no cat and mouse now. The final act had begun.

Mariani did not look over his shoulder. He focused on Scling's back wheel. The descent was nothing but flashes of black, green, brown. Seventy km/h. Pellets of rain stung his face. Seventy-five km/h. A vast black dog barked. A tight corner. Brake, brake, *brake*. The tendons in his wrists straining at the skin. Now go again. His chin on the handlebars and his knees gripping the frame. Eighty km/h. A kid screamed. Eighty-five.

His heart boomed. Breath was yanked from his body and shoved back in. Adrenalin gushed.

They dropped through the air like hawks hunting.

One, two, three, four, five, six riders whished round the final bend of the final descent and onto the dual carriageway. Sixty kilometres away, a white line waited.

FORTY
FOUR

Mariani did not like Trent Mitchell and did not care if whatever relationship the Australian had with his mother was now over: but he knew Mitchell was a superlative bike rider and would always respond to an attack. When Mariani glanced back, the three Feraz-Hi:Gen riders were less than a hundred metres behind. Pulling at the front was Pontu, the ex-world time-trial champion.

Nine men were still in the race. All trying to ride away from their lives, but inevitably riding back towards them.

Volvulus the silent Ukrainian: he knew his wife was screwing another man, because he paid to watch.

Gobder the Scot: he owed a Glasgow gang boss £50,000.

Pronk: two days ago, he'd found blood in his faeces.

Scling: his boyfriend would no longer touch his cock.

Dewbury: had injected steroids before each of his last eight races.

Mitchell: his mother was pregnant.

Pontu: had been cyber-stalking Claudia Banquo for two years.

Van Moolne: had begun cutting his buttocks with a razor blade.

And Mariani.

Into the park for the second time. Mariani looked back. The Feraz-Hi:Gen riders were closing. In minutes they would be all together.

The sodden deer watched the two tiny and desperate-looking children of the huge, fast animal that had surprised them earlier.

Out of the park. Back over the dirty brown river.

Ten kilometres left. The pace slowed. Individuals formed plans they knew could be shattered in an instant.

Mariani did not understand how he was still in this race. For the last twenty minutes, he had been riding on what he believed was nothing. He could sense Dewbury waiting for guidance, but there were no words left.

Scling attacked. The group chased him down.

Volvulus attacked. The group let him go a little while longer and then chased him down.

Pronk and Gobder attacked together, but Pronk would not take a turn on the front and the break petered out.

Back into the great centre of London. The sights reversed.

PRET A MANGER. EAT. SIMPLY FOOD. Museums. Embassies. Hotels. Plastic women in shop windows. Bronze men on pedestals.

One kilometre to go. The pavements crowded now. Mariani crept towards the front.

One day the mysterious energy or force of will or sense of hope that has kept the human race alive for half a million years will be given a name. Mariani found a molecule of it and he pushed it through his body and into his feet and the cranks turned and the bike catapulted forward and the air parted before him and he went past Buckingham Palace into the finishing straight and there were heads and elbows to his left and right and he was leading this race with fifty metres to go, with forty metres to go, with thirty, twenty, ten, five…

When he crossed the line, he kept the pedals turning and his head down.

FORTY FIVE

For once the crosswinds at Airport Central were calm. The plane landed with barely a jolt.

His bike case was already waiting for him at the baggage reclaim and his holdall was the sixth item on to the carousel. In Arrivals, two journalists gave him a light round of applause, and when one of them asked him how he felt, Mariani answered truthfully.

'I was pleased with the result.'

He shouldered his bags and went outside, heading towards the taxi rank. A horn sounded and a taxi reversed back to meet him.

The driver's door opened. Stepan sprang out.

'You could have held back a few seconds longer, but…' He nodded vigorously. 'I'll take third. I'll definitely take third!'

With two old leather belts, Stepan lashed the bike case to the roof rack. Mariani sat in the back of the taxi with his holdall alongside him. Stepan jumped in and started the engine.

'New big end. Sings sweet as a choirboy.'

He put the car firmly into gear and accelerated smoothly away from the airport.

'No *broshkts* today. I'm on a diet – got a new lady.'

Mariani nodded.

'Packed in the chimneys too. So…I bet they're all calling…who's it to be? Deflin-Exo? Cavasoglu? Reckon you could get your old spot at Gazin-Ségur back, no problem. Ask for double the loot, too!'

'We'll see,' said Mariani.

'Nothing to stop you winning that big one,' said Stepan. 'And a few more big ones after that. Hell, why not try for a podium in the Vuelta in August, then go back to the Essence and this time stick to the fifty-three twelve on the time trial…'

Mariani smiled. He tuned out Stepan's words.

Yes, he'd come third in London. Beaten in a photo finish by Pronk and Scling. It was a great result for him and his team. He had congratulatory texts piled up in the inbox of his phone: Grasch, Mr and Mrs Banquo, Serge Hamptons, Slirik Fingh, his Uncle Novtik, Herzy and Flôntina.

Third. All this fuss and none of them knew.

The taxi sped quietly along Road C. The fields were still flat and worn and the weeds that grew in the abandoned petrol station as thick-stalked and oppressive as ever. The sun was low and faint behind dense grey cloud. He had a vaguely disquieting sense of things slipping back into place. His smile hollowed as he stared at the mountains, their edges and angles unchanged for millions of years. Raindrops appeared on the windscreen.

'Hey,' said Stepan, brandishing a copy of *Fair and True*. 'They've arrested some gyppo for – you'll never guess what – dealing human organs on the black market. That lot just get worse, I tell you.'

Stepan threw the paper on to the back seat, where it landed close to Mariani. He looked away, out of the window.

Perhaps it was simply tiredness, but he began to wish he'd come in with the back markers, the *grupetto*. He had not been able to do that however, just as he had not been able to accept what had happened to him in the accident. He had fought and kicked and screamed when it seemed the world he wanted was about to be taken away from him. Some people were allowed to do that and, like indulged children, remain unpunished. Mariani had learnt he was not one of those people. He glanced down then at the newspaper. He took his laptop from his holdall, and when it was powered up removed the email to Keira from the Drafts folder, read it through once and then sent it.

He imagined the words speeding through the air and felt such a definite sense of disappearance, of leave-taking and conclusion, that in some ways what happened next did not surprise him.

'Wounds of God!' shouted Stepan. 'Get out of the fucking…'

He slapped the horn, braked violently and the taxi swerved off the road and went through one of the rusty barbed-wire fences that the farmers used to mark out their parched fields. It hit a ditch and then tipped on to its side and rolled four times over the hard ground. It came to a stop upside down, its wheels in the air and slowly spinning. Mariani's bike case and bike were crushed.

The cause of the crash was a huge feral hog that had been sitting in the middle of the road. Perhaps this was Golgotha. The animal itself did not know what it was and did not care. It had no memory and no concept of the future, no pity and no sympathy. It was alive and it was hungry, and these were the only two things that mattered. It raised itself from its haunches and sniffed the evening air, the sticky mucus coating its respiratory membrane making a bubbling, tearing sound. The new scents it found were rich and pleasing and its bristled tail began to wag. A thin brown stream dribbled from its anus and down the harsh matting covering its hind legs. Thick hot saliva flooded its reeking mouth. Its excited heart pounded, pushing its six litres of blood around its massive body. The beast's empty eyes gazed at the hole torn in the barbed wire. Then it paused for a second, looking at the upended vehicle in the field. With quick, almost dainty steps it made its way to the still and silent car.

Once there, its tail wagged harder, although the twisted, smoking metal and the hiss from the engine meant nothing. It squealed softly.

This was the sound Romain Mariani heard as he came to consciousness for what would be the last time. He found he could move his neck, nothing else. He did that. He was staring into the small pink-rimmed amber eyes of the hog. They showed nothing, just a blank sense of impending action. There was no recognition of the man by the beast, or of the beast by the man, and that, if nothing else, made Romain Mariani happy.

Jonathan Budds has worked in advertising for over twenty years. He has competed
in L'Etape du Tour and the longest cycle event in the world, the 300km,
through-the-night Vatternrundan, as well as numerous UK sportives and triathlons.
He lives in London with a wife and two bikes.
Consumed is his first novel.

Big thanks due to the following.

Michael Potegal Ph.D., L.P., for advice on behavioural aggression.

Laura Slader, Neuro Occupational Therapist for chat on brain injury rehab.

Trevor Byrne, MJ Hyland for critical advice, editing and for being lovely people.

Lynn Curtis for advice, expert proof reading and teaching me how to spell 'peloton'.

Anita Davis for sales, marketing, art direction, packaging, advice, arse-kicking and every minute of the last twenty years.

Information about CJD and Human Growth Hormone taken from Wikipedia

Printed in Great Britain
by Amazon.co.uk, Ltd.,
Marston Gate.